Vicky, we all need someone to [hear me!]

SOMEONE TO HEAR ME

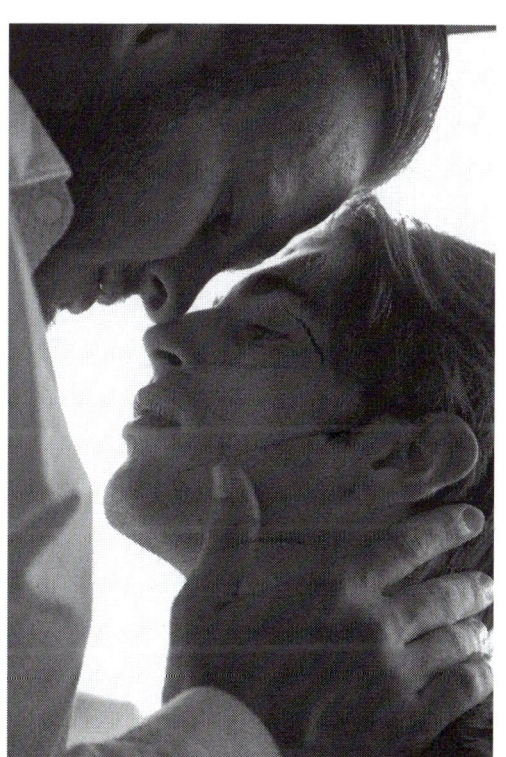

Tru Wray

Someone To Hear Me

Copyright © T.a. McKay, 2017

ALL RIGHTS RESERVED

Cover art by Kari March designs ~https://www.facebook.com/Karimarchdesigns/

Back photograph by Strangeland Photography ~ http://strangelandphotography.com

Formatting by T.a. McKay

This is a work of fiction. Names, characters, places and incidents are either the product of the author's imagination or used factiously and any resemblance to actual people, dead or alive, businesses, establishments, locales or events is entirely coincidental. Any reference to real events, businesses or organizations is intended only to give the fiction a sense of realism and authenticity.

All right reserved. No part of this publication may be reproduced, stored in a retrieval system, or transmitted by any means – electronic, mechanical, photographic (photocopying), recording or otherwise – without prior permission in writing from the author.

Pirating an author's work is a crime and will be treated as such.

Dedication

To anyone who has found the strength to fight.

You are a survivor ~ you are my hero.

Prologue

Ares

Sitting quietly by the window, I watch as the rain falls, creating large puddles on the ground outside. The sky is dark, but the streetlights shine onto the pavement, making it sparkle. I turn my head when a cat runs out from beneath a car, sprinting across the road and under a hedge to escape the rain.

A noise in the apartment makes me jump but I don't turn around to see what it is. I know what, or who, it is and need a moment to compose myself before facing him. I take a deep breath and wipe the tears from my cheeks, avoiding the black eye that he gave me earlier, and I do everything I can to pretend that I'm not upset. Micah puts a hand on my shoulder and it takes everything in me not to flinch at his touch. He hates it when I show him that I'm scared, especially after we've had a fight, but sometimes the reaction is just instinct.

"Are you okay?"

His voice is soft but I don't relax for a minute knowing that he can change in a second, his anger appearing before I have a chance to react. I can feel the lingering pain in the side of my face where he hit me the last time he was angry and I don't want him to do it again.

"I'm fine." I try to make myself sound happy but the tightening of his grip on my shoulder shows that he isn't buying it. I hold in my whimper but it doesn't help keep Micah happy, and he still sounds angry when he speaks.

"I know you're judging me, Ares, and it's unfair. I didn't mean to hit you but you just kept pushing. This is your fault, just like last time."

I'm not sure how I was pushing him because the memories I have from the hour before don't have me doing anything but trying to keep him happy. He had returned home after a day at work to a spotless house and dinner waiting on the table for him. Everything was like it should have been, I'd done everything the way he likes, but when I asked him if he wanted a drink he punched me. It's not the first time he's put his hands on me and I'm thankful that tonight it was only a punch. The last time he was upset he broke my rib and it took me weeks to recover.

I reach up and place my hand on top of his where it still lies on my shoulder, rubbing my thumb over his knuckles. I give him my most convincing smile, one that I don't feel in my heart and I hope that it's enough to placate him. "I know and I'm sorry. Why don't we just go to bed and forget about it."

His hand leaves my shoulders and he walks away from me. I take a deep breath and follow as he walks down the hall to our bedroom. His silence worries me and I can tell by his body language that he's still pissed off. I start to work through a plan in my head on how I can make him relax. Reaching the room, I walk in and start to remove my top. If he can work out some of his anger with sex then there's a better chance of me walking away without getting really hurt. A black eye is nothing when it comes to Micah, so if I can get to sleep tonight without anything worse to deal with I will be more than happy.

I stand in front of him in just my jeans whilst trying to look as happy as I can. The coldness in his eyes tells me that it's not working like I want it to. I reach out and run my hand down his chest, unbuttoning his trousers when I reach them. If I have to get on my knees to calm him down then so be it. "Relax, baby. I'll make you feel better." I kiss his chest, moving slightly lower with each brush of my lips. I think it's working until he grabs me roughly by the hair.

"You think I'm fucking stupid enough to believe anything that comes out your mouth? You said you were here all day but I know you weren't. Stephen told me he saw you in a coffee shop with some guy." He moves in close to my face. "I know you weren't here." His voice is full of fury and my body floods with fear.

I've no idea what he's talking about. I don't leave the house during the day because I'm not allowed to. I can't even pop out to the supermarket without Micah escorting me. There's no way I would go anywhere without permission, especially not to meet someone else. "I didn't go anywhere. Baby, I wouldn't do that to you."

His grip tightens on my hair and I reach up to try and relieve some of the pressure. He uses his other hand to grab me around the throat and pushes me backwards until my back slams against the wall of our room. The impact winds me and I struggle to breathe. The hand on my neck tightens further and he leans in close to my face until his nose touches mine. His eyes are full of rage and I know that tonight is going to be worse than ever before, that tonight is going to hurt enough that I will never forget it.

"See, that's where we have a problem. I don't believe you."

The first punch knocks the breath completely out of me and when his hands release me I collapse onto the floor. The second punch has bright, white lights flashing in my vision and I curl myself into the smallest ball I can.

"I don't know why you make me do this to you, Ares. But you just never learn."

Chapter One

Kohan

I pull open my top drawer and grab the stack of papers that are in there before throwing them onto my desk and returning my gaze to what's left in it. I can't believe that I've lost another tape recorder. I need it for my interview with Mr Hanes and if I don't leave in the next thirty minutes there's a good chance I won't make it in time to interview him, and he's not the type of person to give second chances, no matter your reason for being late.

I rake through the junk in the bottom of the drawer. I know it has to be somewhere. *Where the hell did I put it?* I remember having it when I had my meeting with my boss, Mr James, because I let him listen to a part of a previous interview to check to see if I could use the content. I didn't leave it in there though because I remember putting it onto my pocket before I left.

I grab all the crap from the next drawer down and add it to the already large pile on top of my desk. I don't even know why I'm looking in here. I don't think I've opened this drawer in about six months, and going by the rather dried out orange, I think my timeline is pretty accurate. I've gotten to the point in my frustrations where I'm searching every place I can possibly think of, even if I know that my recorder isn't there.

I slam the drawer shut and sit back in my chair, glaring my anger at the leaning tower of paper that has amassed in front of me. I really should sort through all the crap at some point but I can't be bothered. I've never been the tidiest person when it comes to my office so, true to form, I open the top drawer and knock it all back in with my arm, promising myself that I'll tidy it up when I don't have to find this bloody recorder. *Where the hell is it?*

Leaning my elbows on the desk I drop my head into my hands. I close my eyes and try to walk through my steps after I left Mr James' office. I went to speak to Sophie about a meeting I've lined up for next week, and from there she invited me out to lunch but I told her I couldn't go. She complained for a while but then finally stopped when I told her that I could have a coffee with her in the staff room.

The staff room!

I jump up from my chair so quickly it flies backwards across the floor and hits the filing cabinet behind it. I rush for the door knowing now that I left the recorder in the staff room. I can clearly picture myself putting it down on the table we were sitting at letting her listen to the recording I took of the busker I heard singing in the street this morning. I thought maybe it would make a good 'feel-good' write up because our small town doesn't get many people out of the normal like this guy. It wasn't just his singing that was amazing, he had a smile that would sell sand to the Arabs and I wanted to stand all day and listen to him. I know he was irritating Fred, the owner of the shop he was busking in front of, so I'm hoping a piece in the paper would make people welcome him to the area.

We are a small town where everyone knows everyone, and even though we are kind and like to help each other, strangers always make the majority of the locals uneasy. Even though we aren't too far from some major English cities, the people who live here still don't trust who they don't know. I'd actually heard about the busker, or as I found out later Matt, when I went to The Fly Cup earlier for a takeout coffee. The place was buzzing with gossip about the stranger and I went out of my way to find him. The lone man who arrived with nothing but a sleeping bag and a guitar had everybody guessing why he was here. Was it robbery or murder? There was no way that it could possibly just be that Matt was just travelling through England trying to find the place he wanted to stop and make home.

I spoke to him for at least half an hour about his journey

down from Scotland, living on only what he makes from busking and odd jobs that pays under the table. I sat for longer than I intended to as I listening to his stories and that's when I knew that he would make a fantastic article. It would be a win/win situation: our readers would love to read about his adventures and the people of the town might be more accepting, or at least not cross the road to avoid walking past him. It was his amazing singing voice that I was letting Sophie listen to, and that's where my recorder must be.

I run down the corridor, fully aware that my time is fast running out. I must have less than ten minutes left to get on the road and I still need to grab my bag and get to my car, which is parked on the ground level of the parking lot. *Shit, I'm never going to make this interview at this rate.* When I reach the kitchen I frantically search the table I was sitting at. I can feel my anger starting to rise when I can't find it but I *know* it has to be here.

"What are you doing?"

I look up briefly to see Sophie leaning against the doorframe watching me. Sophie is my best friend but she is also the most annoying person I know. She just has this way about her that makes me want to throw something at her head, but it's also the exact same thing that makes me love her. "I'm building a swing set for the under privileged." My answer drips with sarcasm even though she doesn't actually deserve it. The only thing that keeps me from feeling guilty is the knowledge that she won't take it personally. Slagging each other off is our thing and sometimes it's to the point where people think we hate each other.

"That's nice. I thought that maybe you were looking for this."

My head whips up and I see her standing there with my recorder in her hand. I growl before getting off my knees and marching over to her. I grab the recorder out of her hand and glare at her, hoping she can sense my hate for her in this moment. "I'm so late and I need this. You didn't think of bringing it to me sooner?"

"Your thanks is unnecessary, Kohan. All that gushing will just embarrass us both." Her smile is sickly sweet as she flutters her eyelashes at me, totally ignoring how pissed off I am.

"I hate you." I go to walk past her but she grabs my arm and pulls me towards her before kissing my cheek.

"No you don't, you love me and you know it."

I just grumble as I kiss her cheek in return, pull away and rush back to my office to grab my messenger bag. I barely take a second to catch my breath before legging it out of the building via the back stairs and into my car. I check the clock again and see that if I break a couple speed limits then I'll make it in time. Why did Mr Hanes have to live so far out of town? Well no time to bitch about it now, I just need to drive like Michael Coulthard and get there quickly.

———◇◇□◇◇———

I yawn as I enter the newspaper office through the main door, waving at Tony the night security guard as I walk past. The interview with Mr Hanes went on a lot longer than I expected and I really just want to go home and sleep but I can't. My deadline for the story is lunchtime tomorrow so I need to get at least a first draft done tonight before I think about going home. Before that though, I need to eat because I can't concentrate on an empty stomach. I grab my mobile from my jacket pocket as I enter the lift and lean back against the mirrored wall. Opening up my Whatsapp, I send a message to Helen who owns the sandwich shop next door. Helen is an amazing woman and a lifesaver because she allows us to order food through message and she gets one of the waiters to run the order up to the offices. I try not to use the service too often as it just encourages me to be lazy, but tonight I can't face the idea of going back down to the café, even though I'm not even off the lift yet.

The doors in front of me slide open and I walk forward, fighting with my jacket pocket to get my phone back into it. Instead of successfully returning it, my mobile slips through my fingers and lands on the carpet with a thud. "Fuck." I bend down to get it, not liking the fact I'm having to use energy I don't have to retrieve it. I stand up and head down the corridor again, my focus on my phone to make sure it isn't broken. I turn the corner and walk straight into the body of someone which causes me to drop my phone on the floor for a second time. The momentum of the collision has me also taking a step backwards and I think I'm about to end up on the floor right next to my phone.

Just as I'm sure I'm about to go down, hands grab me around the arms and keep me upright.

"Oh god, thank you." I finally look at the person I walked into, convinced that I'll see someone I know but the man in front of me is a stranger. He bends down and picks up my mobile. He holds it out to me but I don't take it straight away. I notice that he hasn't looked at me yet and even though I don't know why that bothers me, it does, so I wait patiently until he flickers his eyes up to mine. When he does I smile and take the phone from his hand. "Thanks. Are you okay, I didn't hurt you did I?"

The guy doesn't say anything but he starts to shift nervously around and looks like he wants to bolt. His eyes flick back to me again and this time he holds my gaze for a few seconds and it gives me a chance to look at him properly.

His hair is long enough that it sits over the collar of his shirt in dark waves. The curls also sit low over his forehead so he has to look through them to see me, but thankfully I can still see his eyes clearly. They're dark and despite the distance between us I can see that shadows live in them. I don't know what he sees on my face but he looks away suddenly and walks past me around the corner. He moves so quickly that it takes me a few moments to realise that he's actually gone. When it finally registers I go after him because I suddenly want to know who this guy is. I turn the same corner but all I'm met with is an empty space. I'm pulled from my staring contest with the empty corridor by the lift door opening. I look towards it, hoping that the stranger will walk out of it, but it's Rosie from the sandwich shop.

"Hey, Kohan. Helen asked me to deliver this to you. Burning the midnight oil again?" Rosie is a nice girl. She must only be about nineteen but from what Helen says she is a hard worker and is also super sweet.

"It's seven o'clock, Rosie. I don't think that counts as the midnight oil."

Her cheeks colour a little and she looks down at my feet. "I brought your sandwich and soup." She holds out the brown paper bag that's in her hand and I take it from her, my finger accidentally brushing against hers. I hope she doesn't notice but the way the colour on her cheeks deepens tells me she has.

Sophie is forever teasing about Rosie's crush on me and I try everything possible not to lead her on. Even if I was interested in women, Rosie is far too young for me. At twenty-nine I'm looking for someone my own age or older, and obviously someone who has a dick. "Thanks, Rosie." I reach into my back pocket and grab my wallet to take out the money I owe.

Rosie starts to back away when she realises what I'm doing. She never takes money from me for my meals and I always feel really awkward about it. I always go in the day after to pay Helen for the food because I can't have Rosie out of pocket because of a silly crush. "Goodnight, Kohan. I hope your story works out." She smiles and turns away before I can open my wallet, the lift doors close before I can say anything.

What is it with people vanishing on me today? I make a mental note to go in past Lettuce Eat tomorrow and settle my bill with Helen. The smell emanating from the bag has my stomach rumbling at a frightening level so I forget the fleeting visitors and head to my office. The floor is really quiet tonight, which is unusual but welcomed since I have so much work to do in such a little amount of time.

I noticed quickly when I started working here that night times are the quiet times in the office, but still I try to keep ahead of my work so I don't have to take advantage of that fact. I started working at The Daily Conversation nearly two years ago and I love it. It's a small local paper that only covers our town and a few of the surrounding ones but it's enough to keep me and about another dozen people in employment. It's a far cry from working at a tabloid paper in London where I worked before, but I honestly don't miss it or the stress. There was always so much going on there, the offices busy nearly twenty-four hours a day, so the small size of this newspaper was a big seller to me. Will I win any awards for the stories that I write? Not in this lifetime, and I found out very early on that I didn't care. The more relaxed pace and probably reaching my fortieth birthday without a stress-induced heart attack is a huge tick on the plus side.

    I place both my bags onto my desk and pull my jacket off before throwing it over the seat in the corner. I collapse into my desk chair and feel fatigue rearing its ugly head. The thought of finally getting to eat has me perking up a bit and I rip open the paper bag that contains my food, taking the tub of soup and sandwich out as quickly as I can manage. Lettuce Eat makes the best French onion soup and I can't resist ordering it whenever I get food from there. I open the lid and the rich smell invades my nose and my stomach grumbles again. I unwrap my grilled cheese sandwich and instantly dip it into the soup, moaning as I take a huge bite of the orgasmic mouthful. I don't know if it's because I'm that hungry but it tastes a hundred times better than usual.

    I had arrived late to Mr Hanes' farm this afternoon, which he considered bad manners, and it took me nearly an hour of apologising to get him to speak to me. Finally, after promising to give him Mrs Sanderson's, the owner of The Fly Cup's, telephone number, he let me interview him. I know that if I hadn't gotten the interview I would have been able to come up with another story on the fly, but I wanted this one. There isn't much crime around here, so when he had witnessed the local estate agents being robbed, there was no other story I wanted to cover. The article came to me instantly when I heard the news so I was going to use everything in my arsenal to get the story from him, even throwing Mrs Sanderson under the bus. To be fair, I've seen her checking him out the few times he comes to town so I know that she won't mind her number being passed on. What I didn't tell Mr Hanes was the only telephone number I can give him is for the café since that's the only one I have.

I continue to eat but slow myself down a little from the greedy mouthfuls I was taking so I don't give myself indigestion. I start to plot out the story in my head but my mind keeps drifting to the stranger in the corridor. I haven't seen him around before because if I'd seen him before I know for a fact that I would have remembered him, he's not the kind of man you forget easily. I'm not usually someone who's attracted to longer hair but on that guy it just seemed to work. He was dark and mysterious and I have a sudden longing to know what his voice is like. He didn't speak at all during the encounter which is strange, but I imagine that he has a deep voice that makes your toes curl. My dick perks up at the thought and I shake my head. It's been so long since I've been with someone that a two-minute interaction with a stranger has my dick waking up. I really need to get laid but that needs to wait until I've finished this story.

I throw my now empty food containers into the bin next to my desk knowing that I will need to empty the bin before I leave tonight or my office will smell gross by the morning. The company's cleaner left about three weeks ago and Mr James has been struggling to get someone to replace her ever since. It's meant that we've all been dealing with cleaning our own offices to try and keep the mess to a minimum. We're lucky that the cleaner from the library on the bottom floor comes up and cleans the bathrooms and kitchen, because I think there would've been a mutiny if we had to take turns doing that. There was enough bitching when Mr James asked us to empty our own bins because truthfully that's all the cleaner did in our personal offices, the rest was our responsibility anyway.

Grabbing my messenger bag from the floor, I take my laptop out, open it and wait for it to boot up. I go to grab my recorder from the front pocket and I feel my stomach drop when I can't feel it there. *God, this can't be happening again!* I search through all the outside pockets before emptying out all the pads of paper and pens from my bag. I'm just about to go into meltdown mode when it slips out from between two pads. I sigh as I put everything back into my bag. I swear I need to buy a chain for the bloody recorder so I can wear it around my neck.

Chapter Two

Ares

I manage to keep it together until I get home, which in itself is huge progress since I moved here two months ago, but as soon as I walk through my front door I lose it. I slam the door and lean back against it, letting myself slide down until I'm sitting on the floor with my knees pulled to my chest. My breathing is far too fast and I know I need to slow it down before I go into a full on panic attack. I straighten my legs out and drop my head back to the door. I relax my body as much as I can, feeling the muscles soften one by one. I take deep breaths, counting each one for five seconds before blowing the air out slowly. I try to clear my mind of everything but it keeps finding its way back to the encounter with the guy after my interview. Bumping into him was what threw my carefully crafted confidence out the window. If he had just said sorry and walked away I would have just nodded and left, but he looked at me and for reasons I can't explain it feels like he actually saw me. That's why I ran.

Making it to the office on my own had me feeling like I could do this job. It was one of only a handful of times I'd left my house on my own since I moved here so I felt like I was unstoppable. It didn't even bother me that I'd taken the easy way out and walked there since it wasn't too far, because taking a taxi would have been just too much to deal with today. Dealing with strangers isn't easy for me at the best of times, but add in the enclosed space of a car and the panic becomes too much. The meeting with Mr James went okay though and I think I managed to avoid coming across as a complete lunatic. I smiled and remained calm, and I even managed to shake his hand without flinching which is something I was incredibly worried about. He seemed happy when I left his office and I felt the stress of the day start to ease. I didn't apply for this job just for the money, I have a small trust fund from my grandparents that helps me along, but I do need it to try and get back to living a normal life again. I need to get out into the world before I become a complete hermit.

The job isn't much, just a cleaning position at the local newspaper offices, but it's low stress and with the hours being after work hours, there should be less people to deal with. That was actually the selling point for me when I saw the advert. I can tell my therapist that I have a job like he advised, but it's something that will still allow me to keep my distance from people as much as I can. The only other job available was a server at the local coffee shop and after walking past the place a few days ago I knew that I wouldn't be able to cope with it. Too many people, too loud, and way too much happening all at once.

Whistling in my ear pulls me out of my head and I reach up to remove my hearing aids. They've been playing up recently and that inevitably means I need to go and get them checked, but the thought of travelling to the hospital stresses me out so I'm trying to put it off as long as possible. The staff are always so nice when I go but hospitals bring back far too many memories and then nightmares always plague me after I need to go.

I turn them off and lean my head against the door again, letting the almost complete silence relax me. When I lost my hearing I didn't realise what a blessing it would be, but being able to shut most of the world out gives me a chance to decompress. The silence allows me to hide from life when it becomes too much for me, which if I'm honest, is probably more often that it should be. Being able to shut out most of the noise keeps me calm and allows me to pretend that I'm not scared most of the time. The sad fact is that there is nothing left in this life that I want to hear.

One of the first things that I asked Mr James when I arrived at the interview was if it was a problem that I was deaf. I needed to know if I could work without my hearing aids in on a regular basis. He was fine with it as long as I could hear any alarms that might go off but I assured him I wasn't completely deaf. I can still hear high-pitched sounds like alarms and anything that is extra loud like large vehicles reversing or people dropping metal or heavy things.

Getting up from the floor I head towards my bedroom to put my hearing aids into their box since I won't need them for the rest of the day. There's nowhere I need to be and I asked Mr James to text me if he wanted to get into contact with me in case I missed my phone ringing. I don't like using the hearing aids more than I have to, they're uncomfortable and, even more than the hearing loss itself, act as a constant reminder that I'm damaged. Not being able to hear is something I've become used to and I can cope with it, but being reminded physically that I have a disability is a problem for me. It's one of the reasons I grew my hair long. I wanted to hide my ears when I have to wear the horrible things and I thought that it would be one of the easiest ways of doing it. The other reason was to cover the scar on my head because I don't want to see the ugliness every time I look at myself in the mirror.

I feel my pulse rate rise as memories threaten to break through the wall I've built up around them. I need a distraction and only one thing will help. I walk through my small cottage towards the sun lounge at the back of the house. The room is on the opposite side of the house from the one-track road that's runs along the front so it's very private. The windows in this room are the biggest in the house like the previous owners wanted to create a glass bubble that gets the sun all day. It was one of the main reasons I bought this place and it became the natural location for the hobby that soon became my passion.

I walk to the stool that sits in front of my pottery wheel, take a seat and stare at the empty space on top of the wheel. I finished my latest sculpture a few days ago and I've been staring at the empty spot ever since. Sometimes I move straight on to my next project but sometimes inspiration takes a little bit longer to hit. I've heard about authors talking about voices in their heads that tell them how to write their stories, my process is a little like that. I see the face that wants to be shown and I take that and give it life.

My mind has been quiet the last few days but today I can hear the whisper. I can see blue eyes with the long eyelashes, eyelashes that every woman dreams of having, but these frame the beautiful eyes of a man. Short dark hair, strong jaw, and sexy stubble. I can see it all clearly and I rush to grab a clump of clay so I can start creating what I can see. My hands work over the soft clay, the heated material melting through my fingers as they work without conscious thought, sculpting the start of something that I hope will become beautiful.

I feel a burning sensation in my shoulders even though I'm lying flat out on my bed. I sat too long earlier trying to sculpt the vision in my head but I just couldn't get it right. The forehead wasn't sloped enough and the cheekbones weren't prominent like I wanted them to be. I ended up needing to walk away before I lost my temper at the clay, and that's a first for me.

As part of my ongoing recovery my therapist wanted me to take up a hobby that I could focus on when things got too difficult and I chose working with clay. I started with simple things like vases and mugs, but soon I progressed to more complicated sculptures. I tried to sculpt animals and buildings, and I was happy with just doing them until I tried my first human face. That's when it went from a hobby to a passion. I can spend hours creating a face from my imagination, only seeing small sections at a time, which allows me to focus on the tiny details of each area. It's always interesting for me when I finally get to step back and see the finished piece. I love to see the beauty in every single creation, because no matter what they look like, they are perfect to me.

This new face is different though and I can't work out why. It's like even though I don't know what it looks like, nothing fits. I can tell it isn't right without having to see the whole picture. I'm not normally a perfectionist, far from it, I find beauty in all the tiny little imperfections that are created in the clay. It all adds to the final creation, but this time it seems to be wrong. I need everything to be as perfect as I can get it, and that meant that I restarted more times than I should have.

The bedroom ceiling lights up and I turn my head towards my mobile, groaning as the muscles in my neck tighten with the movement. I shouldn't have sat for so long but I lost track of time. My body can't do anything for too long before it starts complaining and I feel like a ninety year old. It's better now than it was a year ago and I'm hoping with my new training regime it will keep improving. I've never really been into exercise but I'm actually enjoying using the running machine that my parents bought for me and maybe one day I'll be brave enough to run outside.

Reaching out I pick up my mobile that's now gone dark, I didn't check it when I came in earlier because truthfully there's no point. The only people that ever get in touch with me are my parents and my brother but I spoke to my mum this morning and my brother usually just texts. I press the home button and look at the email notification that had caused the screen to light up. It's some rubbish from a dating site that assures me that the love of my life is just waiting for me to join. I laugh at it, thinking how fucking little they know about me. I delete the email and I'm about to put my phone down when a message notification catches my eye. I open up the text and smile when I see that it's from Mr James at the newspaper office offering me the job. As nervous as I am about taking him up on his offer, I find that I'm actually excited about the opportunity.

I message Mr James back, telling him I would love to accept his offer, and I get ready to close my phone so I can get some sleep when I take a moment to check my call log. It's a habit I've gotten into just in case I miss a call throughout the day. My eyes freeze on the missed call and a cold feeling instantly spreads through my body, making my heart skip in my chest. My fear is irrational but I have no control over the way it grips me over such a simple thing. I know that there are a million reasons for an unknown number to have called me but I can't seem to get my brain to latch on to a rational thought. All I can see in my mind is Micah's face and that has me scrambling out of bed and into my bathroom. I turn the cold tap on, grabbing handfuls of the freezing water and splash it on my face. I look in the mirror that's in front of me and I'm met with my ghostly white reflection. My skin has gone pale but my eyes are dark, the shadows of past pain clear in them

Memories flash quickly through my mind and a sob escapes me as I'm transported right back where I don't want to go. The need to block them out has me pulling open the medicine cabinet and pushing pill bottles out of the way so I can reach the medication I'm looking for. The bottle is nearly full because I hate taking them, they knock me out completely and leave me to the mercy of my dreams. I'm not worried about that tonight, that's what I want to happen because maybe my mind will settle and the flashbacks will stop. I grab a glass and fill it with the still running cold water, taking the Valium and hoping I will wake in the morning and not remember any of this.

I blink my eyes open but close them quickly when the bright lights overhead nearly blind me. I try to open them again but the struggle hurts so I give up for a moment. Instead I try to move but my entire body screams out in pain making me freeze instantly. A groan works its way through my chest but I can't hear it so I'm hopeful that I managed to stay quiet. Micah hates it when I make a fuss after he's taught me a lesson, and going by the pain I'm feeling, the lesson was for something big this time.

I try to remember what happened before I fell asleep but nothing comes to mind. In fact I can't remember anything before waking up a few moments ago. I take a deep breath and force my eyes open, blinking the tears away as I finally get my eyes to widen fully. I'm met with a bright white ceiling that I don't recognise with strip lighting that doesn't belong in my bedroom. I roll my head to see if I can work out where I am but I'm stopped in my tracks when my eyes connect with my parents who are in the seats next to my bed. They are both asleep in their chairs but they don't look at peace. I can see tension in their face, their foreheads showing lines as they dream, and I worry about what them being here means.

I feel my chest start to rise and fall rapidly as my breathing comes faster and faster when I realise where I am. The horrible peach walls, the rough sheets that are covering my body and the unmistakable disinfectant smell tells me that I'm in hospital, but if I am then why are my parents here? Every other time Micah has gone too far he's either bandaged me up himself or has taken me to an A&E outside the city. I turn to look at the other side of the bed, fully expecting to find Micah sitting there but the seat is filled with the large body of my brother, Roscoe. Terror starts to grow inside me as I wonder where Micah is. There's no way he would call my parents after injuring me enough for a hospital visit and there's also no way in hell he would leave me alone with them even if he had.

I try to sit up but the pain in my head and neck stops me immediately. I try to stay quiet so I don't wake my family up, but when I look towards my parents again my dad's eyes are open wide as he sits up quickly. He shakes my mum awake before walking towards me with tears in his eyes. His lips move and it actually takes me a few moments of watching him to notice that I can't hear anything he's saying. I screw up my face as I concentrate on my dad's face. I stare at his lips as he keeps talking, his hands running gently over my face and shoulders.

Why can't I hear him?

My mum appears next to him with tears streaming down her face and she kisses my face gently, her hands stroking over my cheeks as her lips move quickly. I know she's speaking but no sound is reaching my ears and I can feel the start of a panic attack coming. I look past my parents to the room around me. There's so much going on that I should be able to hear, the television on the wall showing an old black and white movie, the heart rate monitor that I'm attached to that should be beeping, and my brother who is awake and by my side, his lips moving as he speaks in what I know will be a loud volume, but there's just silence. My entire head is quiet apart from my own thoughts that are currently zooming through it at lightning speed. I shouldn't be able to hear my thoughts as clearly as I can when there's so much happening around me. I should be able to hear my parent's voices, the noise of the hospital and I should even be able to hear the annoying buzzing from the strip light above me but there's nothing.

I feel tears on my cheeks as I look at my mum. I can see the moment she knows that something is wrong. I hate that she looks so worried after everything she's already been through but panic has me speaking to them, asking why I'm here. I don't know if they can hear me because the words are silent even to me, and suddenly I reach out to grab my mum's hand. She holds me tight, the look of confusion clear on her face. I want to explain, to take my time so she doesn't get upset when I try to tell her what's wrong, but I cant stop the words from bursting out of me with an edge of hysteria.

"I can't hear anything. Oh god, why can't I hear anything?"

I sit bolt upright in bed, the memories of my dream still flooding my brain. I can feel drops of sweat running down my spine and it causes goose bumps to explode over my entire body. I collapse back onto my pillow as fatigue grabs at me and cover my eyes with my arm to block out the bright sunshine that's flooding my room. The morning after taking Valium always feels like I have the world's worst hangover, and the pounding feeling in my head is another reason that I hate taking them. I haven't actually taken any for about six months and I thought I was doing well without them. So well that I was actually considering getting rid of them, but last night proved that all it takes is one little setback, and I need the safety that the tiny little tablet provides.

I throw the duvet off and sit on the edge of my bed, scrubbing my hands over my face as I try to rid myself of the last traces of sleep. I feel like I barely slept last night and the lack of sleep has me feeling on edge. I often dream about that day when I woke in the hospital, the day my entire life changed, but it never seems to make the incident any easier to cope with. Everything changed that day and when the doctors explained to me about my hearing loss I thought my life couldn't get any worse. I just didn't know that I was wrong, so very fucking wrong.

Chapter Three

Kohan

"Did Robert tell you he finally found a cleaner for the office?"

I go still with my beer bottle half way to my mouth when Sophie speaks. I don't think she realises what she's just said, and no one else would probably notice but I did. "Since when do you call Mr James by his first name?"

It's Sophie's turn to freeze with her eyes wide open and her mouth gaping like a fish out of water. "I… uh… shit."

I knew it. I asked her a few weeks ago if there was something between her and Mr James and she told me I was insane. I should've known better than to be thrown off the scent by her, especially with the way they were looking at each other. People who are just colleagues don't have that amount of heat in their eyes. Dammit, I can't believe that I let her throw me off the scent . "I fucking knew it. You told me I was imagining it and had me doubting myself. I can't believe you're shagging Mr James."

"Will you shut your face? The whole freaking bar doesn't need to know about me and Robert… shit… Mr James." She drops her head to the table and bangs it a few times. I would love to tell her that it's okay and that sleeping with the boss isn't that big a deal, but she gave me so much shit when I hooked up with a photographer we used for an article. She'd gone on and on about me being unprofessional, how I would get a name for myself in the business. She was giving me a hard time just to be a bitch, but now I think it's time to have a little fun with Miss Owen.

"Are you hoping to get a promotion? Has he offered you a special *position*?" It takes everything in me not to burst out laughing at myself. I'm just too funny sometimes.

Sophie raises her head and glares at me in the way that only she can. She might be small with her red hair and freckles that make her look kind of innocent, but get her riled up and you will suffer the consequences. That's actually how we became best friends. We were out with a few work colleagues one night when a random guy took exception to me being gay. I'm not even sure how he knew but when our group got outside the lovely gentleman started hurling abuse in my direction. It wasn't anything that I hadn't heard before and I was a little disappointed that he hadn't thought of something original. He'd just finished calling me a shirt lifter when this blur of red hair came from behind me and kicked him square in the nuts. I stood in shock for a few minutes while I watched this tiny woman beat the crap out of this big bruiser of a guy. When I came to my senses I went in to save the guy before she could hurt him too badly. I had to pry her arms from around his throat but eventually I managed to get her off his back. She gave him a foot in the kidneys before she finally gave up. I'm not sure what sort of classes she took but I'm pretty sure the kidney shot had the guy pissing blood for a while.

I dragged her away by the arm, leaving the stranger to be cared for by the rest of our group. I'd only said a few words to Sophie throughout the evening and most of them were just to be polite, but she was the first to stand up for me when someone started shit. "Feel better?"

She suddenly burst out laughing at me as we continued to walk. "Did you see his eyes when I got him in the nuts? I thought he was gonna puke." She smiled widely at me and I couldn't miss the look of pride that's on her face.

"Are you naturally a thug or was there a reason you handed him his arse?"

She put her arm through mine, cuddling into my side as we made it to the taxi queue. "No one messes with my friends, even if they have the worst dress sense in the world."

That night we became fast friends and she's been my rock ever since. That doesn't mean that I won't use anything I can to wind her up, even if my balls are at risk if I take it too far.

"I said shut up. I'm not sleeping with him, I *slept* with him. It was a one-night thing after the 'Kids with Klass' awards. We both had a few too many drinks and one thing led to another."

The awards were months ago, I can't believe she didn't tell me about it. I always tell her about who I've slept with, usually whether I want to or not. "Hey, that was the night you were meant to come home with me but you changed your mind? What was it you said, you weren't feeling that good so you needed to go home to bed?"

"I did go home to bed, just not alone. Please don't tell anyone, it would cause so many problems for Robert."

I scrunch my face up as I try to work out why it would cause so many problems. I know I joked about her wanting a promotion but she's a fashion blogger for the newspaper, there's no benefit to her job by sleeping with her boss. There might be a few people we work with that would have a little snarky comment about it but no one would really care. "Not that I would ever tell anyone, but you know no one would care, sweetheart. Especially if it was just a one time thing."

"It was. We've seen each other a few times since then but I told him I couldn't be with him again while he was still married."

I choke on my mouthful of beer as I swallow and it goes down the wrong way. I didn't know Robert was in a relationship never mind married and I can't believe that Sophie went there with him if she knew. She hates cheaters with a passion so it's the last thing I'd expect from her. "Married? Sophie, have you lost your fucking mind?"

She holds up her hands to stop me from saying anything else. "I know, okay? It was stupid and impulsive. My only defence is that his divorce proceedings had started a few days before it happened. That's actually the reason it happened. He was pissed off that he got served at work and we started chatting about it. By the time Kids With Klass came around he just wanted to blow off a little steam and I was happy to help. What we didn't expect was to actually enjoy each other's company. We've just been hanging out since." Her face gets this dreamy look on it and it becomes obvious that she's falling for him.

"Wow, you really like him don't you? What happened to no man would ever be able to control you? I thought you were like the wind and can't be tamed?" Okay, she had quoted that rubbish when she was pissed but I knew there would be a time when I could use it to my advantage.

She drops her head to the table again which causes her voice to come out muffled when she speaks. "I know. Please don't be a dick about it."

I want to carry on and act like she does when she gets some ammunition, but the defeated tone of her voice has me moving my chair closer to her. I wrap my arm around her shoulder and lean my chin on the top of her head. "Come on. It's not that bad. I've known lots of people that have fallen in love, and some of them had a happy life."

Her hand comes over to my knee and her nails dig in as she gives me a horse bite. I grit my teeth so I don't cry out in the middle of the busy bar and reach over with my other arm to try and loosen her hold on me. "I'm sorry, okay. Let go." The only way to get her to release her grip is to apologise. I've tried to get her off me before but her hands are like vises. Like I said, she's stronger than she looks. Thankfully she releases my leg and I spend a few moments rubbing the aching muscles. "You are a dangerous bitch, you know that?"

She smiles sweetly at me now that's she's lifted her head off the table. "And you're a dick but I have to live with it."

"I've told you before I can't be a dick … dicks are useful."

This finally gets a real laugh from her. She grabs her beer bottle and takes a really long swallow, finishing it in one drink. "Let's change the subject; there's a new cleaner at the office."

I want more information about her relationship with Robert but I think that maybe a tub of ice cream and two spoons would be the best thing to accompany that conversation instead of a packed bar. "When does she start?"

Sophie signals the passing waitress and holds up her empty bottle. The waitress nods before moving to the bar. "Not she. He. And he starts on Monday night after the offices close."

"Who is it?" I'm pretty confident that I will know the guy because with my job and the small size of the town, I've met the majority of people who live here.

"Don't know him. Apparently he's new to the area and lives out on Smithy Road."

I think about the houses that run along the quiet road down towards the quarry and I know instantly what house it must be. Mrs Brown has stayed in the cottage closest to the town for what I've been told is about fifty years and she has no plans on leaving. The second is owned by Helen who runs Lettuce Eat so that only leaves the house furthest from the town. It's quiet, isolated and has been empty for a long time. I didn't even realise that someone had moved in there. "I thought that place was still empty. When did he move in?"

"How would I know? Robert only said that the guy was starting on Monday, he didn't give me his whole bio."

I resist the urge to give her the finger. She's been touchier than normal tonight and I want to know why. I'm just about to ask her but she doesn't let me speak.

"Don't go there. I'm premenstrual and it's not safe to talk about it. Let me finish this bottle then I'm going home."

"You know I'm going to find out why you're a grump so you might as well tell me. I don't believe for one second that it's because it's that time of the month, that doesn't usually make you this much of a bitch."

"Not happening. Oh, and the guy's name is … shit what was it again?" She looks at the ceiling and I know that she's trying to drag it out so I won't have time to question her about her mood.

"You're easy to read, Sophie. I know exactly what you're doing."

"Andy, no Archie. I can't remember but it was something like that. Robert said he had his interview this week and he wanted to hire him on the spot."

This week? I wonder if that was the guy I ran into on my way to my office the other night? He vanished so quickly I didn't even have a chance to ask him why he was there. Hell I didn't get a chance to find out if he was hurt before he ran off. "I think I saw him."

She turns to look at me. "You did? You didn't mention anything to me, what did he look like?"

Dark haunted eyes invade my mind and heat suddenly spreads through my body without permission. There was something in those eyes that made me want to hold the guy and it's not something I'm able to explain. I've met a lot of people with my job that have been through all sorts of horrific accidents and experiences, and I never wanted to protect them the way I did in that two minute contact I had with this stranger. I pull myself together and shake my head to clear my thoughts. "I didn't mention it because I forgot. I literally bumped into him in the corridor and said sorry. He kept his head down and didn't stick around long enough for me to get a good look at him."

She looks disappointed at my lack of information but there's nothing much I can tell. "Oh well, I guess I might see him hanging around one night."

The thought of seeing this guy actually has excitement fluttering through my stomach. *What the hell?* I saw him for like two minutes, he didn't even speak to me but still I can't wait to see him around the office. It's official, I'm losing my bloody mind.

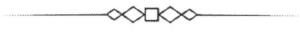

"Did you know, you're my bestest friend ever. You need to find a hot gay man to have sex with. You need to get sexed up until you can't walk properly." Sophie snorts before continuing. "I was gonna say until you can't walk straight but I don't think you can do that anyway."

It's now my turn to laugh because drunk Sophie is a very funny Sophie. She loses her filter when she's drunk, even though she has very little filter when sober. "I can't believe you said that to me."

She stops abruptly and looks up at me in horror. "Shouldn't I have said that? Oh god, was that me being homophobic?"

Is she being serious? I've never met anyone as accepting as Sophie. The only thing she will ever judge you for is being an arsehole. I pull her to get us moving again and lean down to kiss her head. "No, honey. Not homophobic, just funny."

She relaxes against my side again and staggers along the pavement. "Good, cause I love you the way you are. And I mean what I said. You need to go out and find someone to fall in love with. You're too a nice guy to be alone."

It's the same conversation we have whenever we go out together. Every time she has more than a few drinks she feels the need to sort out my love life, and even though I know she means well, the topic gets really boring after a while. It's like she thinks that I don't want to find someone and that I want to be alone all my life but I don't. I want someone to come home to, someone who will share all my highs and lows. I want someone to love me. The biggest problem with it all is that I'm the only gay in the town. Okay, that might be a slight exaggeration but I am the only single gay man here. Okay, again I'm lying to myself, but Lamont is a fifty year old queen who wears more glitter than my niece, so there's no way in hell I'm barking up that tree. He is always very touchy feely when he sees me and I admit, it creeps me out on a cellular level.

"Next time we go out we'll hit up 'Toppers'. We haven't been there in so long and it's the perfect place for you to meet someone hot."

Toppers is a gay nightclub in Greenview, the next city over from Tonbridge where we live. It's the best place to go if I want to hook up but I haven't been in such a long time. Life always just seems so busy lately, but I think Sophie might be right, a night out should be planned soon.

"Yeah, we'll get that organised."

I feel her bounce a little in her steps so I know I've said the right thing. We walk the last few yards to Sophie's front door and I grab her bag to find her keys. I locate them quickly and unlock the door before pushing it open. She turns in my arms and grabs my face with her hands.

"You are too wonderful to be alone. I can't fall in love with Robert if I think you'll be alone." She sounds serious and I feel a lump growing in my throat.

This is what she was avoiding telling me earlier. She's falling for Robert and she doesn't want to. I know Sophie better than she knows herself and if she is falling in love it will be scaring the shit out of her. She doesn't do relationships, or at least hasn't in the time I've known her, and she always swore she wouldn't settle down. The thing is now that I know about it, I think Robert would be an amazing match for her. He's strong willed and probably wouldn't let her get away with her usual crap.

"Find someone. I mean it."

I lean forward and kiss her on the cheek. "Go to bed and I will call you in the morning." I pull her hands off my cheeks and push her into her hallway.

"I'm not kidding here, Kohan."

I pull the door closed making sure I wait until I hear her turn the lock. When it sounds I turn around and make my way back down the path to the street. It was nice to be able to walk tonight and I know that I need to get out more now that the weather is changing for the better. Being stuck behind a desk most of the day writing has turned my once firm body slightly softer around the middle and I'm not liking the change. When I worked in London I would hit the gym next door to my office at least once a day. I needed to look amazing to compete with all the other gay men in the area. God, some of the men in the nightclubs looked like they walked right off a fitness magazine cover. The rest of us mere mortals had to do everything we could to keep up. Here in Tonbridge there aren't any gyms other than the one at the high school and I really don't want to work out with a bunch of teens.

    I really need to get back into running. It's the thing I enjoyed the most when I was a gym bunny and I don't have a decent excuse for not getting outside and putting some miles on my trainers. That's it; come Monday I will cut an hour out of the day just to get out there. Monday will be a new week and things will change.

Chapter Four

Kohan

I stare at my computer screen as my mobile starts to ring. I look at the screen before I accept the call so I know who it is before I answer it. "Hey, Mum. What's up?" I hate to ask her because it opens up a whole world of possibilities. I love my mum, I really do, but she's a touch on the dramatic side. Ever since my dad died it feels like it's been one thing after another and it gets tiring after a while. It started when she was convinced that her neighbour, the one that she's lived next to for nearly ten years, had been taking pictures of her. Turns out he was actually taking pictures of his roses for an online gardening club. Then there was the time that she thought the patch of dry skin on her back was a sign that she had skin cancer. It took three doctors to convince her that she was suffering from contact dermatitis and that she should go back to her old washing powder.

"Did you get the interview you wanted the other day?"

I'm impressed that she remembered that I'd spoken about trying to get a chance to talk to Mr Hanes, usually she doesn't pay that much attention. "Yeah I got a great story out of it. Who doesn't want to read about a robbery?"

"Why do you have to chase these silly stories? You spent all that time studying and all you do is write about school events and people running red lights."

I look to the sky and ask for patience. I've explained this to her so many times but she never seems to hear what I'm saying. I had to leave that life behind me because the stress wasn't good for me and it turned me into someone I didn't want to be. All she saw was my name in the popular paper and in her mind that should make me happy. She loves me and wants me to do something big with my life, and she doesn't understand that I'm happy without all the big accomplishments. "I love this job. It might not win me any huge awards, but I'm happy and that's all I want. I had enough of the big city, Mum, it wasn't good for me."

"I know, I just worry about you. I want you to be happy, maybe settle down and have a family. There has to be a nice girl out there just waiting to meet you."

"Mum."

"Boy, sorry, a nice boy."

She doesn't mean anything by the slip up. She's probably the least homophobic person I've ever met, but sometimes she gets things muddled up in her head. I'm the youngest of five brothers and the only gay one. Her memory isn't working the same as it used to and she's been getting a little muddled about things so I expect a little slip-up now and again.

"Any way, I called to see if you are coming next weekend? Damien is coming with the baby and I know you'll want to see him."

Damien is my eldest brother and he's just had his second child with his wife Heidi. I haven't managed to see his second daughter yet so this would be a great chance to do just that, even if the thought of all my brothers in one place scares me a little. My brothers have made a bit of a reputation for themselves over the years and even though they have grown up a bit and settled down, it still follows them around. The Weston brothers were known to raise hell, and the whole town knew it. It wasn't as if we did anything illegal, but if there was ever a fight to be broken up or an injury to be cleaned up, one of my brothers was usually involved.

"Yeah, I'll be there. It will be nice to finally meet my niece." Damien's daughters are the first girls in the family for a long time, and they are spoiled accordingly.

"That's great. I should let you go, though. Oh, while I remember, did you get the interview with that man about the robbery?"

My stomach churns when she repeats the question. I've noticed that she's forgetting things more and more and becoming confused recently. I've mentioned it to my brothers, but Carey, my older brother who still lives with her, says the doctor isn't worried. I'm not convinced with his diagnosis of stress, but I'll leave it for now. If it gets any worse then I'm taking her to the doctor myself and demanding answers.

"Yeah I did, Mum. It was just what I wanted."

I can almost hear her smile over the phone as she speaks, and it's the only thing that settles my nerves. "That's good, sweetheart. I will let you go. See you at the weekend." She blows me a kiss before hanging up.

I sit back in my chair and stare at the blank wall across my office. My gut says that I should push to get my mum to see a specialist but my brothers tell me I'm being dramatic. I don't think Carey sees it because he sees her every day and it's just become a part of daily life. Maybe when Damien and Emile see her at the weekend they'll see that I'm not just being overly protective and that there is something wrong with her. The only person that's on my side is Jensen but with us being the younger brothers he doesn't say anything. He isn't big on confrontation and will do anything for an easy life.

A knock on my door pulls me from my thoughts of my mum and I shout to come in.

"Hey, Koho."

I look up to see Sophia standing leaning against my office door. "Don't call me that, Soso."

She grits her teeth before sauntering into my office and collapsing into the chair in front of my desk. "I hate it when you call me that."

I laugh because I feel exactly the same way. I hate it when people shorten my name, she knows this but does it anyway. "I wonder what that's like?" I raise my eyebrows and she smiles. "What can I do for you, Sophie?"

"Mr James wants to see you. He said to get your arse into his office ASAP."

I should just leave but I can't miss the chance to annoy Sophie when the opportunity presents itself. "Oh, we're back to Mr

James are we? Did we have a lover's tiff or just trying to be professional?"

Sophie's right eye starts twitching and it's a clear sign that I've got to her. It's also a warning that I should watch my back for a while. "I really don't know why I'm still your friend. Now move you arse before *Mr James* gets pissed off with you, we both know he has no patience." She gets up from the chair and exits my office, shutting the door un-naturally quietly behind her which scares me more than if she threw a fit. Yeah, I really need to watch my back.

I get up from my seat and close over my laptop before leaving my office and heading down the hall towards Mr James' office. With the way my day's going so far, in my mind, Mr James is calling me in to fire me. It all started to go wrong the minute my alarm went off, or should I say the thirty minutes after my alarm when I finally decided to wake up. After getting showered and dressed, I was delayed even longer because I couldn't find my keys. It took far too long to find them, in the freezer of all places, which meant that I ended up driving to work instead of just walking. Add to that the call from my mum and now Mr James wanting to see me. I think today can go down as an epic disaster.

I knock on his office door and wait for him to tell me to come in. When he does, I push the door open and pop my head around to see him sitting at his desk with his head looking down. "You wanted to see me?"

"Come in, Kohan. I was just reading over the article you sent me."

I swallow hard as I take the seat across from him, suddenly worried that I took the story in the wrong direction. "Was it that bad?"

Mr James looks at me, confused for just a moment before he shakes his head at me. "No, God no. It's just not what you usually write. It's really bloody good. I'm running it but not in your usual column, I want it to be on page two."

My heart starts to race as he speaks. My normal column is in the second half of the paper so to make it to page two is … well it's really fucking impressive. I never imagined I'd ever write anything eye catching enough to get the recognition that the main reporters do. I moved here knowing that I would be writing articles that wouldn't get to the front page but that's never been a problem because it means I'm not under the same pressure as the other reporters. If I'm honest with myself now, I remember why I liked my pervious job. The high of getting a story into the paper that isn't just filler. "Page two? Really? Will the other reporters be okay with that?" I don't want to step on anyone toes because this is a friendly place to work and I don't suddenly want to be the dick who steals people columns.

"It's fine. Liam's running late with his article because his contact didn't come through so his story isn't finished. I have space and need something to fill it. I want this story, and I want you to do something similar for next week."

I sit in silence, unsure how to respond, especially when Mr James turns back to his computer and starts typing. He spends a few moments ignoring me before he turns back to look at me.

"Well you won't get a story sitting there. Chop chop."

I stand up mutely now that I've been dismissed and I walk to the door. Just before I leave I turn back to face him. "Mr James?" He looks at me again and I smile. "Thank you." He just nods and I walk out without saying anything else.

I'm still in shock when sit down at my desk. I'm excited to have the opportunity to write another article like the one about Matt, but I have no fucking clue what to write about. The story about Matt pretty much fell into my lap while listening to gossip and I doubt I'll be that lucky again. I could do a follow up story about him to see if he is being more accepted, but I'd need to leave it for a few weeks before I can do that.

I pick up the small stress ball from my desk and lean back in my chair until I'm looking at the ceiling. I throw the ball into the air and catch it as I think about all the possible stories I could cover. Some sort of school achievement? No, that's been done so many times before that it would be boring. What about a scandal involving someone the town knows well? Nope, nothing like that ever happens around here unless you count Mr Lee pretending that the vegetables he was selling were homegrown. What he was actually doing was travelling to a little farm a few miles out of Greenview and buying them there. Not really newspaper worthy.

    I need to get out and start listening to people talk. Tomorrow I should spend the day at The Fly Cup café and pay attention to the gossip. I don't know how some of these women get their information but they seem to know things before anyone else does. These women don't know how invaluable their gossip is to me, its led me to some pretty interesting stories before and I hope it will again.

    I turn off my computer and stretch my hands over my head. I look out the window and see that day has turned into night while I worked on the editorial story that's due on Thursday. Time seems to be constantly slipping away from me these days and I'm not sure how. When it came to work I used to be super organised but these last few weeks I've felt all that slip away. Even the running that I promised myself that I would do hasn't happened, and now I'm going to miss another night of it.

    I put my laptop into my messenger bag and grab my coat, putting it on before pulling the bag over my shoulder so it's sitting diagonally across my chest. After turning off the light I pull the door closed securely behind me. I never lock it because there's nothing in there that anyone could possibly want. I take everything of importance home every night, my laptop and all the stories I'm writing, so there is nothing worth stealing in here. It also means I can work on things at home, which hasn't been happening much recently. *Maybe that's why I'm so far behind?* Sighing I walk down the corridor to the elevator, happy to finally be going home.

    When I turn the corner I see the lift door closing. I pick up my pace to try and catch it so I don't have to wait for it to come back up to this floor, or God forbid, take the stairs. I manage to get my hand between the doors and stop them from closing. I slip my body between them when they are wide enough and when I step inside I see that I'm not alone. Standing in the corner with his eyes facing the floor is the guy I bumped into last week. The cleaning uniform that he's wearing tells me that I had made the right guess when I was speaking to Sophie. I face the doors as they close and try to come up with something to say to break the silence. It would be easier if he would stop staring at the floor, I could just say hi when he looks at me, but he doesn't look up.

Finally the silence gets to me and I can't keep quiet any longer. "Are you enjoying the new job?" I'm met with more silence and as I look at the guy he doesn't even acknowledge that I've spoken to him. It's pretty shitty of him to be so ignorant, especially when he's new to the company. You'd think that he would want to be polite to his new work colleagues. I'm moving before I even think about it, only noticing when I'm standing toe to toe with him. This gets his attention and his eyes open wide as they connect with mine and I see him cower back into the corner. I would feel bad but I'm too pissed off to let it affect me. I don't even know why I'm so annoyed, people have ignored me before, but this is the second time that he's blown me off and for some reason it bothers me. "You know when someone talks to you it's polite to answer them. Pretending you can't hear them is just childish."

He looks at me with a confused expression as I spit the words at him but still he doesn't answer. What do I have to do to get this guy to talk to me? Why is it bothering me so much that he won't let me hear his voice?

I can see the guy from the other night speaking but I took my hearing aids out earlier when I was hoovering and I didn't put them back in. He looks pissed and memories of another angry man has me wanting to bolt from the lift. My palms are sweating and fear has my throat threatening to close up. His lips continue to move and I struggle to read them. I'm not great at that yet especially when the person is talking fast. I manage to make out something about ignoring him and being childish.

He stops talking and stands there just staring at me. He must have asked a question and is waiting for an answer. I get as close to the back wall as I can and look to see what floor we are on, panicking growing further inside me when I notice we that we've stopped on the first floor. The doors behind him open and I'm tempted to make a run for it but he's standing directly in front of me stealing my escape route.

I close my eyes and repeat the mantra that I started a few years ago when I started therapy. It was in hopes that one day I would feel confident enough to believe it. *I am safe. I am strong. Not every man will hurt me. I am safe. I am strong. Not every man will hurt me.* I need to calm down, listen to the words that I'm saying, because if I'm going to work here I'll have to interact with the workers and I need to stop being so scared.

Opening my eyes I reach into my pocket and grab my hearing aids, taking a few moments to put them in and turn them on. When I look up again the guy has lost all the colour on his face and looks like he's going to be sick.

"Oh my god. I am so fucking sorry. I'm standing here calling you all sorts and you can't hear me. I'm such a dickhead. Jesus." He continues to mutter under his breath but the volume is too low for me to hear. At least now I know to be grateful that I missed what he was saying to me. He looks upset at what's happening though, and for some reason that bothers me so I finally speak.

"It's okay, you didn't know. I should wear them when I'm here."

His head flies up and his eyes connect directly with mine. The intensity in his them make me want to take a step back but there's nowhere left for me to go. "So you do have a voice." His head tilts to the side slightly and the edge of his mouth turns up into a smile.

I feel myself relax as some of the tension leaves his face, but I can't calm down fully, it's not in my nature anymore. "I have a voice, there's just usually no-one around to hear it." *Way to sound like a pathetic* loser. I've basically just admitted that I have no friends.

Instead of laughing at me he holds his hand out and I stare at it for far too long. "I promise I won't bite." I know he thinks he's being funny but it's a little close to the actual fear I have. Micah was always fond of leaving teeth marks as a way of claiming me, and I still have scars from the time he bit a little too deeply.

"I'm kidding, don't look so worried. I'm Kohan and I'm a reporter here."

I shake my head at how pathetic I'm being. This is a colleague just wanting to introduce himself and I need to get a grip of my nerves. "Ares. It's nice to meet you, Kohan."

His returning smile lights up his entire face and I find myself smiling without meaning to. Now that he's not glaring at me he looks kind and it helps me relax a little more. The lift pings and a second later the doors open, making me jump a little because I didn't even feel it moving. Kohan turns and looks at them, looking almost disappointed that our time is up. I'm not the person that people want to spend time with, I was taught that a long time ago. Some people are meant to have lots of friends and some are meant to be like me. Alone.

I follow Kohan out of the elevator and towards the main doors, leaving a bigger distance between us than most people would call normal. He waves at the night guard and I feel a little bit of envy that he's the kind of person people seem to get along with. I've been working here for a few nights now and the guard has barely noticed me.

Kohan holds open the glass door for me and I exit, making sure that my body doesn't get too close to his. While I've been working it's started raining, creating huge puddles on the pavements. Shit. I'm going to have to walk home in this without a raincoat. The weather was lovely when I walked to work earlier so I only wore my lighter jacket.

"Do you have a car?"

I shake my head as I pull my collar up to try and protect myself from the rain. I really don't want to get wet; it messes with my hearing aids and it takes a lot of work to get them working normally again.

"Want a lift?"

I can feel the usual worry start to build inside me with this simple question. It shouldn't stress me out so much; it's a simple offer from someone who works where I do. Nothing more, nothing less. I stick my hands into my pockets to try and hide the tremor that's causing them to shake. "It's fine, I don't have that far too walk."

"You'll be soaked by the time you get down Smithy Road. Honestly, I don't mind."

White noise starts to hum in my ears and my sight focuses on Kohan's lips. How does he know where I live? I haven't told him and I don't know him. Did Micah send him to keep an eye on me until … until he's able to come for me himself? I need to run, I need to get away.

Chapter Five

Ares

"What did I say? Why do you look so scared?"

Kohan's hands fly up in front of him like he's trying to calm a frightened animal, and I would laugh if that wasn't essentially what he's doing right now. I'm about a minute away from running down the street screaming but before I make a complete idiot of myself, I want the answer to one question. "How do you know where I live?"

He doesn't look like he's trying to think too hard about his answer and that hopefully means he's not trying to think of a lie. Or maybe he already had a lie all planned out? "My best friend, Sophie works here too, she mentioned that the new cleaner lived on Smithy Road. The only empty house down there is the old Fletcher house so I figured that's where you live."

His answer sounds reasonable but I don't know. It could be a well thought out lie to get me in his car. Maybe he'd planned to try and get me alone all along and the rain has just worked to his advantage. No, if he had been sent by Micah he would know that I was deaf. He didn't lie about not knowing that, he honestly looked ashamed by the way he spoke to me.

"Look we can go in and talk to Chris, you know, the night guard. He'll tell you my address and he'll tell you that I'm not some sort of weirdo. You can also tell him I'm taking you home so you have someone who knows who you left with." He sounds so sincere as he speaks and that helps me to believe him, but I don't know if it's enough to get me in his car. Common sense tells me that if he really was a danger he could get to me without me getting in his car since he knows where I live.

I let out a small snort of laughter when I think about the

direction my thoughts are going. This is exactly what my therapist told me I needed to stop doing. I need to believe that I'm finally safe because if I don't I'll end up spending the rest of my life jumping at shadows that aren't there. It's easy in theory, but now standing here in front of Kohan, who's done nothing to deserve my mistrust, I'm finding that it's easier to talk about than do.

"Is making you laugh a good thing? Look I don't want to pressure you, but I also don't want you to catch the flu. We spent a long time cleaning up after ourselves in there and I don't want to go back to that." That little curl of his lip is back and it shouldn't make me feel comfortable but it does. His entire face lights up when he's being playful and it makes it hard to believe he would do anything to harm anyone.

"Do you promise not to drive me into the woods and kill me?" Even though I try to sound like I'm making a joke, I know the words come out shaky.

Kohan puts his hand on his heart and holds the other in the air like he's taking an oath. "I Kohan Weston, do solemnly swear not to take Ares ... what's your last name?"

"Masterson."

He nods before continuing. "Ares Masterson into the woods and kill him. I swear to drive him home and make sure he gets into his house in one piece. All safe and sound."

His words have me laughing loudly. I don't know what it is about him but he puts me at ease and I've never felt this relaxed with someone this quickly before. Even when I first met Micah I took a while to feel comfortable around him, there was just this air of power about him and I knew that he was in control. Kohan seems to be a genuinely kind man who just wants to make people happy. "Thank you, I would love a lift home."

He smiles as he backs away. "Stay here and I'll grab my car, it's just up the road. It will save both of us getting wet."

I try to tell him not to be silly, that the least I can do is go with him, but he runs off before I can speak. A few moments later a car pulls up at the kerb in front of me and the passenger door is pushed open. I take a quick second to look at the little red Ford before running across the pavement and into the waiting car. When I get in I'm already soaked to the bone even from the tiny distance. I shake my head and cover the car in rain. "Shit, I'm sorry." I look over to Kohan and see the rain dripping off him.

"I think that might be a moot point now. There's a not dry part of me and that includes my tighty whiteys."

A vision of Kohan in his just his underwear comes out of nowhere and I look away, scared that he can see exactly what's going on in my head. I want to pretend to myself that I haven't noticed how Kohan looks, even if he is one of the sexiest guys I think I've ever seen. It's not just his kindness that speaks to me, he has this thick hair that is the colour of straw, slightly golden but with a brown undertone. His eyes are a warm caramel colour and they're what caught my attention the first time we bumped into each other. He's slightly taller than me which should make me shy away from him, but instead it makes me want to feel his arms around me, protecting me.

Wow. I didn't realise that I was still capable of thoughts like that. I haven't wanted to be touched by anyone since the last time Micah hit me, not even my parents can hug me without me flinching internally. This feeling is very new and I'm not sure what to make of it, but I'm sure my therapist will. I need to call him soon to talk.

"Right, let's get you home before we both freeze to death." He reaches out, presses two buttons on the dashboard and a few moments later the seat below me starts to heat and I relax into it.

"Thank you for this. I know I acted weird when you asked but I'm glad you talked me into it. It's really nice not to have to walk home in this because it messes with my hearing aids. You've saved me a lot of hassle in the next few days."

Kohan looks at me briefly as he drives down the road slowly trying to avoid the large puddles. "You're welcome. You're lucky because I normally walk in as well, but this morning I had the worst case of *couldn't be arsed* and slept in. I would have been ridiculously late if I had walked."

"Do you live close to the office?" I want to pretend that I'm just being polite but I find myself actually wanting to know where he lives. I haven't had a friend in a long time and speaking to someone who isn't my family is kind of nice.

"Not too far, maybe a mile or so. Do you know where Murray Park is?"

I nod but forget that he won't be able to see me with his eyes on the road. "Yeah, isn't that across from the high school?"

"That's the one. Well I live on the street next to that. The houses aren't huge but they have pretty big gardens. That's what sold it for me. I like to have a lot of outside space."

That's one thing I love about my little cottage. The back garden opens out into the forest that runs behind my property. With that on one side and a dirt track on the other, it makes me feel like I'm on my own. "I like space. The world can get a little too noisy for me and space usually means quiet." So it looks like I'm going for being open tonight. That's an interesting turn of events, especially when I don't usually tell anyone about myself.

Kohan stares intently at the road as he chews his bottom lip. He looks like he's thinking hard about something and I'm waiting for him to spit out whatever it is that he wants to ask. I've seen people like this before and usually I shut down, but I internally bolster my confidence so I can try and answer anything he throws at me. "Were you born deaf? Shit, sorry. I shouldn't have asked that."

Now I know why he looked so torn. "It's okay. It's actually nice to have someone just ask. Most people like to pretend that it's not a thing and totally avoid any conversation about it." I stop and take a deep breath. Other than my family and the people involved with the trial, no one knows what happened to me and most assume that I was born this way. I'm not going to tell Kohan the whole truth because I'm not sure I will ever be ready for that, but I can give him a little bit of me. "I've only been deaf for about two years now. It was … an accident. Head trauma. When I woke up I couldn't hear."

"Will it ever come back?"

I shake my head again as I speak even though I know he won't see me. "The chances are slim. It might improve a little over time but doctors aren't holding out hope. It's not completely gone, I can still hear anything that's really loud or very high pitched, like car alarms and stuff. It's faint but it's there."

Kohan turns his head towards me a few times, obviously not wanting to look away from the road too long but wanting to look at me. It makes me feel a little awkward and I think he can tell because he takes a sudden change in direction with the conversation. "How long have you lived here?"

"I moved in back in June last year. Just before the summer fete."

He chuckles a little at my answer. "So over six months? How have I not seen you going about?" He stops at the end of my road and checks for traffic before turning down the dirt track. I'm suddenly a little disappointed knowing that I'm nearly home and will need to stop talking to Kohan.

"I don't leave my house much. Actually this job is an attempt to finally get out and maybe speak to another human. God, that makes me sound pathetic."

He stops the car outside my garden gate and turns to face me. "I don't think it makes you sound pathetic. I would say that you are possibly shy but I don't think it's that. I can understand hiding away if the world gets too loud for you, but you can't forget that the rest of us are out here. Maybe you might even make a friend." He winks and I laugh gently at him.

"I will keep that in mind. Thank you for the lift though, I really do appreciate it." I smile before turning away and getting out the car. I run up the path to my front door as the rain assaults me and notice that Kohan doesn't drive away until I unlock it and walk inside. When I wave he turns his car and drives away. I close the door against the rain, pretending that I don't suddenly feel lonelier than I have since I moved here.

I sit at my pottery wheel and let the wet clay mold under my fingers. I gave up on the sculpture about two hours ago, and instead went back to making vases, something that doesn't take much concentration for me. My mind is too messed up for anything more technical. I'm on my third vase with the other two drying out on the side so I can fire them later.

My mind has been full of Kohan since he drove away last night. I just can't get over how relaxed I eventually felt while he was speaking to me or the fact that I wanted to answer his questions. I maybe didn't tell him all of the sordid details of my past but it was more than I've ever given anyone else. He made me feel that I could tell him about myself without him judging me. I know I had no proof of this, and there was a good chance he was thinking I was crazy being so scared, but he just smiled at me gently and that made me not want to run. That's never happened with a stranger before and that's what's messing with me a little.

I spent the first four months after I moved here stuck inside the house because I was scared to go out and meet new people. The only time I came into contact with someone was when deliverymen brought me my groceries and when my therapist came for a home session occasionally. Even meeting with Mr James, my new boss, filled me with trepidation and that was my own decision to apply for the job. Both times I've met Kohan have been a surprise and that in itself should have had me turning in the other direction, instead I accepted a lift and told him a little about myself. For me it's a huge leap of faith even though it would seem minor to most. It almost feels like the first step in becoming normal again and I would accept the happiness what's happening, but normal still seems so far away.

I feel the drag of the clay below my skin so I wet my hands, firming up my grip as I return them to the clay. I use my fingers to press down on the centre of the smooth cylinder to start to create a vase shape by hollowing out the inside. I feel it give beneath my fingers and I feel that sense of satisfaction I always get when I start the creating part of the process. I grab the sponge and run water down the inside of newly formed vase neck, letting it pool at the bottom. I like the shape that's forming and I don't want friction to ruin it. Once I'm happy with the body of the vase I move my hands to the outside, squeezing the clay until it starts to lengthen into a long cylinder. Unlike the other two chunkier vases, this one is heading towards being a bud vase. I grab more water and smooth it over the sides of the vase, enjoying how smooth the clay is becoming.

I never look for perfection with my creations, I just want to let the natural beauty of the clay show through. I don't plan my designs out before hand so each one is unique, showing the natural hues of the bare clay.

There are a few dents at the bottom of the vase but I refuse to fix them. It's pretty in its own way and once it's fired in the oven and painted, the flaws will be highlighted just the way I like. People might not see what I do in the vases, but I've learned that scars don't always make things less perfect.

Happy with the appearance, I grab my cut off wire and sponge. I flood the bat while spinning it slowly, allowing the water to surround the vase, and use the cutters to release the clay. I need to make the vase detach from the wheel so I can allow it to dry out. This is the moment when the clay is at its most fragile and I've lost a few items at this point when I've been too heavy handed. Thankfully the vase moves easily and I slide it onto a wooden board. When it's safely transferred I take it to the sideboard at the side of the room and sit it next to the other vases I made today. I look at them all side by side, smiling when I think about the next stage. The crafting and molding is always soothing, but painting designs onto the fired clay is a release of emotions that I don't get anywhere else. I understand what painters mean when they say they put many emotions into their works because that's how I feel when I design. It's cathartic and I love doing it.

I grab the plastic cover and pull it carefully over the still wet vases. I'll be able to fire them tomorrow but for now they need to dry. I start to clean my equipment when there's a knock on the front door. My heart starts racing as I stand and stare in the direction of the door. I'm not sure how that's helpful since I can't see through walls but I can't seem to do anything else at the minute. I don't have a clue who it could be and it's scaring me more than it should. I should be able to just walk to the door and open it like any other person could but my feet are frozen to the floor.

I wrack my brain to think who it might be but I come up blank. My groceries come on a Sunday afternoon so it's not that, and no one in my family mentioned coming around and they always call beforehand. They wouldn't just turn up because they know how much it freaks me out. But what if there's something wrong with one of them? My brother could be hurt for example and the police or a friend has come to tell me.

That thought is what has me moving to the door, albeit very slowly, and I jump when I hear another knock, this one a lot louder than the first. I start to breathe quickly as I stare at the door wishing it was made of glass.

"Ares, are you in there?"

The voice filters through the wood and it's muffled, but I'm still sure I recognise it. Kohan? Why is he here? I walk to the door quicker this time, wiping my hands on my already filthy apron. Even though I think I know who it is I still look out the peephole just to double check. Standing on the other side is a slightly drier version of the man who said goodbye to me last night and I try to ignore the excited flutter in my stomach.

I put the security chain on before taking a deep breath and opening the door. I know it seems a bit much especially after I spent all day so far telling myself how safe I felt with him, but I've learnt not to trust my instincts, they've let me down before. "Kohan, what are you doing here?"

He smiles as he holds up a white paper bag. "I had the afternoon off so I thought you might want to share a sandwich with me. I got it from Lettuce Eat and they make the best meatball subs

I've ever eaten."

I scrunch my face in confusion. Why would he want to eat lunch with me? We've only spoken to each other for about ten minutes? And why do I want to share that sandwich with him so badly? I close the door and remove the chain before opening it again. "What if I'm vegetarian?"

He looks me up and down, letting his eyes slowly look over every part of me. "Nah, you look like a guy who enjoys his meat."

Chapter Six

Kohan

The minute the words are out of my mouth I want to snatch them back. Bringing a sandwich to share with him seemed like a great idea but now that I can feel the burn of embarrassment on my cheeks, I think I should have stayed at home.

I spent the morning at work thinking about my conversation with Ares in the car last night. Every answer he gave me just made me want to know more about him. I want to know about the accident that cost him his hearing, why he was housebound when he first moved here, and why he looked so fucking scared most of the time we were together? I was tempted to Google him to see if I could find out anything but felt like I was invading his privacy. I want to get to get to know him but I want it all to come directly from him. I want Ares to trust me with his secrets.

"Um, I really don't know how to respond to that."

God, I need the ground to open up and swallow me right now. I'm about to hide my embarrassment by running away when Ares steps back from the door to let me in. It only takes me a second to make up my mind. I'm going in, no matter how big an arse I just made of myself. "I'm sorry, I didn't mean it like that. I just meant that you don't look like a vegetarian." I walk into the small entrance hall and wait as he closes the door behind us.

"And how does a vegetarian look?"

"Hell if I know, but it seemed like a funny thing to say."

"How did that work out for you?" I can see humour flashing in his eyes as I dig myself into an even bigger hole.

"Not great. I just came off sounding like a pervert, and basically called you gay. Sorry." This is not the way I wanted today to go. I wanted to make a good impression since the last few times

I've seen him have pretty much been a disaster.

He smiles and it's the most genuine smile I've seen on his lips, and it makes my heart stutter in my chest. Ares really needs to smile more, it looks good on him. "You have a beautiful smile." *Shit, shit, shit. What the hell are you doing you arsehole?* Not only did you imply he was gay, now you're trying to come on to him.

It's Ares turn to blush and the effect almost has me grabbing him for a kiss. That's something else I've spent the morning thinking about. The fact that the more I see Ares the sexier he is. The first time I barely got a chance to look at him before he ran away, but last night I got my fill as I stood in front of him in the lift and it was better than I could ever imagine.

"Let's go through the kitchen and I'll get cleaned up."

I look down to where he's indicating and for the first time I notice that he's wearing an apron that is covered in … is that mud? He walks away and I follow him. "What were you doing?" The minute we walk through the door into his kitchen I can see what I interrupted. Along one wall there is a shelving unit filled with the most amazing sculpted faces I've ever seen. They are all unique, some smiling and some sad, but all are beautiful in their own way. I look closer at them and see that every single one has a slight flaw. They don't look accidental, they look like they're meant to be there, like they are the whole reason for the sculpture. One woman has a scar running down her cheek and a male figure has a hair-lip scar. It doesn't detract from the overall impact of the pieces, in fact they actually add to them.

On the other side of a large window there is a slightly smaller shelving unit filled to the brim with vases and bowls. The top couple of shelves hold items that are full of colour and light, making the area seem like it's glowing. The bottom shelves are darker, almost like the top vases have stolen all the light from the bottom ones. There's a huge contrast between the two collections and if I was a psychiatrist I'm sure I would have a lot to say about it, like possibly there's a darkness inside Ares that keeps stealing his light. Since I don't want to look too deeply into that just now, I turn to face Ares.

He's on the other side of a breakfast bar in the small kitchen washing his hands. "Did you make all those?" I point behind me with my thumb.

Ares grabs a towel and dries his hands before taking off the messy apron and placing it over a rack that's sitting in front of what must be the back door. "Yeah. I was told I needed something to focus my anxieties into and that's what I chose."

Just like every other time. He gives me information but it just leads to more questions. It's like every little scrap he gives me makes me want to know even more. He has a story and I hope one day he will tell it to me.

He walks around to my side of the breakfast bar and takes a seat, indicating that I should join him. He seems less nervous today and I'm glad. He was like a scared kitten yesterday and it pained me that I made him feel like that. "So where's this sandwich you were going to share with me?"

I take the seat next to him and empty the bag onto the counter. I pass one of the wrapped packages to him and start to open mine. When it's open and the tomato sauce runs out the sides of the sub, Ares gets up and grabs the roll of kitchen roll from under the sink. On his way back he stops at the fridge and collects two cans of Pepsi Max, handing one to me when he sits back down. "Hope that's okay? It's all I have. I may have a slight addiction to it."

"It's great. I drink anything really as long as it's sugar free." I open the can and take a small sip.

"Watching your weight?"

"No, just sugar doesn't agree with me too well. It turns me into the Duracell bunny." I laugh but the talk of weight makes me a little self-conscious of the layer of fluffiness I've put on recently. I pull my t-shirt away from my stomach to make sure I hide my stomach.

Ares eyes watch the movement and redness heats his cheek. "Shit. I didn't mean you were overweight. It was meant to be a joke. You are anything but big, your body is …" He stops talking and his eyes widen. I want to know what he was about to say but he puts all his focus on unwrapping his own sandwich. "So what exactly am I about to eat?"

"The best meatball sub ever. Helen owns the shop next to the office and it's her own recipe. I could eat it every single day, which means I try to avoid the place and save it for a special occasion."

I watch as Ares takes a bite of the sandwich and my breath sticks in my throat as he moans around the mouthful. *Shit, he is so fucking sexy.* His eyes are half closed in pleasure and tomato sauce covers the corner of his mouth. I swore I wouldn't lust after him but it's really hard not to. In my fantasies he's gay and he would invite me to lick that sauce off his lips. I drag my eyes away from him before my mind goes completely to mush and I make a fool of myself again.

"This is so good. Thank you for bringing it over for me."

I nod and take another drink from my can to buy myself some time. I need some blood to start flowing to other parts of my body so I can talk to him without looking like I have some problem forming sentences. When I still can't think of anything to say I take a bite of my own sandwich and concentrate intensely on chewing. I don't want there to be an awkward silence but I honestly don't know what to say. Thankfully Ares takes the lead, even though he confuses me when he does speak.

"I am by the way."

I look at him and see that he's picking at the top of his roll, crumbling it between his fingers. "You are what?" I'm thrown by the confession, the last thing we spoke about was sugar and my body.

"I'm gay. I don't know if that's a problem for you or not?"

It's a huge fucking problem, but not for the reason he thinks. The only thing that was keeping my hormones under the slightest amount of control was the idea that he was straight and now that he's confirmed he isn't, there might be a problem with my dick. "Not a problem."

"Look if it is, just go now. No hard feelings. I know that some guys aren't comfortable with it."

I smile and turn my full attention to him. "Seriously, Ares, there is no problem." He still doesn't look convinced with what I'm saying. "I'm gay."

His eyes widen in shock and I swear his eyebrows touch his hairline. His reaction makes me laugh hard, so hard that I can feel the tears running down my cheeks. This finally has him glaring at me in a *I want to punch you right now* sort of way.

"Laugh it up."

I finally calm down but at least the awkwardness between us has been broken and I look back over to the faces on the shelves. "Why do you make them all have flaws?"

He chews his lip for a minute and I think he isn't going to answer me. Just as I'm about to tell him it doesn't matter he speaks. "The world is obsessed with beauty, but only a certain standard of it. Perfect teeth, flawless skin and a body that is tight and smooth. But who said that's what beauty is? Who told the people that had imperfections they weren't beautiful? I just see those imperfections differently and want others to embrace them. Celebrate them." His eyes are full of passion as he talks and I'm slightly in awe as I listen to him.

"I agree. The world is full of beauty that people miss." I rub my stomach again. "And very few of us fit the perfect title."

"You are pretty perfect." As he speaks he gets up from his stool and goes into the kitchen to grab another can of pop. I know it's a distraction because he hasn't opened his own one yet and I have only had a few mouthfuls from mine.

"You seem to be passionate about the subject." I'm hoping to find out a little more about him, and I think this might be a way to see under that carefully crafted veneer. I know I've only spoken to him a couple of times but I can already tell when he's holding back, there's a lot he doesn't like to talk about.

Ares walks around and takes his seat again, putting the extra can in front of me "Lets just say I have a very unique perspective on the subject."

Again, so much information but so little at the same time.

"I'm sorry. I know I'm probably not making sense just now. I just … I don't normally tell people things about me. I have a past that isn't pretty and I keep it to myself. But then I haven't had a friend in about five years." His voice goes quiet and he looks down at the sandwich he's slowly destroying. "I know that sounds really pathetic, but it is what it is."

I want to reach out and touch him but I can tell he wouldn't be comfortable if I did. I might not know his past, but he has a *don't touch me* vibe that comes off loud and clear. "You don't need to tell me anything, but I want you to know, I want to be your friend. I want you to know you can trust me with your secrets, but I understand that it will take time for you to get to that point. Let me bribe you with a few more sandwiches and see how it goes." I smile gently at him and my heart breaks for him when he finally looks up at me. His eyes are filled with pain and I want to know what put it there. My mind goes over every possible scenario it can come up with and I hope it isn't some of the things I can imagine.

Ares takes a deep breath and pushes his hair away from his forehead. His eyes won't meet mine as he moves a little closer. I focus on his forehead since that's obviously where he wants me to look. A thick white scar runs diagonally from the hairline in the middle of his forehead to the outside edge of his eyebrow. The scar is thick with smaller scars criss crossing it at certain points.

"What happened?"

He drops his hair back into place, blocking my view of the scar. "Let's just say I was in a relationship that didn't follow the conventional rules."

My stomach churns and I feel anger build inside me. He won't say it but between the scar and the fear he thinks he's hiding so well, I know exactly what he means. I can't believe that someone would put their hands on Ares, and hard enough to leave permanent marks. I'm so caught up in my anger that I flinch when fingers touch my forehead. Ares is leaning in towards me and massaging the frown that has appeared between my eyebrows.

"You'll give yourself wrinkles."

I take a deep breath and try to let the anger melt out of my body. "Sorry." I don't even know why I'm apologising but I don't know what else to say.

"No, I'm sorry. I've ruined a lovely lunch with my baggage. Let's change the subject. What do you do for fun around here?"

I spend the next hour telling Ares about the severe lack of nightlife apart from Westies, and how I'm being dragged to Toppers by Sophie. He laughs when I tell him all about my crazy best friend, and I notice that he sits quietly and lets me monopolise the conversation.

"Tell me a little about you, Ares. Do you have any siblings, hobbies, bad habits?" I leave the questions open so he can tell me whatever he's comfortable with. I want to get to know him but I don't want to push.

"I have a brother called Roscoe. He's married to Tina and they live in Birmingham where we grew up. My mum and dad still live just a few streets over from them. I have a few cousins but they live in Scotland so I don't see or speak to them much."

"One brother? Shit, you don't know how lucky you are." I groan to emphasise my point. People from smaller families just don't understand the struggle of coming from a big family, especially if you are the youngest like me.

"Big family?"

"Understatement. There are five of us. All boys. And to make matters worse I'm the youngest."

"Shit. I bet that was interesting growing up. Tell me about them."

This could take a while but truthfully, talking about my brothers is actually a pleasant thing for me. As much as I bitch about them, I love them more than anything. "Damien is the eldest at thirty four. He's married to Heidi and has two daughters, Darcy and Milly. Milly is only four weeks old and is as cute as hell. Darcy gets her attitude from her dad, which is funnier for us than him. Carey is thirty-two and Emile is twenty-nine. Emile has been married to Maya for about 2 years. Jensen is twenty-seven and he's been married to Thea for about six months. Thea has a son called Henry and he's five. He was so shy when he first met us but he's just another member of the family now. Then there's me, the baby of the brood."

Ares smiles as he listens to me talking again and I realise that he's turned the conversation away from himself again. He has a skill for being able to do that and I'm about to ask him another question when my mobile rings in my pocket. I take it out and see Sophie's name on the screen. Before I answer I check the time and see that it's a lot later than I realised. I suddenly know why she's calling. I cancel the call and type out a quick text telling her I'm on my way.

I start to pack up the remains of my sandwich and throw the rubbish in the bag it came in. "I'm really sorry to eat and bail on you. I totally lost track of time and I need to meet a photographer at the office." I'm brushing up some crumbs when I feel Ares hand on my wrist, stilling my movements.

"It's fine, just go. I can tidy up the little bit of mess you made, it's the least I can do." He gets up from his stool and starts to walk to the front door and I'm relieved that he isn't making my sudden departure awkward. He opens the front door for me and I go to walk through it but stop just as I'm about to pass him. My eyes flicker down to his Adam's apple as he swallows nervously and it takes everything in me not to lean forward and run my tongue along it. He has a sexy neck and I want to feel it under my skin.

"Thank you for lunch."

I meet his eyes when he speaks. I need to stop seeing him as anything other than a friend because I have a feeling that's what Ares needs. He doesn't need me lusting after him; he needs me to be there for him and to listen to him. "Anytime. Hopefully you will let me do it again."

He laughs and I just spend a moment to enjoy the sound. "I didn't give you permission this time, but yes, that would be nice. Maybe I'll cook next time."

That thought makes me smile. Just knowing that he wants to see me again makes me happier than it should. "I would like that. I wasn't lying when I said I wanted to be your friend, Ares. I want nothing more than that."

He blushes slightly but his smile is relaxed, showing none of the worry I normally see in his face. "Have fun with your photographer."

I walk away from him and when I reach the garden gate he calls my name, causing me to look back at him. "Use the doorbell next time. I don't always wear my hearing aids in the house. The doorbell will flash a light so I know you're there."

I nod and watch as he goes back into the house. Taking food over was a spur of the moment decision, but as I practically skip back to my car, I know it was the right one.

Chapter Seven

Ares

    I knock on Kohan's office door and wait until he calls for me to enter. For the last two weeks this has become our new nightly routine, eating dinner together before he goes home for the night and I start work.

    It all started the first night after we had lunch and I found a packet of jellybeans along with a note on my cleaning trolley. The note told me to go to Kohan's office before I started working so I did. He had more food for me, this time a grilled cheese sandwich and a cup of tomato soup, and a can of Pepsi Max. Remembering my favourite drink was a sweet touch, but I refused to think too much about that. As we ate he told me that he expected me in his office every night for dinner, and even though his demands should have had me freaking out, they didn't. It was actually something that I wanted to do; but if it hadn't, I know that Kohan never would have forced me. I've known Kohan for roughly two weeks but I feel safe around him and it's a strange concept. Micah was the man I loved but when I think about our relationship now, I can see that he was always surrounded by an air of anger. I learned quickly to tread carefully around him so I didn't set him off because that never ended well for me. Kohan doesn't make me feel like that; he's more relaxed and centered, and it makes me want to spend time with him.

    When Kohan calls I open the door and peek around the edge of it. He's sitting back in his chair with his feet propped up on his desk, holding a notepad in his hand and he's wearing glasses. Shit, this is the first time I've seen him with glasses on and I'd be a liar if I said it did nothing for me. The more time I've spent with Kohan the more attracted to him I've become. It's not just his smile and gentle eyes, it's his kindness and humour that speaks to the part of my libido I thought had died. No one has ever made me laugh the way he does, and I feel so relaxed in his company that sometimes I forget that I was ever scared around him.

"You brought food. Come in and save me from the hell I call editing."

I can only smile at his dramatics as I enter his office and close the door behind me. Every night he complains about one thing or another that he hates and I need to save him from.

"What did you bring?"

I chew the inside of my cheek as I place the plate down in front of him. Normally we have some sort of take away but tonight I wanted to do something different. After our first meal together I told him that I would cook and up until now I haven't. This afternoon I had the sudden urge to cook an old favourite. I haven't cooked in a long time, because cooking for one isn't much fun, but tonight I wanted to make something for Kohan.

He stares at me through narrowed eyes and I can only guess that the lack of takeaway container is confusing him. "What is this?"

"Open it." I bite my cheek harder trying to control the urge to tell him to forget it and that he doesn't need to eat it.

He takes so long to open it, almost like he's dragging it out on purpose just to tease me. Eventually he takes the lid off and a waft of steam escapes and I'm happy that it's still hot. He sticks his nose over the bowl and sniffs, his stomach rumbling in response to what I hope are pleasant smells. "What the hell is that?

"Mushroom and bacon Penne."

"Shit, that smells so good." He doesn't waste a second before he grabs one of the forks I packed and spears a piece of pasta. He groans and mutters something around the mouthful before diving back in for more.

I sit down in the seat opposite and watch him as he digs in. My nerves have been replaced by pride as I watch him devour my food. It doesn't even bother me that he's eating it all himself without offering me any. I would happily go hungry if it meant being able to watch him enjoy something I made.

He continues eating for a few more minutes before he stops and looks at me with his mouth full and a guilty look on his face. He tries to say something but it comes out garbled thanks to the mouthful of pasta. I don't know why it strikes me as so funny but he looks so much like a kid caught with his hand in the cookie jar that I start laughing. It's not just a little chuckle either, it's a full on belly cramping, snorting laugh that has tears running down my cheeks. I try to stop but the harder I try to the funnier I find the whole thing. It doesn't help when Kohan looks at me as though I've lost my mind.

I've spent the last three years either in pain or terrified, and to be able to let my guard down like this releases so much pent up emotion. Unfortunately along with the laughter comes other emotions that I can't control either. Within a few seconds my laughter has turned into heartache and my tears are no longer happy ones. I cover my mouth as gut-wrenching sobs escape from me. My therapist warned me that I was bottling up my emotions and one day they would break free, I just didn't expect it to be in front of someone I barely knew.

Kohan is out of his seat in seconds and around the desk. He kneels in front of me and pulls me into his arms. The contact should have me pulling away, but instead I wrap my arms around him and hold onto him like my life depends on it, letting my pain escape in my tears. He doesn't push me away or say anything; he just lets me take my time, almost like he knows that I need to let it all out.

What feels like hours later I pull back from him feeling lousy that I've left a huge wet patch on his shoulder and cheek. I reach out to attempt to dry his skin but he grabs me by the wrist to still my movements and holds my palm against his cheek.

"Are you okay?"

I don't trust my voice yet but I nod. I actually feel a lot lighter, like a weight's been lifted from my chest and, even with my snotty nose, I can breathe deeply again.

Kohan gets up and leaves the office. I'm not sure what to do but a few minutes later he returns with a box of tissues and hands them to me. He returns to his position in front of me and rubs his hands over my thighs as I wipe my nose and eyes. The movement of his hands is soothing and when he stops I almost ask him to keep going. "Come on, let's get you home."

I look at him in confusion. I still have a full nights work to do so there's no way I can leave. He seems to have forgotten this fact though as he packs all his stuff away and puts his jacket on. He pulls his bag over his shoulder and walks to the door. I'm still sitting there looking at him like he's gone insane but he just motions for me to move.

"I told Mr James that you weren't feeling well and needed to leave. I'll walk you home since I don't have my car, but you need to get your jacket first."

I'm still a little confused but I get up and follow Kohan to the cleaner's storeroom to grab my belongings, and within a few minutes we are walking side by side towards my house.

It usually takes me about twenty minutes to make it home, but tonight it takes a little longer, not that I'm not complaining. Chatting with Kohan about nothing and everything is settling my frayed emotions and I love to hear him speak. He seems to find joy in the simple things and listening to him talk about how his nephew Henry got on at his first day at karate lessons has me cracking up. I didn't think it was possible for a kid that age to break his instructor's pinky on his first night but apparently it can happen. Oddly Kohan seems really proud of the kid and it's cute to watch his face light up as he speaks about him. I think Kohan would make a fantastic dad, he seems kind and patient which is what all kids need.

"Well that's you home my fair prince."

I look up, shocked that we're already outside my garden gate. I hadn't been paying attention and now that we're here I suddenly don't want to be alone. Kohan hasn't been in my house since he first brought the sandwiches weeks ago, but tonight I can't face the silence that being by myself will bring. "Do you want to come in for a drink?"

He looks a little hesitant and I realise I've made a mistake. I shouldn't have asked him.

"Forget I asked. I'm sorry. Goodnight, and thank you for walking me home." I turn and walk away without giving him a chance to speak. I make it half way up the path to my door when he grabs me by the arm. I know it's him, everything in me knows it is, but it doesn't stop me from flinching and tripping on the edge of the grass. I land on my arse with a thud that has my teeth jarring.

Kohan is in front of me instantly but he doesn't touch me. He looks worried and I don't blame him. Why can't I keep my fucking fear under wraps? Every part of me knows that Kohan wouldn't hurt me but still I react like a scared child when he touches me unexpectedly.

Tears burn in my eyes but this time it's out of sheer embarrassment. I struggle to get up and I can see that Kohan wants to help but he's sensible enough to keep his hands to himself, and I don't blame him. Who would want to touch someone who loses their shit from simple contact?

"Are you okay?"

I nod and wipe the grass off of the back of my jeans. The ground is wet and I can feel the soggy patch on the back of my jeans sticking to my skin the longer I stand there.

"I'm so fucking sorry. I shouldn't have grabbed you like that. Did you hurt yourself?"

His apology makes me feel even worse because he shouldn't have to. It's not his fault, it's one hundred percent mine.
"I'm fine. I'm sorry I overreacted, it's just … it's just me. Don't feel bad, you didn't do anything wrong."

"I shouldn't have grabbed you, Ares. I just wanted to stop you and say I would love to come in for a drink. My only hesitation was because I was meant to meet Sophie tonight for a drink but I can do that another night."

"No, don't do that. Go have fun with Sophie. You shouldn't change your plans for me, I was stupid to ask." I give him a weak smile and start walking away again. I just want tonight to be over.

I've made a fool of myself multiple times, and I wouldn't blame Kohan if he doesn't want to see me again. It's been so long since I had a friend and I was really excited about having Kohan in my life, but just like Micah used to tell me, I'm fucking useless.

Kohan appears in front of me with his arms out to stop me but this time there's no touching. I hate that he's reluctant to put his hands on me now, especially after we'd formed a comfortable bond. "Don't do that. Don't act like you aren't worth spending time with. I want to come in and have a drink with you, I was just trying to think where Sophie would be so I could call her. I wasn't meeting her for anything important, just shooting the shit and catching up. We see each other all the time. Ares, I would rather spend the night with you."

He sounds so sure of what he's saying, so even though I want to just go inside and allow him to leave, I grab his offer with both hands. I don't want to be alone tonight, and the need to spend time with him is more important than my need to hide from him. "Are you sure?"

"I'm more than sure. Ares, would you like to have a drink with me … in your house?"

I laugh and I can feel the tension between us diminish. "I would love to go into my house and have a drink with you."

"Well hurry up and get the door open then."

Playful Kohan is back and that makes me really fucking happy.

"Kristoff … no, the Beast."

"The Beast? You into hairy men?" Kohan snorts and takes another drink of his vodka and Pepsi max.

When I invited him in earlier I didn't really put much thought into it but I was lucky that Kohan drinks vodka. I'd only planned to have one to try and calm my emotions from earlier in the evening, but that one soon became two and then that became three. I'm now sipping my fourth glass and feeling the effects of it right down to my toes. We're both sitting on my couch, our heads leaning on the back as we slouch comfortably close to each other. We started off with a large distance between us but as the hours passed we got closer, and now our arms are within touching distance as we chat.

I don't know if it's the alcohol or Kohan but I feel pretty good right now and I'm glad that he agreed to come in. "I don't like them hairy, just growly. Not angry growly because that scares me, but powerful growly. I'm pretty sure that would be you by the way." *Did I just say that out loud?*

"I can be toppy when needed."

Oh yeah, I said it. "Toppy is very different than growly." I snort and Kohan rolls his head in my direction. Our noses end up only inches away from each other and I stare into his beautiful eyes. God I wish I wasn't so fucked up; I would be all over Kohan like a cheap suit.

He seems to be fighting the same urge as me and his eyes continually flicker down to my lips. His tongue brushes over his lips, leaving them wet and I want to be brave enough to lean over and kiss him. I just keep thinking that Micah was soft and sweet until I let him in and as soon as I gave him everything I had, he used it against me to cause me pain. Nearly every part of me is confident that Kohan would never do the things that Micah did but the cautious side of me can't shake of the fear.

"I want to kiss you so fucking badly, Ares."

My breath hitches and I let my tongue trace over my lips, wetting them like Kohan did to his own a moment ago. "I can't." I don't know where the words come from but they're out there now and I can't take them back. I'm actually glad that part of my brain is still working because kissing Kohan would be the wrong thing to do. It would mess up the comfortable friendship that we've formed. Micah told me that I was no good at relationships, that I made things hard when they didn't need to be, and that's why he got so angry with me. I don't want to do that with Kohan; I don't want to ruin what we have.

"I know, but it doesn't stop me wanting to." His fingers trace over my cheek bone and down to my jaw. The gentle touch has my eyes closing as I enjoy the intimate brush of his finger. I remember when touches like this meant someone loved me, but eventually each one led to pain and bruises.

I flinch away from his touch as the memories of pain sear through my brain. I can tell that Kohan notices because he quickly drops his hand and I see a look of sadness in his eyes. "Please tell me who hurt you. What did he do to you?"

"Micah. He took the love I had for him and turned into something I dreaded. He hurt me more than I thought anyone could, and it took me too long to get away." My voice cracks as I finish speaking but I'm proud of myself for finally getting it out. After only two weeks of knowing Kohan I trust him enough to give him a painful part of my past, even if vodka helped me.

Kohan doesn't say anything but reaches out and takes my hand. He's letting me take my time and decide what I tell him and what to hold back. I down the last of my vodka and face him, finally ready to share a little bit of my darkness. "I want to tell you what happened the night I lost my hearing but I've never told anyone other than family. I'm scared; I don't want you to look at me differently because of it."

"Why would I look at you differently?" His hand tightens on mine and it gives me the confidence to carry on.

"Because I went back to Micah after it happened. I believed his lies and ignored my family's pleas to go back to their house. I'm weak and pathetic, and I don't want to see disappointment in your eyes. You're the first friend I've been allowed to have in forever and I don't want to lose you."

Kohan moves even closer to me on the couch until he is practically lying on top of me. The position is comforting and the pressure of his body makes me feel safe. Safer than I think I've ever felt before. "I promise there's nothing you can tell me that would make me think you're less than strong. I'm your friend, Ares.

Nothing will ever change that. If you don't want to tell me that's fine, but I'm here to share the burden if I can. Two weeks or two years, I'll be here for you."

I look deep into his eyes and see nothing but understanding. If he's lying to me then he's hiding it really well. My therapist says that it's time to let people in and that I need to stop spending my life thinking I'm not worthy of people caring for me. Tonight is the time to shit or get off the pot. "I met Micah after I started going to a local gym. He was charming and swept me off my feet. For nearly six months he was the perfect boyfriend and we moved in together pretty quickly. For another two months after that things continued like we were straight out of a romance story. The first time he hit me was a shock but he convinced me that it was because he was stressed at work. That stress must have continued because slaps and punches starting coming more often after that."

Kohan's grip tightens on mine and I can see him trying to control himself. I know he's not angry at me, but I hate that he's feeling like that because of me. I don't stop talking because now that I've started I want to tell him the whole story.

"Before I knew it I was cut off from all my friends and family, and I was no longer working. I wasn't allowed to leave the flat without him and that meant not being able to talk to anyone without permission. It all happened so slowly that I didn't really notice until it was too late. I was lonely and scared, bruised and broken but I kept myself sane by thinking that it couldn't get worse ... but then it did."

Chapter Eight

Ares

    I stir the tomato sauce for the Bolognese whilst swaying to a song that's playing over the radio. The window's open wide because the sun is shining and the sound of the city below me is relaxing. When I moved to the centre of Manchester I wasn't sure how well I would settle. The area of Birmingham that I grew up in was quiet and friendly, and it always felt more like a small town to me. It didn't take me long to get used to living amongst the hustle and bustle of city centre life and quickly the sounds became as soothing as the countryside. I enjoy nothing more than sitting at the window and watching the world moving below, and when I get permission to go outside I absorb every experience I can.

    I check the clock and see that it's nearly time for Micah to come home. I smile as I grab the colander to drain the pasta. He has been so attentive and caring recently, making me feel special and important. I love when things are going well like they are and I've been working hard to keep him happy. I've just put the colander in the sink and grabbed the pot when the front door slams. I smile to myself again as I wait for him to come into the kitchen. I'm just starting to pour the boiling water from the pot when I hear footsteps behind me.

    There's no warning, no hint at anything being wrong, when Micah's fist suddenly connects with the side of my head. I drop the pot but the water splashes up and covers my hands. I cry out with the combined pain in my head and hands as I collapse to the floor. My ear is ringing as I try to control the tears that are threatening to fall. I don't know what I did to deserve this lesson but I can't cry or it'll make him angrier. I turn onto my side and watch Micah walk to the freezer and grab a bottle of vodka from inside. He doesn't even bother with a glass and just drinks straight from the bottle.

My hands start to throb as the skin blisters where the boiling water scalded. I want to get up and run them under a cold tap but I can't move, I haven't been given permission.

Micah finally looks in my direction and I wish he hadn't. I see a hatred in his eyes that I've never seen before and a darkness that makes it look like he has lost all his humanity. I don't know what happened today but I'm more scared of him than I've ever been before. I've had bruises and broken bones, but never once has Micah looked so detached.

I take a deep breath before speaking. "I'm making your favourite for dinner." I'm hoping that'll pull him from the rage that's simmering just below the surface but his stare cuts through me.

"I thought I told you not to talk to anyone?"

I stare at him blankly because I have no idea what he's talking about. I wrack my brain but I know that I haven't spoken to anyone without his permission. The last person was my brother but Micah was standing right next to me monitoring the call. There's been no one else. "You did and I haven't spoken to anyone."

"You're lying!"

I flinch at the volume of his voice but force myself to stay still. If I show any indication that I'm scared it will only make this worse. "Baby, I haven't spoken to anyone since my brother. You were there. You have my phone, I can't speak to anyone. Why don't I finish dinner and you can relax the rest of the evening?" I speak with the happiest sounding voice I can muster, smiling as I get up on my feet and move carefully to stand in front of him. I keep my aching hands at my side even though I want to put them in front of me for protection.

Micah is practically vibrating with anger now so I take a chance and reach out to touch him. It takes everything in me not to flinch as I connect with his skin, but I swallow down my fear and show him love. I quickly look down at my hand to see what damage the boiling water caused and I have to stop the sob that builds in my chest when I see the blisters. I don't know how he's going to patch them up, but I suppose we can tell the emergency room that I had a cooking accident.

I'm concentrating hard on my injuries and it must anger him because he reaches out and grabs me by the throat, pushing me backwards until I collide with the kitchen unit behind me. I can't hold in the cry when the worktop catches me in the base of the back. The grip on my throat tightens and it takes absolutely everything I have not to reach up to try and loosen his grip.

"Are you calling me I'm a liar? I know what I fucking read today. Your mum text you to ask if you had decided whether you're attending your brothers graduation. That *means she's asked you before. I'm not fucking stupid."* The sudden calmness in his voice scares me more than his shouting.

I want to tell him that Roscoe had asked me about it when he called and my mum must be following up for numbers, but I can't get any words past the hand that's still wrapped tightly around my throat. I shake my head in the hopes that he'll loosen his grip if I give him a response.

"You've spoken to her so don't lie to me. I told you what would happen if you lied to me." I don't get a chance to answer him before he drags me away from the unit and towards the bedroom. I know what will happen if he gets me in there and I'm barely recovered from the last lesson he gave me. My body clenches at the memory and I can feel the pain throb through my rectum at the action.

Panic has my eyes flickering over to the open window and I wonder how loud I would need to scream for someone to hear me and come to my rescue. He follows my line of sight and must figure out what I'm thinking because his grip tightens.

"You want someone to hear you, is that it? Come on then, I'll help you get some attention." He drags me over to the open window and leans me backwards until the only thing keeping me from falling to the pavement below is his hands.

My body shuts down completely and tears start falling from

my eyes as I realise that this is how it all ends. I don't want to die, not like this.

"Come on, Ares. Why don't you yell for help? That's what you wanted to do, I'm giving you the chance."

"Please, Micah." I manage to get the words out as he moves his hands to grab the front of my t-shirt. He drags me back into a standing position and relief has me sobbing. I need to move away from the open window, I'm still only one push away from falling.

"Please what, Ares? Please provide for you and protect you? Please love you like no one else can? Please do all that and only expect you to follow my rules? That's all I want; for you to know your place, Ares. Why can't you just do that?"

I'm feeling guilty by the time he's finished speaking because I don't know what to say to him. I know this is all my fault and I don't know what to say to him to stop him from getting angrier with me.

"Not going to answer me? You are so pathetic standing there and crying like a fucking girl. I have no idea what I see in you any more, Ares. There's the real problem, I don't want you, but I don't want anyone else to have you."

Deep, dark fear spreads through my body as I stare at him. His anger has been replaced with an emptiness that I've never seen before. It's almost like everything that made Micah has vanished, gone along with all his emotions. There's just nothing there, no anger or fury, and no love.

I'm still taking in the sight before me when his head connects with mine. Holy fuck. Bright, white lights float in front of my eyes and I blink quickly to try and clear them. He's never head-butted me before and I'm glad he hasn't. I barely have a moment to compose myself before he grabs me and drags me across the floor. When it registers where he's dragging me I try to stop him. The cupboard in the hall is where he puts me when he feels I need time to 'reflect and think about what I've done'. Being in there scares the shit out of me and I find myself begging as we move towards it. "No, Micah. Please don't put me in there. I'm sorry, I'll be good."

I barely slow him down but I know I've pissed him off when he suddenly stops walking and turns towards me before backhanding me again. I hit the wall and something wet instantly flows down the side of my head. Without his hands holding me up, I slide down the wall. I hold my head to try and control the ringing in my ears that intensified with the impact.

"Why do you make me do this? Why can't you just do as you're told?"

His words are punctuated with a kick to my ribs and the air from my lungs whooshes out of me. I sit there winded and struggling to fill my lungs as he screams at me.

"Just once I would like you to treat me with the respect I deserve but instead you go behind my back and do whatever you want."

Another backhand across my cheek has me collapsing onto my side on the floor. The ringing in my head has progressed to a pressure that feels like it's going to make my head burst open. His yells are now muffled and I'm a little thankful for that. I blink a few times and look up at him. His lips are moving but I can't hear him properly which makes him even angrier.

His face reddens with each passing second and he crouches down to my level, spit hitting my face as he continues to rant. I don't know if he asks me something or if he's just letting his fury bubble over, but he lashes out, his fist connecting with my cheek. My head rolls to the side and my vision blurs as I stare at the ceiling. I want to lie here and sleep but Micah grabs me by the front of my shirt again and drags me to my feet. My legs feel like jelly as I struggle to stand and when Micah tries to pull me towards him I stumble and fall against him.

Micah cups my face and brings it close to his. I blink as I try to focus on him but it's a battle I lose. I can feel blood dripping down my face and my cheek throbs. I just want painkillers and a warm bath but I doubt that's going to happen any time soon. My eyes roll back into my head but Micah's shaking me brings my attention back to him. His lips are still moving and I want to tell him

I can't hear him but I've lost the ability to form words.

A second or an hour, I'm not sure which one, but that's all it takes for me to experience the worst pain I've ever known. I'm moving backwards and before I have the chance to gain my feet, my head is slammed into the hall wall over and over again. As the world slips away from around me all I can feel is sharp, shooting agony and I suddenly pray for the death that I didn't want earlier. Anything to save me from the torture I'm suffering.

Kohan

I sit and watch Ares' eyes glaze over as he tells me about his past. It's obvious that he's reliving the whole thing as he speaks and I want to tell him to stop but the words just keep spilling out of him. I don't know if it's the alcohol or not but he's giving me more information than I thought he would and I feel nausea creeping up my throat as he explains what he's been through. I knew Ares had experienced something terrible but never would I have guessed just how bad it was.

When he finishes the room falls silent and I just sit there, not sure what to say to him. What can you say to someone who survived an attempt on their life like that? Now I know where the scar on his forehead came from, and as I sit and stare at him I want to reach out and touch it, try to sooth any pain that might still be there.

Ares gets up from his slouched position, sitting forward and putting his elbows on his knees. He rubs his hands over his face and I can only imagine what's going through his head just now. To survive that ordeal makes him the strongest person I've met. To know that's how he lost his hearing and that his life was changed by someone's anger, fuck, I just can't comprehend it.

"Ares?" His name comes out strangled and I swallow, trying to get rid of the lump in my throat. I'm trying to hide how much his story affected me because he was worried I would see him differently. Nothing can be further from the truth. I still want to be his friend and spend time with him. All this does is explain why he looks frightened most of the time.

"Please leave."

My eyes widen in surprise. I don't want to leave him alone right now because I know he must be feeling raw and exposed. I can help him though this feeling if he would just let me, but instead he's asking me to leave. "Ares, don't ..."

"Kohan. I can't do this right now. Please just leave." He doesn't look at me as he pleads with me and I wish he would. I wish I could see his eyes but he doesn't raise his head.

I want to argue with him, tell him that he'll have to try harder to get rid of me, but it wouldn't be the best approach after what he just told me. He spent a long time being abused by some arsehole and I don't want him to be scared of me. I get up slowly and turn towards the door. As I go to move past him, I reach out and put my hand on the back of his head. "I'm here whenever you need me. Call me and I will be here within minutes." I leave it at that and walk out the front door, grabbing my jacket on the way.

When I reach the quiet road outside Ares' I turn back and look at his cottage. All the lights have been turned off and if I hadn't been in here a few moments before, I would think he wasn't home. I button up my jacket and start slowly walking towards town. I could call someone to come and get me but I want to take the time to work out what I'm feeling. I don't know if I should feel so numb after hearing about his experience but I do. I don't think there's a human out there that wouldn't feel something after listening to that.

Knowing that small part of his past has opened up so many more questions but I'm not sure if I will ever be able to ask them. I want to know how he was found? Did Micah call an ambulance after he nearly killed him? And, most importantly, where is the son of a bitch? Did he lie about what happened and is out there somewhere lying in wait for Ares to wander by alone? Is that why Ares is here, is he hiding? He did say that he didn't leave the house for a long time when he first moved here. Is it because he's still scared that Micah could get to him?

I look around me into the darkness, suddenly very aware that I'm alone and very vulnerable. Am I putting myself in danger by hanging around with Ares? Micah did say if he couldn't have him then no one would. I put my hands in my pocket and grab my keys, spreading them between my fingers to use as a weapon just in case. I know it's stupid but after a few drinks anything seems possible.

My mind goes back to something that Ares said before he told me about the incident. He said he didn't want me to think less of him because he went back to Micah. *Shit. He actually went back to that psycho after what happened?* I've read reports on abuse victims saying that they go back to their abusers because they are so broken down that they believe what they're told. Was that the case for Ares? Did Micah convince him to go back and then hurt him when he did? Where was Ares family while he was suffering?

I have so many questions flooding my mind and I have a feeling the list is only going to get longer. The most important question I want answered is whether anyone knows where Micah is now? I'm going to Google that fucker and make sure he's very far away from Ares, and if I'm really lucky he'll be dead. Ares might not want me to be around him tonight but I'm not giving up on him. I am going to keep him safe, even if I have to do it from a distance.

Chapter Nine

Ares

"So why the sudden need for an appointment, Ares?"

I look at Adam, my therapist, sitting in his usual seat with a neutral expression on his face. This is his normal routine. He lets you lead the session and I always find myself telling him more than I had planned to.

I called him this morning looking for an emergency appointment because I was still freaking out after last night. I needed to talk to him to try and make sense of what's happening between Kohan and me. I want to think that it's just the start of a fantastic friendship but I think it might be more. I told him part of my deepest, darkest secret after just two weeks of knowing him and I don't know why. I want to understand and I need Adam to help me. "I needed to speak to you."

"I figured that much. I didn't think that maybe you missed me. I'm also a little worried because you have called for an appointment outside of our regular schedule. Has something happened?"

I rub my nail over the knee of my jeans and chew my bottom lip. When I called Adam this morning I knew that I needed to talk it all out, to give him all the information so he can help me; but now that I'm here it's difficult to find the words to explain everything. It's probably better just to come out with it, act like it's a plaster and rip it off in one go. "I made a friend."

"That's great. Where did you meet them?" He makes a note on the pad and then looks back at me, giving me all his attention. I spent far too many hours when I first started coming to see Adam wondering what was in his notes, but now I don't care, figuring it's probably better that I don't know what he really thinks about me.

"I met him at work."

Adam's eyebrows lift slightly before he writes something else on his pad. "A job? That's even better. It's been an eventful week hasn't it?"

I laugh without humour. "You don't know the half of it." I get up from the couch and walk to the large window that's behind it. I've always loved the view from up here, being able to see the whole City spread out in front of me. I used to miss living in the city, the hustle and bustle of the whole place, the people and the craziness. Now I don't think I would be able to cope with the exact thing that I used to love.

"I can't help you if you won't tell me what brought you here. Let's start with something easy, is it the job or the friend?"

I keep looking out the window but I do answer Adam's question. "The friend. I haven't had one in a long time and I don't know …" I turn and walk back to the couch, collapsing onto it. "I don't know if I'm doing it wrong."

"I'm not sure how you can do friendship wrong?"

"I told him about Micah."

The statement is met with silence but I can feel the surprise radiating from Adam. I don't blame him; it took me months to admit to him what happened to me, so to tell Kohan so quickly is a little shocking. "Well, that's unexpected."

"That's one way to describe it. I don't know why I did it."

"Yes you do."

I hate that he knows me so well and can tell what I'm thinking before I do. I go back to rubbing over the knee of my jeans again, letting the rhythm sooth my nerves. "I do." *God, I wish my voice had come out louder than the barely audible whisper.*

"Then explain it to me."

"I trusted him. I don't know why because I barely know him, but he makes me feel safe in a way I haven't felt for a very long time."

"Do you really think time has anything to do with feeling comfortable with someone?"

I bite the nail on my thumb as I think about my answer. The short time of our friendship is my biggest stumbling block and I don't know if I can get past it. My brain keeps telling me that it's far too soon to trust Kohan, but my heart wants me to tell him everything. "It should. How is it possible to feel so comfortable with someone you barely know?"

"How is it possible to feel so uncomfortable with someone you have known for years?"

I know he's talking about Micah. I'd known him for years and as time passed, I'd felt less relaxed than when we'd first met. My initial impression of Micah had been completely wrong though, and this is the cause of my fear. "I know what you're trying to say and I know that I've fallen into that trap before. What if I'm doing it again?"

"What did he say when you told him about it?"

The guilt of asking Kohan to leave hits me again and I want to go back in time and give him a chance to speak. I just couldn't though, the burn of humiliation was raging through me and I didn't want to see disappointment on his face. "Nothing."

"Well in that case then, maybe he isn't the right friend for you to have. If he can't handle your past then I don't think he would be able to support you."

Anger rises inside me as he puts Kohan down. Adam doesn't know what happened, he doesn't know that I was the one who chased him away, so he doesn't get to judge. "He didn't walk away so don't talk about him like that. He wanted to stay but I kicked him out and he had enough respect to leave without making a fuss. I could see the hurt on his face though, as he stepped out the door. So it wasn't him, it was all me."

Adam sits in silence after my little rant but he has that annoying smug look he gets when he's forced me to make a breakthrough.

"Fine, you win. I'm broken and fucked up, I admit it. That isn't much of a surprise, though, is it? We've known this all along."

"I don't think you're broken, Ares. I think you blame yourself for what happened when you had no control over someone else's actions. This makes you cut yourself off from people who might be good for you. People who might give you exactly what you need but you're too scared to see it. Tell me why you trust this friend."

"I don't know." My voice has gone quiet again, the anger that I felt a few moments ago draining quickly from me. "There's something about him. When I look into his eyes I can see only kindness. It's not like it was with Micah, he always wanted to be the one in charge, even when we first started dating. Kohan's different. He's willing to let me lead the way and take my time. He has never pushed for anything, even when I can see that he's dying to ask questions. I don't know how to explain it, he just feels … nice?"

"I think you're explaining it just fine. What I don't see is the problem with you two being friends. Tell me, am I missing something?"

I think back to when Kohan said he wanted to kiss me, he warned me instead of just taking what he wanted. My heart melted with his words and I wanted to kiss him so badly but I just couldn't find the courage to do it. "I think he likes me."

"That's always a good thing in a friendship."

I roll my eyes. *He can't be this dense*? "I don't mean like that. He *likes* me. He told me he wanted to kiss me."

"But he didn't kiss you?"

"No. I told him I couldn't and he didn't go any further. He wouldn't push me into doing anything I didn't want to."

"He sounds like a great guy. I'm still trying to see the problem, Ares. Why don't you explain it to me?"

I don't want to explain it. I want him to tell me what I should do and how I should be feeling. I don't want to examine my emotions because if I do I might have to admit things I'm not ready to, like the fact that I like Kohan and I would like to be more than his friend. "You suck as a therapist. I thought you were meant to tell me how to feel so you can fix me?"

Adam laughs, it's not the first time I've said this to him. Whenever he forces me to actually analyse my feelings I tell him he sucks. "We both know that's not how this works. Only you know how you feel. And, if you've finished stalling, how about answering me."

"I don't like you just so you know. The problem is I don't know how to be friends with someone. Before I met Micah it just came naturally to me, but now I just don't know how to let someone in. How do I ... be a friend? Can I trust him enough?"

"It sounds like you already do. And where does it say that you have to give him everything straight away? Becoming friends is give and take. You don't have to bare your soul before he gives you a little bit back."

Adam always makes so much sense when we talk and I really need to come to him before I do stupid things. Jumping straight in with the worst thing wasn't the most sensible of options. Maybe I should have started with my favourite movie or music. I want to claim ignorance as to why I told Kohan but I know exactly why I did it. "I think I told him to scare him off. I thought that if he walked away before I became too attached it wouldn't hurt so much and I could blame it all on him."

"That makes sense, but it also sounds like a destructive coping mechanism. Why do you need to prove he will leave? What if ... and just think about this for a second ... what if he doesn't leave?"

"I think that scares me more than if he does."

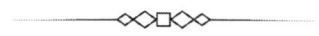

"So did your guy shrink your head like he's meant to?"

I stare at Roscoe as he tries not to laugh at himself. My brother's an arsehole but I do love him. "Yeah, it's all shrunk now you dick."

His laughter finally breaks free and I can't help but join in. There are very few moments in my life now that I feel at ease but I always do with Roscoe.

"Seriously though, is everything okay?"

"Yeah. I just needed to chat about something."

"Glad we had this discussion." I can hear the sarcasm dripping from his words. Roscoe doesn't like to pry too much, or at least that's what he pretends. He has a way of asking for details without actually asking. This is one of those times so I should have known he would say something like that.

"Fine. I met a guy and I didn't know what to make of it."

"When you say met you mean ...?"

"A friend. A guy I've been spending some time with and it's a little bit confusing. I told him about Micah."

Roscoe swerves across the lane he's in as his head whips around to face me. He corrects the car and stares out of the windscreen as he grips the steering wheel. "You told someone about *him*? I'm not even sure what to say to that."

"Now you know why I needed to speak to Adam."

I see Roscoe's knuckles turn white as he grips the wheel tighter and I start to worry that he's going to break it. He hates how much I suffered because of Micah but he hates how much it still affects me more. There were times when I was worried that Roscoe was going to go after Micah, the hate and anger so strong that he needed to do something. My biggest fear with that was that Roscoe would kill him, and I would lose someone I loved so much. I begged him not to go after Micah, using his love for me to guilt him into staying away, and it wasn't for Micah's benefit, it was for Roscoe's. "I hate that that fucker still has you so messed up. You can't even meet a new person without talking to your therapist about it. I swear if I got my hands on him."

"I know, Ro, and thankfully that's not possible. And it's not really his fault, a lot of people go through what I did without turning into a fucking freak." I hold on to the edge of my seat as the car suddenly swerves towards the hard shoulder of the motorway. I brace myself against the dashboard with my other hand as Roscoe slams on the brakes, bringing us quickly to a complete stop.

He turns towards me, resting one hand on the back of my seat and the other on the steering wheel. He looks pissed and I find myself inching away from him. "You listen to me, little brother. Don't you fucking dare put yourself down. You are not a freak, you are a survivor. I can't even imagine having to deal with what you did, so the fact you walked away from it shows your strength. He made you fucking deaf for God's sake and here you are carrying on with your life. So don't you think you are anything other than my hero."

Tears build up in my eyes as I sit and stare at him. My brother has never gotten angry at me before and he's never said anything like that. I always thought I was a burden to him. He had to give up so much to get me through the court case after I finally decided to press charges against Micah - new job, a relationship with the woman he thought he might marry, and the new apartment he'd just moved into. He never once held it against me and supported me one hundred percent through the sleepless nights and break downs. Back then I was so scared to fall asleep, convinced that if I did Micah would be there when I opened my eyes. He threatened to kill my family if I ever left him and even though he was incarcerated, I was sure he would get to them. I would never have forgiven myself if he hurt them.

Now hearing Roscoe telling me I'm not broken, that I'm a survivor, has my heart nearly exploding in my chest. He's the strongest person I know and if he believes in me I should trust him, but I can't. He thinks he still knows me but the boy he knew growing up is gone. He's been replaced by a hollow shell that's scared of his own shadow. I can't tell him that, I can't take his words and throw them back in his face like they mean nothing to me, because they do. It settles me to know that he will always have my back no matter what. "Thank you."

He reaches over and grabs me by the back of my neck before pulling me into his chest and wrapping his arms around me. I hug him back tightly, needing him more than he will ever know. Roscoe has always been there for me, to give me advice whenever I needed it, and maybe now I should listen to what he's told me in the past and embrace the friendship with Kohan. He met Tina a month after my trial ended and within a month married her. He told me that when you know something is right then there is no point in wasting time.

I sit back into my seat when Roscoe lets me go and he doesn't say anything as he pulls away from the hard shoulder and heads for home again. This is how we do things. We aren't afraid to show our emotions to each other, but once we're done we don't talk about it. I smirk as I sit in silence and Roscoe calmly raises his middle finger in my direction. I burst out laughing and it feels like the release we both need.

"So tell me about this friend."

"His name's Kohan and he's a reporter at the offices I clean. I literally bumped into him at work and he gave me a lift home because it was raining." I remember that night and how I was convinced that Micah had sent him.

"You got into a car with him?"

I chuckle at the surprise in Roscoe's voice. Three months ago if you had tried to get me into a car with a stranger I would have freaked out and collapsed into a heap on the floor in a major panic attack. I don't know why cars had such an effect on me because it's not like Micah did anything to me in one, but I just couldn't handle being in one with someone who wasn't family. That's why I relied so much on Roscoe to drive me places. "I got in a car with him. Aren't you proud?"

"Closer to shocked I'd say. Have you been in a car with anyone else yet?"

I shake my head violently, just the thought of it makes a cold sweat break out over my skin. "I just can't do it yet. I nearly got in a taxi a few weeks ago but when it arrived I paid the driver and made him leave. But with Kohan, he made it seem easy and I just got in the car. I know I'm not explaining this well but I'm all fucked up about the whole thing. It's confusing me."

"Don't over think it little brother. Not everything needs to make sense. Me and Tina don't make sense but fuck do I love that woman. Go with the flow for a little bit and find the fun in life again. You have spent the last few years being kept in check; it's time for you to live again."

Roscoe makes it sound so simple. Can I just hold my middle finger up to the world and enjoy myself again? Maybe he's right and it's my time to find out.

Chapter Ten

Ares

When Roscoe dropped me home just over a week ago I'd felt amazing. I was going to take his advice and start to live my life like the twenty-five year old I am. That lasted for about four hours and then reality hit with a bang.

Determined to get out and meet new people I had decided to take a walk into town. The walk down my dirt road had been fine, stress only started to show with sweaty palms as I reached town. Taking a deep breath, I'd stepped onto the pavement that would take me along Main Street but as soon as I started along it I knew I'd made a mistake. People stared at me as I passed and I was barely a hundred yards into my walk when real panic started to creep in. It started subtly, my breathing picked up and I felt a little out of breath, and then I started sweating more than normal, so much that I felt it running down my back. I tried to convince myself that I wasn't struggling with my anxiety, that this was all normal for someone who had walked from my house, but all too soon I knew I was lying to myself. I could feel everybody staring at me and it made my imagination go into overtime. There were too many people around me, too many strangers, and I was scared one of them was sent by Micah to hurt me.

Just as I was ready to turn and run for home, a car backfired and the noise echoed through the street loud enough to make my ears throb. I collapsed to the ground in terror, shuffling myself backwards until my back connected with a shop door. I buried my head under my hands on my knees and sat there rocking back and forth. I could hear people trying to talk to me but I couldn't hear them. I was too far gone, too convinced that someone was going to hurt me. All I had wanted to do was hide from the world until everyone disappeared. When someone reached out and touched me I freaked out worse than I was. The scream surprised me but it made people move away from me and when I saw a gap in the crowd I ran and didn't stop until I was at my front door.

That was nine days ago and was the last day I put my hearing aids in. I'd decided that I would rather live with the silence if it would block out my fear. And it's that decision that has me sitting on the floor of my living room at this moment with my back in the corner so I can't be seen by anyone outside. The overhead lights are flashing and I know it means that Kohan has rung the bell again. I can't hear the bell but the visual is enough to have me wrapping my arms around myself. It's Friday night and the third night in a row that Kohan has tried to get me to open my door.

After my panic attack I decided that I wasn't interested in changing. Stepping out of my comfort zone was too stressful so I wasn't going to do it. I asked Mr James if I could clean the office first thing in the morning before people arrived instead of at night. He said that he didn't care as long as it was done before eight thirty. It meant getting up at four thirty each morning but it was worth it to avoid seeing Kohan. Although after a few days I noticed him coming in earlier, almost like he was looking for me, and it became a game of hide and seek between us. I've spent the last four days alternating between going in early or really late so he wouldn't find me, and I'm getting really tired.

I'm tired of hiding.
I'm tired of staying away.
I'm tired of being me.

It doesn't help when he keeps trying to talk to me. Every time I go into work he's been there, leaving packets of jellybeans on my cleaning trolley so I can find them. I don't know how he found out I love them but he did somehow, and now I have a ready supply of them. He's been texting too, asking how I'm doing and asking if I would meet with him. Every single one had me wanting to reply but I knew that it would drag everything out and hurt more in the long run. The first night he came to the door I nearly answered it just so

I could see his face. I'd hoped that he would give up when I didn't speak to him but he came back again last night, and tonight. I should be panicking, possibly call my brother and tell him that Kohan won't leave me alone, but I know that will never happen.

That's why I'm sitting here crying, because he's making it so hard to ignore him. I want him to give up and leave so I don't have to try and be strong. He needs to see that it's better for him if he stays away from me. He needs to understand that I'm not worth this attention, that I ruin everything I touch. Micah taught me that I was like a disease that eventually destroys everything I touch.

Adam and my family have tried to tell me that he only said those things as an excuse for what he did he did to me, but I'm not so sure now. What kind of person can't walk down a street without falling apart? A damaged one, someone who would infect anyone who was good and caring with their darkness.

That's why I can't let Kohan in.

The only problem is I can feel my resolve starting to crumble with every press of the doorbell. He's not giving up like he has previously. *Why won't he just leave me alone?*

I bury my head in my hands to try and block out the flashing lights but it's not working. Every time I think that it's stopped I look up to see if it has, panic seizing my heart as I worry what will happen if Kohan finally decides to walk away.

That's what's going through my head as I get up from the floor and rush towards the front door. I must look like shit with tears running down my face and my hair messed up from dragging my hands through it, but I don't care. The thought of Kohan walking away is more than I can cope with tonight.

When I open the door he's standing with his hands on the doorframe and his head dropped forward. He must hear me though because his head whips up instantly. His eyes widen as he takes the sight of me in and in a heartbeat he has me wrapped in his arms. I should fight against him and tell him that I'm fine and he can leave now but I'm selfish and I don't want him to go. I want him for as long as he is willing to put up with me, no matter how much it hurts when he inevitably walks away. I can feel his jaw moving and I know he's talking but without my hearing aids I have no chance of understanding him. I should pull back and tell him that I can't hear him but I don't want to lose the feel of his arms around me. He's holding me tight and the pressure from his arms is making me feel complete for the first time in over a week.

I don't notice we're moving to begin with, but when I feel the breeze from outside being cut off I open my eyes and see we're both now inside with the front door closed. Kohan relaxes his hold on me slightly and I reluctantly step back from him but he doesn't let me go far. I can't bring myself to look up at him, the shame burning deep in my gut, but he cups my jaw and tilts my face up. When I raise my eyes to meet his, he slowly mouths something at me and my heart literally melts with how much he cares even though I've don't nothing but push him away.

Nodding my head I squeeze his wrists before walking to my bedroom. I grab my hearing aids and look at myself in the mirror as I fit them. That's what Kohan had mouthed at me in the hall; he wanted me to put my hearing aids in so we could chat. After placing the hearing aids I grab a wipe from the packet in the drawer and try to make my disaster of a face look a little better. I wipe over my cheeks to try and get rid of the mess from the tears but it's a lost cause.

I look up to find Kohan leaning against the doorframe, his arms crossed over his chest. "Can you hear me now?"

I turn and lean back against my dressing table. I nod as I stare at him.

He goes to move but stops before he enters my room. "Is this okay? Can I come in?"

I nod again and he enters my small room. I wait for the panic to hit me but it never comes, even when he stands right in front of me. He just looks at me, his gentle eyes taking me in like he's making sure I'm not hurt.

"Was it you that had the panic attack?"

The memories of that day make me blush. I felt so weak

even though I had convinced myself that I could be strong. Admitting to Kohan that it was me is embarrassing. Me knowing that I'm broken is different than admitting it to him, but I nod my head, refusing to lie to him.

He starts to raise his hand towards me but stops before he makes contact. I take a deep breath, pretending to feel more confident than I do, and take a step towards him. It must confirm to him that I'm okay with him touching me, so he raises his hand the final distance and cups my cheek. His skin is warm against my skin, his finger rubbing over my day old stubble. "I knew it and I was so scared. I wanted to talk to you but you ran away from me. You told me something so painful and then you were gone."

"I'm sorry." I lean into his hand, absorbing the heat from his skin.

"Don't be sorry, Ares. I want to be your friend but I can see how hard it is for you. Tell me what I need to do for you to let me in. I promise I won't hurt you. I just want to help, give you someone to talk to when you need it. Please let me be your friend."

His words sound perfect and I spend a moment basking in the feeling before reality sneaks in unwanted. Why does he want to be my friend, I'm no good? "I don't know what to do, Kohan. I can still feel his hands hitting me and I swear I expect to see him around every corner. How can I give you everything you deserve when he stole so much of me? You deserve better. You deserve someone who isn't so fucking broken. I just don't understand why you want me. I'm disgusting. I'm worthless. I'm nothing."

Kohan's grip tightens on my cheek slightly and he uses his hold to push me backwards, turning us until my back hits the wall. Again, I wait for the panic to hit me but it never comes. I was in this position with Micah so many times and none of them ended well for me. But with Kohan holding my head away from the wall and him slowing us so my body barely bumps the wall, it feels different. He must see something in my eyes though, something that I didn't realise I was showing, because his eyes widen and he leans closer to me.

"I don't think you're broken. Did he tell you that? God I wish I could get my hands on him. I know I haven't known you long but that means nothing. I can see who you are, Ares." His lip curls up and his finger strokes over my cheek. "And you should ask Sophie, I only have the best people as friends. No arseholes allowed."

I laugh despite myself and it's a relief. The tension seems to dissipate and I can tell that Kohan notices it as well. The smile I'm granted makes my heart swell in my chest, giving me hope that we might be able to do this friendship thing.

Kohan

"Were you hiding from me on purpose?" I look over to Ares from where I'm leaning against the headboard to where he's leaning with his back against the wall. He's holding a pillow against his chest like he needs protection from the conversation we need to have. After finally getting him to relax in my company I asked if he wanted to move to the living room but he sat on his bed, surprising me into silence until he asked me to join him. We've been sitting here for about twenty minutes just talking about random things but now I want some answers.

"I wouldn't call it hiding."

"I would. So it was on purpose?"

"I'm sorry."

He keeps apologising but that's not going to work for me. I get that he has a lot of baggage, and if he wants to share it then I'm here for him, but if we are going to be friends he will have to realise that I need the truth. "Not accepting your apology this time. I want you to talk. I don't need everything but I want the truth. Why were you avoiding me?"

He sighs and pulls the pillow closer to his body using it like a barrier between us. "I didn't know what to do and that's the truth. When I told you what happened to me with Micah I panicked. I didn't want to see how disappointed you were in me so I made you leave before you did it on your own. People always leave because I make them. I'm stupid and people get frustrated and angry. It was easier to make you leave before it hurt too much."

I want to grab him and shake some fucking sense into him but I don't think that'd be the right approach with Ares. "Do you remember having dinner with me every night?"

He nods, his eyes so wide that he looks like an innocent child.

"Well I don't know what you got out of that, but I have to tell you, those nights meant everything to me. I don't know what you've been told in the past but you are kind and funny, passionate and smart. I loved getting to know you and yes, you told me some heavy shit, and guess what? I'm still here. Not only am I here but I'm chasing you. Thought I would mention that since you seemed to have missed that bit and I don't just chase anyone. Actually … I don't chase people at all."

"I don't know why you are, but I promise I'm going to try harder. I loved the time we spent together; it was nice to speak to someone who didn't know everything. I can't promise that I'll be able to give you the whole Ares because I don't remember who he is."

I want to reach out and touch him. I've found that touching Ares has become an addictive habit that gives me more comfort than it probably should. I'm here preaching about friendship and all I can think about is how soft his skin is and how much I want to kiss him. Unfortunately that isn't something that he can give me, and because I'm a glutton for punishment, I'm willing to accept whatever he is willing to offer. No matter what Ares has been told in the past, he's worth spending time with and I need to convince him of it. I know it wont be an easy task since he's obviously spent years being told the opposite, but I'm feeling up to the challenge.

"I'll give you time to find him again. I'm not here to pressure you for anything. I want you to know that you can be whoever you need to be. You can laugh or cry or whatever you need; I can cope with anything you throw at me. I'm friends with Sophie, and if I can handle her crazy arse then you will be no problem at all."

"Why does she sound like she would scare me?"

I laugh as I imagine poor Ares meeting Sophie. As much as I would love for them to get to know each other I don't think it should happen straight away. Sophie's been bugging me about meeting Ares properly, especially since I can't stop talking about him, but I think he needs to be a bit more confident in himself before I set her on him. Sophie is, well let's call her an *acquired taste* and that taste isn't for the faint hearted. "I think Sophie would scare the shit out of you. Why don't *we* get to know each other a bit better before I put you through that?"

Ares laughs but I can see a little bit of panic flash in his eyes.

"Don't worry. When you do meet her I'll be there to take care of you. She'll like you and she's the most loyal person I've ever met. Once she becomes your friend no one will be able to hurt you. She once attacked a six foot brick shit house because he called me a shirt lifter."

Ares laughs again but this time it seems more genuine, losing the edge that the last one had. When he's happy he looks like a different person. His entire face lights up and he loses the darkness that's always deep in his eyes. I want to keep seeing him like that, to keep him smiling. I spend the next hour telling him stories about Sophie and everything she gets up to. I don't even notice the time as it passes until Ares has to get up and turn on a light. Spending time with Ares is effortless, and it makes me realise how much I missed him while we were apart.

Chapter Eleven

Kohan

"Pass the potatoes will you, Ko?" I pick up the bowl of mashed potato and pass it across the table towards Carey. We're all visiting mum for Sunday dinner, and as usual, it's complete chaos. The only person that couldn't make it this afternoon was Jensen because Henry, Jensen's stepson, isn't feeling well. They suspect he might be getting chicken pox so they kept him at home so he wasn't around Damien's month old daughter, Milly.

"So how's the fast moving world of journalism these days, Ko?" Damien goes back to helping Darcy eat her sweetcorn after he speaks.

"It's not too bad. I'm writing more important articles now so that's a good thing."

"So they promoted you from writing about the local pet shows? I'm impressed little brother."

I look down the table at Damien and see him looking at me with a smirk on his face. The fucker loves to get a reaction out of me and I don't disappoint him this time as I raise my middle finger. His laughter is loud and lasts until Darcy mimics my movements and gives her dad the finger. His face instantly falls and he reaches out gently and covers her hand as colour works up his cheeks. Now it's my turn to laugh. *Serves the fucker right.*

"Laugh it up, arsehole."

The little voice next to him pipes up with 'arsehole' and that earns Damien a death glare from his wife, Heidi.

"What did I tell you about swearing in front of her? It was bloody embarrassing last week when she told the nurse," She reaches out and covers Darcy's ears. Darcy doesn't even flinch so she must be used to this. "That fucking hurt." She removes her hand and puts more sweetcorn onto Darcy's plate. "I told you that I refuse to take her anywhere with that mouth of hers, but keep going, Damien. I will make sure you take her to every future appointment."

By the time Heidi has finished scolding Damien the rest of us are almost crying with laughter. With Damien being the eldest he always was the biggest and the strongest. He used that against us even when we all grew up and almost matched his size. The day he met Heidi there was a definite shift in the force and we all witnessed the gradual retirement of Damien's balls. Now his wife is in control and it's a beautiful thing to see.

"And that right there people is why I will never get married."

"No, Carey. You won't get married because no woman is stupid enough to have you."

A slight blush creeps over Carey's cheeks as Damien retorts, but I have a feeling that it's not what Damien said that elicits that reaction. Carey's eyes flick over to mine but he looks away quickly. I make a mental note to speak to him before I leave tonight. Carey is the second eldest but he's the one I've always felt closest to, even over Jensen who's barely a year older than me. Carey still lives here with mum and as much as he wants us to believe that it's because he doesn't have life sorted out, I think it's so he can keep an eye on her. He's more sensitive than he likes people to know and tonight he's been quieter than normal, making me think that something is going on with him.

"How's Maya doing, Emile?" Mum looks down the table towards my brother as she scoops some more chicken onto my plate. I didn't ask for it but that's never stopped her in the past so I doubt it'll ever change. She is such a typical mother.

"She's good, mum, wishes she could be here today but her shifts have been chaotic recently."

"She'll have to slow things down a bit when she gets pregnant. A woman shouldn't be working when she's having a baby."

The colour drains from Emile's face as he stares slack jawed at our mum. I actually didn't think it was possible for someone to look so green without actually vomiting. "But we aren't trying."

"Oh pish. I give it six months and you'll be sitting here with a lovely pregnant wife. You've been married for two years now, it's time that Thea was adding to the family."

The whole table goes silent and we all turn to look between Mum and Emile. I don't know if she realises what she's said but I reach over and pat her wrist gently. When she looks at me, her face is completely relaxed and I know that she doesn't know she's made a mistake. "Mum, Emile is married to Maya not Thea."

She looks at me as though I'm the one that's losing my mind. "I know that. I told him that Maya needed to get pregnant."

My heart aches for her as she looks around the table, looking at everyone's face for support. I've been trying to tell my brothers for months that there's something wrong with mum but no one would listen to me. "You just made a mistake, it's okay."

She pulls her hand away from me and glares around the table. "I didn't make a mistake. I said Maya. You need to pay better attention." She pushes back from the table and walks from the dining room.

We all sit quietly looking at each other until Heidi gets up from the table, huffing as she does. "You guys are pathetic. You just sit there and look like idiots, I'll go make sure she is fine."

We all sit in silence as Heidi leaves the table, the only noise in the room is the sound of Darcy hitting her knife against her plate. Damien takes it out of her hand and kisses her head. "Go and play in the den now, honey. I'll call you back for dessert."

She smiles up at her dad and my heart melts. I have always loved children and I've always though of maybe starting a family of my own one day. She slides off the side of her chair and skips towards the bedroom that was turned into a den for the kids.

It's Emile that breaks the silence and I'm glad that it's not going to have to be me. I felt I was the only person who had seen it but thankfully I'm not. "Mum's getting worse."

"I don't know what you're talking about, she made a simple

mistake. I call Milly by Darcy's name all the time." Damien's going to be the hardest out of them to crack and it will be nice if the others have my back to try and convince him.

"Damien, she needs to see a doctor."

He glares at me and on a normal day that look would have me dropping the subject but I refuse to this time. This isn't about what present we're buying someone or where we're going to eat, this is my mum's health and I will push it until we're all on the same page.

"Kohan's right, she's getting worse." Carey's speaks up and maybe living here will give him a little bit more weight in the argument against Damien. "I'm scared to leave her alone because when I do I'm not sure what I'm going to come home to. She keeps calling me Joe, and for the first few times I thought she was just having a moment, but these moments are becoming more regular. She forgot she was cooking last week while I was out. When I came home there was black smoke filling the house and she didn't even notice. She could have killed herself."

My stomach clenches as I listen to Carey tell us what's been happening. Thinking that there might be a problem is very different to having it confirmed, and hearing how dangerous it has become to leave Mum on her own, that just makes me all the more determined to make my point with Damien. "I'll make a doctor's appointment for her, but we need to talk to her before we take her. It's not fair to just spring it on her."

Damien grunts at us but at least this time he doesn't argue.

"I don't want to throw anyone under the bus here, but I think it would be better coming from Damien. You're the eldest and Heidi can help you. I think if we all do it then she'll feel like we're ganging up on her. Kohan can take her to the doctor but she needs to be on board. I'll go with them so I can give extra insight into her everyday living." Carey has always been the voice of reason out of all of us, and today is no different. He's also the one person that Damien won't argue with.

"I don't see why I should talk to her about it. I don't think there is anything wrong with her." Damien's such a hardheaded fool and sometimes I just want to smack some sense into him. I'm about to tell him just that when Carey speaks up.

"Then you still have nothing to lose. If we take her to the doctor and he doesn't see anything wrong, then you were right and we saw something that wasn't there. Wouldn't you rather that than not doing anything and there being something wrong that is too late to do something about?"

Damien pushes back from his seat and huffs as he stands. "Fucking hell. Watch the girls and I'll go talk with her." He doesn't wait for us to say anything before he storms out of the dining room. He loves to act as though he's put out but he, like the rest of us, would do anything for family.

Emile gets up from the table and starts to clear away the dishes. I think we have all lost our appetites so there is no point in hanging around in here.

"Emile, why don't you take Milly through to the den and keep an eye on her and Darcy?" Emile looks between me and Carey, thankfully realizing that I'm asking for privacy to talk to Carey.

"No worries." He goes to the large window that looks over that back garden and lifts Milly from the moses basket that's always there. He snuggles the baby into his chest and I smile when I see how natural he is with her. Mum's right about one thing; Emile would make an amazing dad.

I pile up the plates from the table and follow Carey into the kitchen. I fill the sink with hot water and soap, and start hand washing the pots and plates. Carey moves to stand beside me and grabs a dish towel. We're quiet while we clean up but I can tell that Carey wants to say something.

"I'm ready whenever you want to talk." I look at Carey out of the corner of my eye and see the small smirk on his lips.

"No one likes a smart arse you know." He grabs the frying pan from the draining board and concentrates on drying it. I start to think that maybe he doesn't have anything to say when he starts talking. "Were you ever attracted to women?"

Okay, not exactly where I thought he was going to go but I run with it. "I think that there might have been one girl I liked, but it was more that she brought Monster Munch to school each day for break time snack."

Carey stops drying and stares at me in confusion.

"Don't look at me like that. I was seven and loved Monster Munch. But to answer your question, I think I always knew I was different than my friends. I didn't know it was because I was gay, but then it became quite clear when showers after PE were like a boner minefield."

He stays quiet and I allow him to have his moment of silence. He's obviously working through something in his head and I don't want to rush him. "I think …"

I try not to look at him but when he stops talking I can't resist any longer. I wipe the bubbles off my hands and lean back against the unit so I can see him.

"Don't stare at me. This is hard enough without you being all judgy."

I laugh at him, knowing for a fact that he's talking shit. There is no one in this house less judgmental than me and Carey is well aware of that. I see what he's doing, deflecting his unease onto me, but instead of calling him out on it I just stay silent. The only outward sign of any kind of reaction from me is a slight raise of my eyebrows.

"God, stop pressuring me to talk." He walks over to the kitchen door and closes it.

Shit, this must be serious.

"It's just … fuck it. I'm having feelings for someone and I'm not sure what to do with it."

Now I'm really confused. Carey has always had an open door policy when it came to the women that's he's *dated*, so I'm not sure what he's being so shy about. "If you're trying to tell me your straight, Carey, I already know that."

"I didn't say it was a woman."

"Oh …OH! Shit."

He rolls his eyes at my reaction but he can't blame me. Carey is thirty-two years old and I've never had a single inkling that he was anything other than straight. "Don't make a big thing out of it or I won't tell you anything else."

I mime locking my lips and throwing the keys away because I want to hear this more than just about anything else in the world.

"There's this guy at my gym and we got chatting. It was nothing more than grabbing a smoothie and talking. It happened so gradually that I didn't notice anything until he kissed me."

I struggle to keep my lips sealed tight but I can feel my eyes go wide. The thought of Carey kissing a guy is … strange?

"It's not the kiss that threw me, it was the fact that I didn't push him away. I didn't really participate, but if I'm honest, I enjoyed it more than I would have expected. It was so completely different to kissing a woman and I can't think of one bad thing about it."

This time I don't hold in my smile. *Look my big brother enjoying what I have all these years*. "Do you like him? I mean sexually?"

"I think I do. Since he kissed me I can't seem to get my dick under control whenever he's around. I just don't know what to do about it."

"I say go for it. I could tell you all the joys of loving dick but until you experience it you won't believe me."

Carey laughs and kicks my shin gently. "Don't be so bloody crude. I'm scared to do anything more though, what if I like it?"

"Then you like it. Maybe this is the person you have been waiting all your life for."

He still doesn't seem convinced so I keep talking hoping to say something that will make him feel better. I don't want this to become a huge hurdle for him. "What've you got to lose? If you don't like it you can say stop at any time. That's the fun of it all, finding out what you enjoy."

"I want to try, I really do, but I'm scared of disappointing him. He's been so understanding with everything, listening when I explained how inexperienced I am and none of it bothered him. He said he would let me decide how far we go. He's pretty damn perfect."

My heart soars as he describes this guy. I haven't heard him talk about any woman like this and I've always thought it was a shame that he hadn't found someone. "Does he have a name?" I want to find out everything about the guy that's making my brother so happy.

"Duncan. He lives in Greenview, quite close to the gym. I don't think he's been in the area long, he mentioned moving from Manchester after a bad break up."

The bad break up is a bit of a red flag to me. An ex coming back into the picture is never a good thing for the new love interest, but if he's over it then I'm happy for my brother. "When do I get to meet him?"

Carey chews his lip, looking nervous again. "I don't know. I'm still too unsure about what to do with all this."

"What do you want to do? In your heart you must know where you want this to go."

Carey looks down at the floor and I move over to stand next to him, putting my arm around his shoulder. He looks so torn and I want him to know he has my support no matter what. "I want to see where this goes. I don't know what will come of it and I don't know if it's men or just him that I'm attracted to. I do know that want to kiss him again." Carey's voice is low and he sounds like a really confused teenager trying to work out his feelings. I can relate to that and I'm glad I knew myself before I reached my thirties. It must be really fucking hard dealing with this at his age after spending all those years thinking he knew who he was.

"Then kiss him. If it doesn't work out then you decide how you move on. It might be another guy or a woman. Do you still like women?"

He nudges me with his shoulder. "Of course I do." He scrubs is hands over his face. "Why is this thing so fucking hard?"

"It isn't, big brother. You just need to do whatever makes you happy. Stop thinking about all the other stuff. This family will be here to support you no matter what. So go out and get laid. But remember I want to meet this Duncan, see if he's good enough for my brother."

"I hate you a little right now." He pulls me close and kisses the top of my head. "But I love you so much. And just so you know, if you embarrass me in front of Duncan I will return the favour when you find someone special."

I laugh and move back to the sink. "You'll have a long wait." I wish it wasn't true, but the only guy who has caught my attention recently isn't in the position to want anything more than friendship. I wish he was but I'm just not that lucky.

Chapter Twelve

Ares

 I pop some jellybeans into my mouth as I lean against the wall and look at the face I've spent the day working on. It might not seem like a fun way for most people to spend a Sunday, but after finally getting over my creative block, it was the only thing I wanted to do. I chew as I stare at it sitting on the potter's wheel, wondering why I haven't left a flaw into this face. I'm also trying to convince myself that it isn't Kohan's face that I ended up sculpting. *No, it's just someone that looks really, really like him.* Unfortunately I know I'm lying to myself because even over this distance I know its Kohan's eyes staring at me. I'm pretty sure that's why I couldn't put a flaw onto it, because it would be marking the most beautiful thing I've ever seen.

 I decided to create something today even though I didn't really need an outlet for my anxiety. No today I was calm, I just needed to do something with my hands. Ever since Kohan made me open my front door, I've felt happy and in control of myself. It's the first time since I woke up in the hospital and decided to press charges, that I think I might be able to be normal again.

 I'm not naïve enough to think that one hug from Kohan will cure everything, but it's a starting point where I can try and get my life back. Kohan has been nothing but supportive up until this point and I need to give him the benefit of the doubt. I need to stop looking for him to do something bad to me.

 Now if I could get my brain on board with that then everything would be great. All I can think of though is how Micah was the sweetest guy I'd ever met at the beginning. He was kind, attentive, gentle and loving. Six months of nothing but pure romance that swept me off my feet. That's why I married him so quickly. Micah was moving to Manchester for a new job and I wanted to go with him. He told me that if I was moving with him then he wanted to make it official and make sure people knew I was his. At the time I thought it was romantic, he wanted to spend the rest of his life with me and wanted everyone to know. What he was actually doing was showing everyone that I was his property and that no one should come near me.

My parents begged me not to marry him and told me to move if I needed to but not to commit myself to him in such a permanent way. I thought they were being over dramatic and that they just wanted me to have a long engagement like they did. They told me later that they had always seen something in Micah, something that made them worry for me, but because they didn't have any proof of it they couldn't say anything. I wouldn't listen to them though when they told me to slow down a bit. No, I had to be a hardheaded idiot, and a few weeks later I walked out of the registry office as Mr Ares Henley. The night before we got married was the first time Micah let his anger show and it should have warned me enough to walk away. I was in love though so I gave him his way and took his name, telling myself that he was just old fashioned and wanted us to share our surnames. If only I knew then what I know now, I could've saved myself from a lot of harm.

That was nearly four years ago and it's time to finally put all that behind me. I've let Micah have a hold on me for all this time and it's giving him power he doesn't deserve. I need to take that power back from him and it needs to start now. Micah's in jail and can't get to me anymore. The thoughts of him sending someone to watch me are crazy. I need to get through my head that he isn't a danger to me. He can't touch me anymore.

Now I just have to gather enough courage to actually get out there and grab life by the balls. I spoke to Adam on the phone this morning, giving him the outline of the new plan to change my life. He was cautiously excited about my sudden decision, telling me to take it slowly but keep moving in the right direction. He's worried that there might still be moments when the past sneaks into my mind and it makes me freeze. Adam's tried to explain to me that I suffer from PTSD but I refuse to accept that diagnosis. Soldiers who have survived through some of the worst experiences in life experience that so there's no way I do. He tried to explain that I went through hell at the hands of Micah but my mind struggles to believe him. I just nodded at him and told him I would get over it eventually. Little did I know that three years later I would still be fighting with my demons.

I gave up on everything when I left Micah. To begin with I told myself the reason I had no interest in anything was because I was healing, but once the marks faded and the scars became paler I convinced myself it was because I was dealing with the court case. After the court case it was because I was wanted time to be by myself to find out who I really was. Now I have no more excuses other than the truth. I'm scared of my own shadow, but not anymore. This is my last day that I'm going to be stuck in my house. Tomorrow morning I'm going to get up and start as I mean to go on. I will go for a run down by the quarry and then I will go to work with a smile on my face. I will not live in silence, I will put my hearing aids in and become part of the world again.

I step forward and run my finger over the prominent cheekbones on the head sculpture of Kohan. Friendship aside, I have to say that Kohan is really beautiful. He's what I would class as traditionally handsome. With high cheekbones, full lips, sparkling brown eyes, and a jaw that I want to run my tongue along, he looks a little like an old time actor. Shit, that's not really how I should be thinking of Kohan. Nearly three years since Micah put me in hospital for the last time and that was the last time I felt the loving touch of a man. Now I'm falling for the first man who showed me the slightest bit of affection, but I just can't escape the need to touch him and have him touch me in return so badly. In my mind he's a gentle lover who would take care of me and make me feel like the most important person in the world. He wouldn't demand anything from me that I didn't want to give and for that I would want to give him everything. The only problem is that I can't give him anything.

I put another handful of jellybeans in my mouth and head towards the kitchen. I haven't eaten proper food all day and I'm starting to feel a sugar high. I need to get some real food in me before a sugar crash hits because those are never fun. I wash my hands and stare out the window as I go about my task. It's a beautiful day out there and I didn't notice. The sun is shining through the trees in the garden, highlighting the seating area I organised last week. I'd wondered from when I moved in what to do with the small patio area in the centre of the grass, a cement circle with a path leading to it, but I found a seating set online that I fell in love with. It isn't a traditional garden set of table and chairs, instead it's a comfortable curved sofa with large padded cushions. I might actually get a fire pit for the cooler evenings but at the moment I'm happy with what I have and I can't resist going out and sitting in the sun any longer.

I remove my apron after drying my hands and head towards the side door that leads to the garden. As I walk past the fridge I open it and grab a can of Pepsi Max, opening it and taking a drink as I let myself outside. The warmth hits me instantly and I smile to myself. The summer is arriving quickly and I can't wait to spend it here. As I sit on my new garden chair I look out over my garden as I take a large drink. I need more colour out here. I should go to the local garden centre and see if they have anything that would brighten the place up. Maybe plant some pots for the patio that I can keep topped up with bright new flowers, and hanging baskets, I need some of them too.

Making plans feels a little strange. I'm usually a day at a time kind of guy, just wanting to get through the hours as quickly as possible. This feels like a step in the right direction. To continue with the positive vibes I grab my mobile from my pocket and open up a new message window. Kohan gave me his number the other day and told me to use it anytime. Maybe it's time to reach out to him and finally make the first move. I bite my lip as I start typing.

I was thinking that this garden needs colour. The problem is I can't drive and I don't fancy walking with all those pots. Do you have the number of a good taxi company?

I purposely don't add my name to the end because I'm feeling good for a change, and with that good feeling comes playfulness. I lock my phone but keep it on my knee so I can feel it vibrate. I didn't put my hearing aids in today because I wanted to concentrate on my pottery, so I won't hear my phone if it pings. I close my eyes and lean my head against the back of the chair. The heat of the sun feels good against my skin and it relaxes me until I sink into the cushioned seat. If this is what the summer is going to be like then I might actually get a tan this year. I'll need to up my workouts if I want to be ready to bare my body to the sun.

That thought has my stomach dropping. I haven't gone topless in front of anyone since Micah, not even in front of my family. I always hide it under a t-shirt so people don't see the scars that Micah left on me. They are the result of Micah losing a business deal and using me to work out his frustrations. I honestly don't think he was meant to whip me enough to leave scars, but it was inevitable since he refused to take me to the hospital. God, the pain was unbelievable but it didn't last long since I passed out not long after the punishment started. The weeks after are when I knew what real pain was. The burning pain as the injuries healed was worse than the initial attack. It actually stopped me from leaving my bed for nearly a week. Micah was there with me the whole time, telling me he was sorry and that he loved me. By the time I was able to move again I had forgiven him and was happy to move on, that I understood that he'd had a bad day. Now I'm left with the reminders every time I get undressed. Maybe I wont need that beach body because I'm not sure if I can let other people see them.

My mobile vibrates on my leg and I open my eyes to read the message.

There's a company called Weston Taxis and they are really

reliable. They are cheap too, all they ask is for you to have dinner with them ;)

I laugh at his reply. He knows it's me and that makes me happier than it probably should. I'm thinking of something to write back when another message comes in.

Don't freak out! You didn't answer your door and I saw you out here. Look up.

My head whips up when I finish reading and I see Kohan standing just inside the garden gate waving at me. Panic seizes me when I realise how easy it was for him to gain entry into my property. Anyone could have got to me without me knowing and I'm just sitting here like a sitting duck. *Shit.* Being out here minus my hearing aids isn't the best idea I've ever had. Kohan sits on the step that leads down from the patio and types on his phone.

I can hear you panicking from here.

My fingers shake a little as I type out a response.

I'm just ... I shouldn't have been out here without my hearing aids. Anyone could have gotten to me.

Kohan's head scrunches up as he reads my message, obviously confused by it and I don't blame him. He only knows a tiny little portion of the Micah story and that's completely my fault. He doesn't know that I still fear for my life, constantly worrying that my ex-husband is going to find me and finish the job he started the last time he saw me.

I have a past that you couldn't imagine. The little bits I've told you are just the tip of the iceberg. I will tell you one day I promise, I just can't do it all now. Just know that my ex wasn't a nice man at all and the last time he saw me he swore he would kill me.

I chew my lip again as I watch Kohan read. I know when he's finished because he looks at me, sadness clear in his eyes even at this distance.

I'm here whenever you are ready. But know that no one will touch you again. I will kill anyone who lays a finger on you.

My stomach flutters as I read his text. There's so much in those few words and they mean everything to me. Maybe having a friend isn't such a bad thing. To have someone who isn't family to confide in, to let them help me get through this burden, maybe that's what I've been missing all this time?

"So how's your weekend been so far?" We're both now sitting on the couch in the living room, catching up on everything that's happened since we last saw each other. I now having my hearing aids in and, as always, conversation with Kohan is so easy.

"Let's just say *interesting*. I think my brother came out to me … well kind of."

I'm a little confused. *How can you kind of come out?* I remember when I told my family I was gay in high school. I worried myself sick for weeks before I worked up the courage to do it and it was the most anticlimactic event of my life. I waited until we were all at the dinner table and after I told them they just smiled at me and went back to the previous conversation. Apparently everyone knew I was gay before I was ready to admit it so it wasn't really needed. When I came out though, I came out. There was no kind of. It's an all or nothing sort of thing. "I'm confused."

Kohan laughs and moves a little bit closer to me on the couch. I try to focus on what he's saying but the heat from his arm next to mine is making it really difficult. I remember what it feels like to be wrapped up in his arms and I want to be there again, just not because I'm crying like last time. I want him to hold me tightly while he drops his lips to mine and kisses me until I can't breathe anymore. "You aren't even listening.

Where did you go, Ares?"

My cheeks burn as I turn to look at Kohan. I missed everything he just said and I was the one who asked the question. "I was ... um ..." I have nothing. All my excuses have vanished along with my brain cells.

"I'll be kind this time and not ask you what's causing that blush." Kohan touches my cheek gently and I'm sure the redness increases. The rush I get from just his fingertip has me a little light headed but I concentrate, determined to hear what he's saying. "And to repeat what I said, my straight brother has fallen for a guy."

"Oh ...wow. Did you have any inkling that he was bi?"

"Nothing. As far as everyone knew he had a revolving door on his bedroom and women were entering. I can't wait to meet Duncan because he must be one hell of a guy to turn my brother's head."

I sit up to take a drink from my can before lying back against the couch again. Hearing about Kohan's brother is nice, it makes me realise that there's a huge big world out there that I need to get back into. There are so many people I can become friends with and I need to start soon. "I want to go out. Will you come with me?" I turn my head to face a shocked looking Kohan.

"Are you sure?"

I nod my head but stay quiet, not trusting my voice to sound as confident as I want it to be.

"Then there's no way that you are going out without me. Any ideas on where you want to go?"

I blow out a breath because I haven't thought that far ahead. Going out itself was a bit of a spur of the moment decision and I don't actually know what's around here. "Something quiet to begin with."

"That I can do. Are you up to meeting some new people … or one in particular?"

"Sophie?"

He nods his head. "Yeah, she's dying to meet you. We could go to the local café and have coffee. It will be easier to handle her if there's no alcohol involved. I'll save you from drunk Sophie for a little while longer."

Kohan shivers dramatically and I laugh at his reaction. A coffee shop actually sounds perfect and I love that Kohan knows exactly what I need without me telling him. He understands that it's going to be baby steps until I build up my confidence and he's not making me feel stupid about it. "I think that sounds perfect."

He snorts and shakes his head. "Let's see if you're still saying that after you meet her."

Chapter Thirteen

Ares

My leg bounces under the table as I sit and wait for Kohan to return with our drinks. We arrived earlier than we told Sophie to come so I could get used to being here before she invades us. Kohan's words not mine.

I felt confident when we first arrived but people are starting to notice me now and I'm convinced they remember me from my stupid panic attack. The table next to us is filled with little old ladies and they aren't making it a secret that they're talking about me. It's pretty obvious as they turn their heads and nod in my direction. I want to get up and leave but I just bounce my leg quicker to try and get all my nerves out without running.

Thankfully Kohan returns with our mugs and puts my hibiscus tea on the table as he slips into the seat right next to me at the small round table. The smell of coffee from his cup hits my nose and I have to stop myself from turning up my nose. "Did you just hate on my coffee?"

I take a sip of my tea, closing my eyes as I savour the sweet flavour. "Yeah, I'm sorry. I just hate coffee."

"There's no way you can say that about my caramel mocha with extra shot of fudge."

Even hearing what it's called makes my teeth ache just imagining the sweetness. My tea itself is sweet but all those added flavours and sugars would make me so hyper. Micah didn't like it when I consumed anything that contained anything other than natural sugar. He told me he didn't want me to put on weight so I had to avoid anything that contained refined sugar, carbohydrates or too much fat. The only thing I managed to sneak without him noticing was jellybeans and that soon became an addiction I couldn't break. I'm surprised that Micah never noticed because I would gorge myself on them until I was practically bouncing off the walls. I still struggle to eat sweet foods and drinks, but I'm getting better.

Kohan holds the cup under my nose and I back away from it quickly. "Come on, try it. If you don't like it I'll buy you another one of those boring teas." The smile on his face makes it difficult to say no but I hold my ground, not giving in to his seductive voice. I lean into him, pushing the mug out of the way so I can get close to his ear.

"There's only one thing I put in my mouth that's warm and sweet, and it doesn't come out of a cup." I don't know where the bravery came from to say that. I would never normally dream of saying something that sounded so suggestive but as I pull back and see Kohan's face I'm glad I did it.

His eyes are big as saucers and his mouth is hanging slightly open. I want to giggle at him but there is an underlying heat in his eyes that makes my breath catch in my chest. He's staring at me with lust in his eyes, and I can't help the fact that my dick is hardening in my jeans.

Just as things are becoming a little awkward the seat between Kohan and me is taken and arms are thrown around him. I blink and focus on the world around us again, looking to see who's joined us. It's actually a little worrying how wrapped up in Kohan I get, especially since you know, the whole friends thing.

"You must be Ares. It's so nice to finally meet you. This guy here hasn't stopped talking about you for weeks," She cups her mouth like she's trying to keep a secret from Kohan. "I was actually starting to think he made you up."

I snort at what she's saying; actually I don't think that's what I'm laughing at. It's probably got more to do with the look that Kohan's giving her. It's a mixture of *I want to throttle you* and *please stop talking right now*. She takes no notice and holds her hand over the table at me. I meet her half way and shake her hand gently. Her smile is infectious and it doesn't take me long to smile back at her.

"This pain in the arse right here is Sophie. Feel free to ignore anything she says, most of it's rubbish anyway." Even with his harsh words I can see the affection Kohan has for his best friend.

"And I was going to tell you how awesome you look today."

Kohan points at her and then looks at me. "Sometimes she speaks sense."

Sophie gets up from the table and slaps Kohan's head as she walks passed him. "Be right back. I need caffeine desperately because work is … god it's work." She practically skips away and I can't help but watch her as she moves. She's caught the eye of nearly every male in the place and I can't blame them for staring. Even if her long red hair and nicely rounded hips don't do it for me, her bubbly personality appeals to me.

"She's something else isn't she?"

I turn to look at Kohan and nod my head. "She appears to be a lot of fun?"

Kohan bursts out laughing and the deep sound vibrates right through me, making my earlier problem make itself known again. "Well that's one way of putting it. She's crazy and a little bit hyper, but there isn't a better person out there. Once you have her as a friend no one can mess with you, so be prepared for that."

"She might not even like me."

He laughs again and his face softens as he looks at me. "Could never happen."

If I were sitting alone I would sigh but because that would probably appear a bit pathetic to Kohan, I pick up my mug and take a drink of my tea.

"You really can't handle compliments can you? You know you better get used to it."

I'm saved from answering when Sophie takes her seat again. "Sorry for interrupting the flirting but I couldn't stand up there on my own any longer, people were thinking I was some kind of weirdo."

I blush as I get my first taste of Sophie's lack of filter but I end up laughing when Kohan drops his head to the table and Sophie pats the back of it.

"So, Ares, tell me a little about yourself. This guy here wouldn't give me anything, told me I needed to ask you myself."

I look over to Kohan who shrugs his shoulders and in that moment he gains a little bit more of my heart. I always try to tell myself that Kohan's a great guy who wouldn't do anything to hurt me, and then he does a simple thing like keep my secrets and I know that I can trust him. If he hasn't told his best friend anything about me then maybe I can trust him with my past?

"There isn't much to tell really." I'm hoping to get away with that pathetic answer but when Kohan shakes his head and laughs I know that I'm not getting off that easily.

"Oh come on, spill it. Age?"

"Twenty Five.

"Siblings?"

"One brother, Roscoe."

"Parents?"

"Both alive. My mum, Grace, is a nursery school teacher and my dad, Andy, runs a garage."

"Hobbies?"

"Pottery and running."

"Favourite movie?"

"Um ... don't really watch them."

"Favourite book?"

"Twilight."

"Dick size?"

The questions come so quickly I just answer them automatically, that is until she hits me with the last one. I nearly answer but catch myself before I do. I look between her and Kohan and wonder what the hell that was about.

"Soph. Really?"

"Oh come on, Kohan, I know you are dying to know."

Kohan face instantly reddens and his eyes flick to mine. The move has my pulse racing and I suddenly need to be somewhere else.

"Um, I'm going to the loo. Be back in a minute." I don't wait for them to say anything before I get up and move quickly across the café towards the toilet. I manage to keep from falling apart until I get the door closed behind me. As soon as it's locked I lean back against it and drop my head backwards until it bumps against the wood. I take deep breaths as I try to get my body to calm down. Between all the blood in my body racing to my dick and struggling to breathe I feel light headed. I don't want to think about what Sophie said; I can't believe that Kohan wants to know things like that about me. If I let my thoughts go in that direction then I might want more than what Kohan's willing to give, or what I think he's willing to give.

I bump my head against the door a few times trying to knock some sense into myself. Friendship, that's all there is between Kohan and me, no matter how much I want to see him naked. I don't know when that realisation came to me but it's true, I want to see him under me naked and preferably working his way towards orgasm. I've imagined it a couple of times when giving myself some relief in the shower, the vision of Kohan's face as he comes is always what sends me over. I've gone from having absolutely no interest in anyone to having orgasmic fantasies about someone. *Shit, when did this become my life?* Is this what it's like to actually fancy someone? I jump when someone knocks on the door I'm leaning against. I put my hand to my chest and let out a strangled nervous laugh.

"Ares, are you okay?" Kohan's voice is quiet on the other side of the door and I sigh knowing that my time alone is up.

I take a deep breath and open the door. Kohan doesn't wait for an invite as he slips in through the gap. Having both of us in here is a tight fit, but instead of it making me feel uncomfortable, it's making me feel hot. My temperature is rising with Kohan's proximity and sweat starts to run down my back.

"I'm sorry about Sophie, you get used to it after a while. I'm sorry she embarrassed you with that question, she just has no filter."

I feel bad that Kohan thinks that I'm embarrassed or anxious. This has nothing to do with that, it's purely because of the feelings I'm having, but I can't tell him that. "It's fine. I just needed a minute. I'm not used to that many people and then all those questions. She has a knack of getting you to tell her stuff."

Kohan leans against the door and puts his hands in his pockets. The move has his jeans pulling tight against his thighs and groin and I struggle to keep my eyes from looking down. I know he's seen me when that damn blush colours his cheeks again. He stares at me and I start chewing my bottom lip under his scrutiny. There are so many things in his eyes: curiosity, kindness, but the most glaring thing is lust. Even after all my years of neglect and fear, I can see the passion as clear as I can see him standing there in front of me. The silence between us drags but I can feel the rising tension. It's not a frightening tension like it was with Micah. I'm not anticipating when Kohan is going to hit me, but I am wondering if he's going to kiss me. I lick my lips like I'm preparing myself for him and his eyes zone in on the movement.

"Um … maybe we should get back to Sophie?" I don't know where the sudden clarity comes from but I'm glad that some of my common sense is returning. Kissing Kohan would be a big mistake and could cost me a friendship that I think could become really important to me.

"That's a good idea." He coughs and turns to face the opposite direction. He pauses a moment before opening the door. I think he's going to say something but he shakes his head and pulls the door open, holding it so I can step out into the busy café. I walk slowly to the table and sit in my seat.

Sophie looks nervous as we both sit down and I wonder what Kohan said to her while I was gone. "I'm so sorry, Ares. I didn't think about what I was saying. Kohan is used to my motor mouth and I should give you some time before I lose my filter."

"Don't be silly, Sophie. I was just feeling a little overwhelmed and needed a minute. It was more the people around us looking at me. I don't know if you heard but the last time I tried to come to town I had a little bit of a panic attack. I think everyone's remembering that because they're staring. It just gets a bit much sometimes."

Both Kohan and Sophie look around at the tables next to us, noticing for the first time that people are actually watching me. Sophie is the first to speak up and I have to bite the inside of my cheek to stop myself from laughing. I don't know where she gets her confidence but I wish I could get some.

"Keep staring people and I'm gonna give you an eyeful of something you won't like. Actually, I think you," She points to a lady two tables away who has been the most obvious in her staring. "I think you might like it." She finishes up her loud statement by blowing her a kiss. The woman huffs as she gets up from the table, places some money on her side plate and leaving the café. "You should have told me, I have a way with people."

This time I do laugh. Sophie is a firecracker and I am so glad Kohan introduced us. She's the kind of person that will have me forgetting about my own problems and concentrating on her. She is just what the doctor ordered.

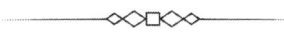

Kohan and I are quiet as we walk side by side down the dirt road towards my house. We decided to leave his car in the little car park next to the café since the weather is still warm. You never know how long the nice weather will last in Britain so I'll make the most of it while I can.

"She didn't put you off too much did she?" His voice is light but I can see real concern in his eyes. He shouldn't worry though, after the embarrassing start we were soon talking like we were old friends. She is easy to like and I'm relieved because it could have caused a problem between Kohan and me if we didn't get on.

"I like her. She has a lot of energy but I think that's a good thing. I doubt it would ever be a challenge to keep conversation going."

"You're right there, and you don't even have to be involved in it, she'll just keep talking."

We both laugh and walk a little further in a comfortable silence.

"What are you up to the rest of the week?" It's Monday afternoon and other than work I have nothing on the rest of the week. I'm hoping that I can get some gardening done but Kohan hasn't mentioned taking me to the garden centre since I asked on Sunday.

"Well after this lovely day off I have to work late for the next four days. There's a big project I'm working on and between the photos needed and traveling for interviews, it's going to be manic. Next week should be a little slower but I do have a doctor's appointment with my mum." His voice changes as he says the last part and he suddenly sounds worryingly sad.

"I hope everything is okay."

"That's what we are going to find out. She is getting really forgetful, and no matter what Damien tries to tell us, the rest of my brothers don't think it's just normal forgetfulness. I'm hoping we're just being over protective but I'm not convinced."

God, I haven't heard him sound so down and it makes me do something very out of character. I reach out and take his hand, squeezing it to try and offer him some support. "She'll be fine, and if she isn't you aren't alone. You have lots and lots of brothers … and I'm here."

He tightens his hold on my hand and pulls me closer until my arm is pressed completely against his. "Thank you. That means more than you can imagine."

We don't move apart as we get closer to my house and I savour his warmth. The more time I spend with him the more comfort I get from the simple things he does. A little touch, a smile, or listening to him giggle, these are things that make my heart flutter and my palms sweaty. Yeah, I think its safe to say I have a crush on Kohan. The biggest problem now is going to be keeping him from finding out. He must get so many men asking him out that I can't imagine that he would ever think of me in any sort of sexual way. I know he's looked turned on a few times we have been talking but those times have been when the air was charged and it would be hard for anyone not to be aroused.

"What are your plans?"

"Well I was thinking of heading into Greenview and picking up a few guys, bringing them home and having a private party."

Kohan stops moving and I come to a halt a few steps further on. I turn to look at him and he has a strange look on his face. Its like he's trying to work out if I'm being serious or not and as funny as it is that he thinks I'm capable, I decide to put him out of his misery.

"I'm kidding, Kohan. The chances of me even getting to Greenview without having a breakdown are slim, and picking up men. Nope, not happening. Once bitten and all that."

Some colour comes back to his face and he starts walking again. He laughs and I'm impressed with his attempt at making it appear natural. "I was worrying there that I was going to miss my chance to see you dance."

"I'm so far away from being ready to do that, but when I am you will be the first to know."

He seems happy with that answer. "Do you think you will ever go out and meet anyone again?"

I look at him but he is concentrating hard on the ground and his steps. "I don't know. I went through hell with Micah and there were days I didn't think I would survive, but he wasn't like that when we met. He was sweet and caring when he introduced himself at our local gym. He took his time and we became friends before he finally kissed me. How can I trust my instincts with a new man? My judgement is apparently flawed."

"Don't do that, don't blame yourself for what he was like. You trusted him and he ruined that with his behaviour. You will find that trust with someone again."

His words are ones I've heard before but coming from him I

try to believe them more. I want to be able to let people in, to go out and not be scared when I'm surrounded by strangers, but I can't see me being at that point. One thing he said is true though and I know it deep in my heart, even if my head has to catch up a little. "I trust you."

Those three little words were totally worth it when Kohan's smile beams at me. For not the first time today, and probably not the last either, I just stare at him because he's gorgeous. Bright eyes, rosy cheeks and the happiness just oozing out of him. I never want to see any sadness on his face because he's the kind of guy who deserves only happiness.

Chapter Fourteen

Kohan

"Are you going to tell me at any point?" I've been sitting on Sophie's couch for about an hour now and she hasn't said a single word about Ares. I walked Ares home after the coffee shop before returning to her house to watch a movie. Work is going to be crazy for the next week or so, and I wanted to catch up with her before it did. I feel like I haven't seen her in a long time, not since I started spending time with Ares.

Now I need to know what she thinks about him, because life will get really difficult if she doesn't like him. Sophie's my best friend and no one could ever replace her, but Ares is just … more. I want them to like each other because I'm greedy and I don't want to have to give up either one.

"Tell you what?" She fills her mouth with ice cream after speaking, not taking her eyes off the TV screen. I lost interest in the film shortly after it started, my mind wandering continually to Ares.

"Don't play dumb, Sophie, it's not a good look."

She finally looks towards me with the spoon still in her mouth. She grabs the remote and pauses the Tom Hiddleston movie we're watching. "Not playing over here. What the hell are you talking about?"

I want to throw my own spoon to knock some sense into her. I can't believe she's going to force me to actually ask her. I haven't felt like a teenager with a crush since … well since I was a teenager with a crush. "Ares. What did you think of him?"

"Oh that, yeah he was all right."

All right? Only all right? What the actual hell is she talking about. Ares is funny and sweet, and so fucking sexy. How can she only get that out of their meeting? "Wow, don't go overboard with the praise."

Her face is completely neutral and I can't get a read on her which is annoying the shit out of me. Sophie's usually an open book but I feel that she's holding something back.

"What do you want me to say?"

"I want you to tell me what you thought of him. I mean you spent the afternoon with him so I don't believe that you didn't think he was great. Did you miss how funny he was? He might not say much but when he speaks he's amazing."

She slowly takes another spoonful of ice cream and it's infuriating to watch. When she finally swallows she puts the ice cream on the table in front of us. "Does it really matter what I think of him?"

My heart is racing and I have this horrible feeling that she's about to drop a bombshell that I don't want to hear. "Yeah it's important. I need you to like him."

She stares for a few seconds but it feels like it's been hours before she speaks again. "I like him, he's a really nice guy."

The churning in my stomach settles and I let a smile onto my lips.

"Don't get ahead of yourself there. I think he is great, but I'm not sure he's the guy for you."

The churning returns and along with it comes sweaty palms. "We're only friends so that doesn't matter." I should feel bad for lying to Sophie, even though it's technically not a lie. I am only friends with Ares even if I want to be so much more. I want to be something very special to him, the person that he comes home to every night, or at the very least the guy who gets to give him pleasure until he screams for me to stop. I close my eyes as that vision invades my head and I can feel myself start to harden. Shit, I need to get myself under control because I'm not going to help my cause by having a hard on when I try to convince Sophie that there's only friendship between Ares and me.

"You forget who you're speaking too, Kohan? I know you better than almost everyone else in this world and I can tell that you're falling for him. There is way more than friendship in your eyes when you look at him."

She's right but I can't admit it. If I say it out loud that means that it's real. "I don't know what you're talking about."

"Don't bullshit a bullshitter. I know exactly how you feel about him, and I just want you to be careful. Ares is a lovely guy, but I can also tell he's been through something big. He's like a scared rabbit and I don't think that's because he's shy, I think he's scared of something and I just want to make sure you're safe."

Sophie doesn't know what Ares has been through in the past and I'm not in the position to tell her. No one has the right to give away Ares' experiences apart from him, but its now obvious she could see the same fear in him that I did. "I know his story, well at least a part of it, but it doesn't scare me off. And I'm trying to be his friend because that's what he needs."

"So you don't want anything else with him?"

"I didn't say that, but he needs a friend more than he needs me trying to put moves on him. I want to be there for him when he needs me, make sure that no one can hurt him."

Her eyes open slightly wider and I can see all the questions that she wants to ask running through her head. I know she gets the gist of what I'm telling her, or what I'm not telling her in this case, when she asks. "Is he safe?"

"As far as I can tell, but I know that he's running from something. I can't tell you any more because it's not my place and I don't want to betray his trust."

She bites her fingernail which is her tell that she's worried about something. "That doesn't make me feel any better."

"I know, but believe me when I say that I'll make sure nothing happens to him."

She looks like she's going to scoop up some more ice cream but instead she points the spoon at me. "Fine, but if he needs anything you let me know. Now that we have that out the way, want to tell me all about how you want in his pants?"

I groan and let my head fall back onto the couch. "Oh god, I want that man so much. Did you see him? I mean seriously, have you ever seen anyone as gorgeous?"

"He's not really my type, but he's very much your type."

I turn my head and look at her. I didn't realise I actually had a type so this surprises me a little. "I have a type?"

"You haven't noticed? Shit, and I thought you saw everything. Dark hair, sexy eyes, shorter than you and a body that's slim but tight. He likes you too by the way."

Right on cue my heart starts racing at her comment. I want to pretend that I can see the attraction in Ares eyes but then I put it down to wishful thinking on my part. "I don't think so. He's sworn off men, and even if he hadn't I don't think he would want me. As I say, he's looking for a friend."

"Oh my poor, little, deluded friend. The pair of you are tip toeing around this attraction you have for each other, neither of you wanting to admit your feelings. It would be cute if it wasn't kinda pathetic. You need to just kiss him and put you both out of your miseries."

"Like you're an expert in the ways of love?" I know it's a low blow but I can't have her saying shit like that when my heart is already fighting not to fall in love with Ares.

"Don't take your hormones out on me. I might understand it a little bit more than you realise." She looks sad when she finished speaking and it's the perfect opening for me to finally ask about Robert.

"Things not going so well with Robert?"

This question has her groaning and eating more ice cream. "I swear I don't know what's happening between us. It's like one minute he seems like he wants something special with me and the next we're barely speaking. I don't know what to think and I don't want to be one of those people."

"One of those people?"

She rolls her eyes, obviously not happy that I don't know exactly what she's talking about. "A clinger. I don't want to be the kind of girl who's hanging around and waiting for any attention that

I can get. This is what I get for liking someone, I should have just followed my own rules."

Okay this is new to me. I didn't know that Sophie had rules that she followed and now I'm intrigued to know what they are. "Please enlighten me with these famous must follow rules."

She puts the ice cream down again and raises her fingers, putting one up with each passing rule. "Number one; don't be stupid enough to fall for a guy. Number two; make them do all the chasing. Number three; again, don't fall for a guy. And number four; hit it and quit it, no feelings allowed."

My heart aches a little as Sophie tells me her all important rules. I know I'm a guy and I should believe fully in not letting emotions get involved with fun, but I'm not like that. I'm the guy who wants to settle down and have a family. "Do you not think you're missing a lot by not letting emotions get involved?"

She glares at me before grabbing her glass of wine. "I think we've maybe got our roles mixed up. Isn't it the woman who's all about love and emotions, and the guy is out to see where he can stick his dick?"

"It's two thousand and seventeen, I'm pretty sure we share gender roles now. All I'm saying is maybe you should see where this thing with Robert is going. You never know, it might be something really good."

She drinks the last of her wine before refilling her glass almost to the rim. I want to tell her not to drink so much on a work night, but it's not me that has to deal with the hangover tomorrow. "He's just coming out of a marriage, albeit a really shitty one. He's told me that he can't jump straight into another relationship so this whole thing is going nowhere."

Now I understand her mood the last few weeks. I asked her a few times what was wrong but she told me that it was nothing. I didn't believe her but I didn't want to press her to talk at work, and being the shitty friend I am it's taken this long to get her alone. "I don't know what to say, that sucks big time."

"It is what it is. Now that my love life is officially in the crapper, lets talk about yours."

"I don't have a love life, as sad as that may sound. I can't remember the last time I had sex, actually I can and it wasn't exactly great." I shudder when I remember that encounter over a table in the break room where we were working.

"The photographer?"

"Yeah, and lets just say that I was never gonna go back for seconds even though he kept calling."

Sophie laughs and it's my turn to glare at her. "Oh come on, you made out that it was great. Not once did you tell me that the experience was shitty. So out with it now, tell me all the unsexy details."

I close my eyes so I don't have to see her face as I speak. There's a reason that I didn't go into detail about my time with Ronnie, and that reason was the experience was really bloody embarrassing. "It started with so much potential, I mean you saw him, he was fucking gorgeous. I soon realised that it was his looks alone that probably got him all his action. When he kissed me I swear I thought he was trying to swallow me whole. I know I sound like a dick, but he just wasn't very good and pretty much licked my entire face."

I stop talking to let Sophie get herself under control because I'm not sure she'll be able to hear me over her laughter. When she calms down enough I continue my story.

"I decided to ignore his lack of kissing skill and that was a huge mistake. A piece of advice, if a guy can't kiss there's a good chance he doesn't know what to do with his dick. God, the whole thing just ended up being a mess of his fumbling hands and lots of thrusting. And the worst part?" I turn my head and open my eyes to see Sophie sitting forward eagerly awaiting my confession.

"I faked an orgasm so I could leave."

The burst of laughter from Sophie is almost deafening and it only takes a few seconds for tears to fall down her cheeks. She tries to speak but just sucks in a few cackled breaths before bursting out in laughter again. She holds her hand up in front of her and takes some deep breaths trying to calm herself down. She finally gets control over her giggles but I wish she hadn't when she finally speaks. "How exactly does a guy fake an orgasm?" Her question elicits another bout of laughter from her and I reach over and take her glass of wine from her, taking a huge drink from the glass.

"Laugh it up, bitch. I hope the next time you have sex it's really, really bad."

This just causes more laughter and I sit back and wait for her to finish.

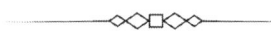

The phone on my desk goes off and I'm tempted to let it go to my voicemail but that means I have to call whoever it is back. I grab it before it rings off, and tuck it between my chin and shoulder as I continue typing. "Kohan Weston."

"Hey, little brother."

I stop typing at the sound of my brother's voice, leaning back in my chair and giving him all my attention. "Hey, Carey, how's things?"

"Not too bad. I was just calling to check that everything is still okay for Monday?"

I've told Carey that I'll drive both him and mum to the doctors for her appointment, and have taken the full day off work to make sure that I don't have to rush off afterwards. "Yeah everything is still fine on my end. How's mum doing?" Carey's been texting me every other day with progress reports on mum but it's been a few days since I heard from him.

"She's not having a good day. She woke up early to make breakfast for dad before he went to work and she wouldn't listen when I tried to explain that he died. I can't explain how heartbreaking it is to keep telling her that her husband is dead."

Carey's voice goes quiet towards the end and I feel for my brother. Not only must it be hard for him to tell mum about her husband, but also to constantly have to explain that his dad is dead must be taking it out of him. I don't think I would be able to cope reliving it over and over. "I'm sorry, Carey. I wish I lived closer so I could help more."

"You have your life there, Kohan, and no one expects you to move here for this. There are five of us in total and we will all take the slack."

The only thing is we aren't all taking the slack. It seems to be falling mainly on Carey at the moment. "I still feel like I could do more."

"Let's just get Monday out of the way and we can make decisions once we know what we're dealing with."

It makes sense to wait before we make our next move, but it doesn't make me feel any better. "How is everything else?" I haven't spoken to Carey since we had dinner together and he told me about Duncan. I was meant to call but works been crazy, and by the time I get home every night, I just want to sleep.

"Same shit, brother, same shit. Work's boring and I don't have much time for a social life. You know how it is."

"And how's Duncan?" I know I might be opening a can of worms by mentioning him but I want to know.

"He's good." I can hear the smile in his words and I finally manage to relax. "We haven't seeing a great deal of each other because of mum, but the little time we get to spend together is fun."

"I'm glad to hear that. Maybe after Monday we can organise that night out. Don't think I've forgotten."

He groans down the phone and I laugh at his response. I've never met any of the women that Carey's dated in the past. Actually, maybe dated isn't the right word, had one night of hot monkey sex with is probably more appropriate. This thing with Duncan definitely seems different than anything else my brother has described and I want to be able to give him all the support I can, and that means meeting the man in question.

"Why did I have to tell you about Duncan?"

"Because you love me and you want me to meet him. Its

okay, Carey, wanting your family to meet your boyfriend doesn't make you a bad person."

"I need to go."

"This conversation isn't done, Carey." I have to shout that last bit down the phone because I know he's about to hang up on me. I love to wind my brother up and it's so easy to do, especially over the phone. I hang up the phone and turn back to my computer with a smile on my face. I might tease my brother about his new relationship but I want him to know that I support him one hundred percent.

Chapter Fifteen

Kohan

I can't keep my knee still as I sit in the waiting room with Mum and Carey. We arrived in plenty of time for her appointment but as always the doctor is running late.

"We should just go. This is a waste of time and someone else could use the appointment, you know someone that actually needs it." Mum gathers her bags like she's ready to leave now that she's spoken, but Carey puts a hand on her wrist to still her.

"If you leave then it's a waste because they won't be able to fill the appointment. We're here now so let's just talk to the doctor." I'm glad that Carey's here to be the grown up because I'm struggling to deal with this. My mum has been the one constant in my life and the thought of something being wrong with her is scaring the shit out of me.

"Mary Weston please."

This is it. I hold Mum's hand as we walk along the hall behind the doctor and help her to a seat. Carey and I sit across the room for moral support.

"Hi Mary, I'm Dr Allcroft. What can I do for you today?" He seems too young to be diagnosing my mum but I keep my opinions to myself. It wouldn't help Mum to piss off her doctor.

"I'm fine, but my sons seem to think I'm having a problem with my memory."

Dr Allcroft looks behind Mum at us, almost like he's looking for confirmation from us but he doesn't ask anything. "What sort of problems are you experiencing?"

"You know the usual sort of things. I'm a busy woman and I just get a little muddled sometimes." She smiles like she's indulging the doctor in his questioning and I'm about to step in but Carey takes my arm and shakes his head. I bite my tongue but if the doctor doesn't do anything I will be saying something.

"Oh I know how that is, but why don't we just do a little memory test to see how things are. It's just a few questions and a list of things to remember."

My mum smiles again, probably convinced that she'll pass the test with no problems. Part of me hopes that she does do well, but a bigger part hopes the doctor actually sees the issue." "That's fine, doctor. Anything to appease my boys."

He takes out a notepad and writes something on the top. "I want you to remember these five words and I will ask you at the end to repeat them back to me. Chocolate, elm, sparrow, train and twenty-four Rochester Way. Did you get all them?"

"Chocolate, elm, sparrow, train and twenty four Rochester Way. See, no problems at all."

The doctor writes something else and then turns back to my mum with a smile. "Okay, Mary. Just answer these questions, nothing too hard. You said you had sons, how many?"

"Five for my sins. They kept me on my toes as they grew up."

He looks at me and I nod to confirm she's right. "What date is it?"

"It's March ... no wait." She stops and her face screws up as she thinks about it. My heart crumbles as I watch her stumble over something so easy. "April ... it's April twenty-seventh."

"Close, Mary. It's the twenty-eighth. Can you tell me who came with you today?"

She turns and looks at Carey and me. "That's Kohan and Joe."

The look of pain on Carey's face has me reaching out to grab his hand. He does look a lot like our dad but since he's been dead for five years now and it must hurt to be called his name. "Mum, this is Carey."

The doctor makes more notes and I know that this can't be good. He picks up a stapler and holds it in front of mum. "Do you know what this is, Mary?"

She sniggers before she answers. "Of course I do, it's a stapler."

He returns it and picks up his stethoscope. "And this?"

"That's a …" The same look of concentration comes on mum's face but she doesn't give an answer. He pats her on the knee and puts the stethoscope down.

"Can you remember the words that I told you when you arrived?"

I repeat them in my head like I can help her answer but she's on her own. Seeing her struggle like this has made it scarily obvious that there's a bigger problem than even I thought.

"There was … um … elm and train. Then there was …" Her voice breaks and I want to rush over to her and hold her.

"Don't worry, Mary." The doctor soothes her with his words but it won't last for long. He's about to change the Weston family forever and I hold my breath as I wait for it. "Going by your results here I think that there is a little cause for concern. Memory loss is normal as you get older but yours is a little more pronounced than most. What I would like to do is send you to a neurologist at the hospital as they are experts in this field. They will be able to further investigate this and give you a proper diagnosis."

I hear Mum sniffle and I move forward to wrap my arm around her. Carey moves next to her and takes her hand.

"What does this all mean, Dr Allcroft?" I'm glad Carey is thinking to ask questions because my mind has gone completely blank.

"I think there may be a slight onset of dementia, but without further testing there's no way to determine that. I don't want anyone to worry though, there are lots of things that can be done to help if this is the case. The most important thing is to get an accurate diagnosis. I will get an appointment for her and she should be seen within the next fourteen days."

"Fourteen days? Why so bloody long?" The anger in my voice is clear and my mum puts her hand on top of mine.

"The hospital is busy, son. They can't drop everything just for me." Why is she the one making so much sense and I'm losing it. She should be screaming and crying, demanding to be seen immediately but she's still thinking of others before herself. "You get that appointment organised, Doctor, and we'll take it from there." She stands and brushes off her trousers. "Come on boys, I need to get to the supermarket before your dad gets home. He doesn't like it when his dinner is late."

I look at Carey and the sadness on his face matches mine. The news from the doctor isn't great but the hospital appointment is going to be worse. Now to tell the rest of the guys about what's happening. This isn't going to be a happy conversation.

"What do you mean? Couldn't the doctor just tell you what's happening?" Damien is pacing back and forth with Milly in his arms. He picked her up when we all arrived at his house and I think he did it to keep himself in check.

"It's a difficult diagnosis for a GP. He wants Mum to be seen by an expert so she can get the proper diagnosis and care."

"But what will they do at the hospital?" He keeps asking questions that I can't answer and it's frustrating me as much as it is him.

"I don't know."

"Then why didn't you fucking ask?"

Heidi walks into the room and takes Milly from Damien's arms, kissing him on the cheek before leaving again.

"I didn't ask because I didn't think of it." I'm glad the baby's gone because this conversation is going to get more stressful and louder.

"You went to get all the fucking information. Did you actually find out anything?"

I stand up from the chair and walk in front of Damien, getting right in his face and not backing down. Damien used to be the tallest and would use that to his advantage, but I grew a lot in my teenage years and I can easily get nose to nose with him when needed. "If you are so fucking good at this then maybe you should have gone instead of being a fucking chicken. I didn't think of it because I sat there and watched Mum struggle to tell the doctor today's date and then she called Carey dads name again. For fuck's sake, she couldn't remember the word for stethoscope. So forgive me if I wasn't exactly full of relevant questions to ask." My voice breaks as I finish my rant and tears finally falls from my eyes and roll down my cheeks. The first tear barely drips off my jaw when I'm wrapped in Damien's arms and pulled tightly against his chest.

"I'm sorry, Kohan. I'm worried and I'm taking it out on you. I'm sorry." He continues to talk to the others while I take comfort from him. "So what do we do next?"

"We wait. After the hospital we'll know what's happening and we can come up with a better plan. I do think that she needs someone around as much as possible." There goes Carey making sense again.

"We all have lives and it will make Mum angry if we stop living to look after her."

I pull back from Damien and become part of the conversation again. "I agree with Jensen about us all having lives, but we also need to spend more time with her. Carey lives with mum but that doesn't mean it should all fall on him. She has a lot of clubs and friends so she's out a lot of the time, it would only be certain times someone should be there. I'll struggle to get here a lot though, traffic isn't great when I finish work." I know it's a pathetic excuse but the hour drive can take at least double that with rush hour traffic. Just the thought of doing that after a full day at work tires me.

"No one expects you to come here to babysit. Let's take it one step at a time. Mum has been fine on her own up until now. Things are getting worse but she's still able to take care of herself. I don't think we should jump to worst case scenario just yet. I'll be home every night and if I'm not I will let one of you know."

"It shouldn't all be on you, Carey. The rest of us can help."

"You all have wives and kids at home. The only people without any commitments are me and Kohan, and he lives too far away. There's nothing in my life that I can't put on hold for a while."

I glare at Carey because I know that he does have something that he shouldn't put on hold. Carey avoids my eyes as he speaks and turns towards the rest of our brothers. He knows that I won't say anything in front of the others, but if he thinks I'm keeping quiet about this then he is very wrong.

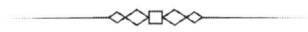

I collapse into bed and let out the biggest sigh. Today was a long arsed day and I need it to end right now. I grab the bottle of beer from my bedside table and take a large sip. I don't usually drink on a work night but after today I more than need it. I'm just returning the bottle when I hear the message tone on my mobile going off. I grab it and open the new text.

How did it go today?

I smile despite myself. Ares has a way of making everything seem less horrific, even with just a text.

Long story but no happy ending. Will tell you about it when I see you, easier to tell than type.

The next message throws me a little bit, because I didn't expect Ares to be so forward.

I could FaceTime you?

I never would have thought of doing that but now that he's mentioned it there's nothing else I want more. I want to tell him about my day, clear my head of it all, and I want to see his face while I do it. I don't bother texting him back, instead I just open the Facetime app and press Ares' contact details.

It only rings twice before the screen is filled with Ares' smiling face. I relax back against the headboard and take him in. He must be in bed as well because I can see a pillow behind him. The screen aimed at his head but it doesn't stop me from seeing his naked shoulders, and the sight makes my stomach clench. It's the only part of Ares' body that I've seen and I have to admit that I'm kind of hoping he drops his phone.

"Hi."

"This was a great idea and one I would never have thought of."

His eyes flicker down and I can see he's feeling a little awkward. "I found it was easier to talk to people this way. My hearing aids can be a pain in the arse sometimes when I'm on the phone."

That makes sense I suppose. I don't know exactly how they work and I suddenly wonder if he gets feedback from them. I haven't actually given his hearing loss a lot of thought, just accepting it as a part of him, but now that he's brought it up I want to know more. "Was it terrible? Losing your hearing I mean?"

"Yes and no. When I woke up and I couldn't hear anything I thought my life was over. Once I went back to Micah I realised it was a blessing because I couldn't always hear him shouting."

I have to control the urge to growl when he mentions his arsehole ex because I don't want him to stop talking. He doesn't often tell me much about his life before moving here and I want to hear it no matter how angry it makes me. "Didn't you have hearing aids to begin with?"

"By the time I left the hospital I did but I found that sometimes they made the pain in my head worse. It was the trauma of the attack that caused the hearing loss and sometimes I felt like my head was going to explode. Once I fully healed, I still didn't tend to wear them because I was back by Micah by then and he didn't like me to wear them. If he saw me with them he would accuse me of trying to make him feel guilty for the accident. He also thought they made me look broken so he eventually banned them. The funny thing is that he used to get so angry because I couldn't hear him."

Don't get angry. Don't let it show you want to kill the fucker. I keep repeating those words in my head as Ares continues to speak. I don't know what I imagined his life to be like but the more I hear the more in awe of him I become. How can someone go through all that and still function? "How long did you stay with him when you went back?"

"Two months. I didn't mean to go back but he convinced me like always."

"How could he convince you after everything he did?" I don't mean to sound judgmental but I obviously do because his face falls and he flinches. "No, don't do that. I didn't mean it like that. I just want to understand the hold he had on you. I think you are nothing short of amazing."

He doesn't acknowledge what I've said but he does continue talking so I stay quiet. "You have to understand that I met Micah when I was eighteen and we quickly moved in together. The way he treated me became the norm. I mean I knew the abuse was bad, but when he apologised and told me he loved me more than anyone else, I ate that shit up. He was attractive and successful and he *wanted* me. I vowed to stay away after I lost my hearing but when I went back to get my belongings he was there. No one had seen him for a month so I thought he'd left and I went alone. That was my first mistake. My second one was listening to him when he begged me to stay. He told me he felt like he had lost the best part of his life and that he couldn't believe he'd done that to me. He then went on to tell me that if he couldn't win me back he would hurt himself. I bought it all and actually, I felt bad for leaving him."

"What made you finally leave?" I hope he doesn't mind these questions but I have to ask. He's been a closed book about his past that I need to ask as much as I can whilst he's willing to talk.

"My family were so mad when I went back; told me I was

stupid and that they were scared for me, but I didn't listen. I mean they hadn't seen the mess Micah had become. I wish I had listened because it took less than a month for him to hit me again. What he didn't know was that the previous head injury he gave me had left me with more problems than just the hearing loss, so when he hit me again, especially so soon after recovery, he caused a bleed on my brain. I was in an induced coma for two weeks to protect my brain and when I woke up I decided to press charges. Between that and the previous injury I had enough evidence to put him in jail."

My mouth drops open as I try to work my way through everything he just said but my mind gets stuck on little detail. "You put him away?"

He laughs a little and I see him visibly relax. "On November tenth, Micah Henley was sentenced to seven years in jail for two counts of ABH, two counts of assault with intent to harm, one count of attempted murder and two counts of threatening behaviour."

I can't stop staring at the small smile on Ares' lips. I've never seen him look so happy whilst talking about his past. Normally he looks scared and nervous, but tonight he looks like he's proud he did something so important. I genuinely don't know what to say to him. I want to tell him how fucking brave he is and that he showed more courage than most people would in that kind of situation. I want to ask a hundred other questions like when does Micah get out and what prison is he in? I need to know what the court case was like and if he was scared while going through it, but I keep all that to myself and tell him the most important thing I'm thinking. "You are my fucking hero, Ares."

He blushes and looks away from the camera. I love it when his face goes red because that's how I imagine he would look when he comes. Flushed but happy, yeah, that image has starred in my fantasies way too often. I shake my head to clear those thoughts because now is so not the time. Thankfully Ares' voice pulls me from my musings.

"Anyway, I didn't call to talk about me. Tell me how today

went. How are things with your mum?"

I groan and lean my head back. "Are you sitting comfortably because this might take a while?"

Ares shuffles on the screen a little until he's lying down. "I am now and I've nowhere to be tomorrow so I'm all yours."

God, how I wish that was true. "Well let's just say that it didn't go well." True to his word, Ares spends the next two hours listening to my horrible day and he doesn't look bored once.

Chapter Sixteen

Ares

"I'm thinking of going out, like to a pub or nightclub."

Adam's pen stops it's scribbling and his head rises slowly until he's staring at me.

"Oh stop it, it's not like I've never gone out."

It's just his eyebrows that rise this time but he makes his point.

"Okay so I've never gone out but I want to. I'm sick of being locked up inside for nothing. Okay, so it's not nothing, but it's time to get over the fear. Micah can't get me anymore and I need to stop using him as an excuse to avoid the world. Yeah, I know you've been telling me this for years but I think Kohan's made me see that I can trust people. Well, he's shown me that I can trust him so that's a start, isn't it?" The word vomit finally stops and I can see that it's amused Adam far too much.

"Well I don't know if I should charge you for the hour now because you pretty much did all that on your own." He leans forward and puts his pad and pen on the little table in between us. "Do you want to discuss it or is your mind sorted?"

"No let's chat."

"Okay, so why do you want to go out now?"

"I met a girl." It's kind of accurate but I mainly say this to see Adam's reaction. I'm not disappointed when his eyes widen and he stutters something I don't catch. I take pity on him and explain before he bursts a brain vessel. "Kohan's best friend to be exact. Sophie is a freaking force of nature and she made me realise that people looking at me isn't always a problem. We met for coffee and she didn't give a shit what people thought about her. I want to be like that, not caring what people think."

Adam looks a bit more composed when he speaks. "That wasn't funny, even if I was planning my new extension with all the new appointments you would need." He winks at me and I laugh at him. This is why I wanted Adam to be my therapist, he knows exactly how to deal with all my shit but he's also funny and down to earth. I've never felt like he's judging me so I've always felt able to talk to him and he feels more like a friend now than a therapist. "I'm happy that you've decided to take some positive steps in your life. I've been telling you for a while that putting everything on hold has had a negative impact on your life. Micah's been in jail for a year so I think you are allowed to feel safe now."

"I know you're right but I think I needed to see it myself. Between Kohan and Sophie I'm seeing the life I can have."

Adam sits back in his chair and crosses one leg over the other as he studies me. He stays silent for too long and when I can't bear it any longer I speak up.

"What?"

"I'm just thinking that this Kohan's had very a positive effect on your life."

He doesn't know half of the ways that Kohan has improved my previously sheltered life. He's stripped away so many layers of my protective coating that I use to keep people away. "Yeah, he's bringing the best out in me."

"Why do you think that is?" Adam can never just take what I say at face value, always pushing me to dive deeper into everything I'm feeling.

"I don't know. I just get this feeling that he's completely safe. I know it doesn't guarantee that he won't hurt me, but it makes me want to find out."

"Are you attracted to him?"

I'm a grown man and I like to pride myself in my maturity, but when he asks me that I can't help but giggle. I cringe when I hear the noise because it reminds me of a teenage girl.

"Should I take that as a yes?" There's far too much humour in

Adam's voice for my liking.

"Shut up. But yeah, if I was to find any guy attractive it would be someone like Kohan."

"And are you going to allow yourself to find someone attractive or is that still too much?"

I bite my nail as I think about my answer. I keep telling myself that I can't find Kohan attractive because I don't want to ruin any possible friendship, but what if it's something more? Is it possible that I'm scared to find him attractive? "The honest answer is I don't know. I think about him all the time and I want to know what it's like to kiss him, but I can't make the move that'll take it further."

"What would you do if he tried to take it further?"

"I want to say that I would go with the flow but I don't know if I can. I'm scared of freaking out and making a fool of myself. What if it makes him leave? Isn't it better to keep him as a friend than try to take it further and fucking it all up?" I rub my face as I try to clear my head. Every time I think I've made a break through it opens up hundreds of more questions and problems.

"What if it doesn't fuck it up? Is he the kind of person who would run if you freaked out, would he not understand your past?"

"He wouldn't run. He would probably hold me until I felt better. I … I actually told him about the last two attacks and the court case. He knows Micah is in jail as well."

"That is fantastic. I'm glad you have someone who knows what you went through. What did he say about it?"

I laugh when I think about our FaceTime conversation the night before. I thought that he was disgusted with me for going back to Micah and I was ready to hang up to avoid his disappointed face. Then he spoke and I knew that he understood, or at least he wanted to. "He told me I was his hero."

This has Adam smiling and he drops his foot to the floor and leans towards me. "I'm telling you this next bit as your friend, or at least, not as your therapist. Grab life by the balls and enjoy yourself. I'm not saying it will be easy, and I'm sure there will be moments where you freak out a little, but you *will* come out the other side. It sounds like you are building a good support system. I don't want you to be still second-guessing yourself in another five years. So, go out, try new things and maybe fall in love. The chances of you meeting another Micah are slim, and you might miss something amazing in the mean time."

"I think I want to go out one night."

Adam sits back and crosses his arms over his chest as he looks at me with a happy expression on his face. "And I think that's a bloody good idea."

"When are you free next?"

"What do you mean? Do you need something?"

I take a deep breath and force the words out of my dry mouth. "I want to go out and I want you to take me."

Kohan's silence makes me a little nervous. Maybe I got it wrong and he doesn't want to take me out. A night in a pub is different from an afternoon at a café. "Are you sure?"

"If you don't want to that's fine, I understand. I just thought it might be a fun thing to do." *Could I sound any more pathetic?* I'm tempted to hang up and turn my phone off but then he would just turn up my door.

"No, no. I want nothing more than to take you out, I just want to make sure that you are okay with it. But I will totally go with you. Do you want to go to Westies? It's nice and close so if you want to leave and it will be less busy than going to Greenview."

I hadn't actually thought about where I wanted to go but he's making some very good points. "That sounds like a good plan. Do you think Sophie will want to come?" I'm thinking that the more people I have around me that I know, the more relaxed I will be.

"Try and stop her." Kohan suddenly becomes very quiet and it's a little worrying. When he does speak I bite my lip to try and stop the sigh that wants to break free. "And um ... this is just an idea ... Westies isn't far from my place and you could maybe stay over to save you from having to get a cab home."

He's so damn cute when he's unsure of himself. He's usually so confident about everything, that to see him stutter over something just melts my heart. It shows a vulnerable side to him that makes me feel that I'm right in my assessment of him. "That's another great idea. I'm off on Saturday and Sunday, do any of those nights suit you?"

"Let me text Sophie and I'll let you know. Sunday will be quieter but with having work on the Monday, Saturday might be better."

I didn't think of them having to go to work the next day. Either is suitable for me because I don't have to clean until later in the evening. "Say Saturday then, make it easier for both of you."

"I'll text her and let you know straight away. If she can't make it are you happy to go out with just me?"

L*et me see, would I be okay with just going out with a gorgeous guy?* "I don't think that would be a problem."

Kohan's laughter warms my entire body and I suddenly can't wait to go out in three night's time. I just hope I can follow Adam's instructions and have some fun.

I shake my hands in front of myself and try to calm the fuck down. You'd think that I had never been out before, but as I wait for Kohan to pick me up I feel like I could be sick. *Get a grip Ares.*

I walk back to my room to check myself in the mirror for the hundredth time. I decided a simple outfit, not wanting to be too dressy for a small town pub, dark blue denim jeans and a simple fitted black shirt, simple but classic. I tuck the shirt into my jeans and check myself out again. I can't decide if I should leave it hanging out or not. *Shit, I'm over thinking this.*

Just as I'm about to untuck again the light in my room flashes and my stomach explodes with nerves. Kohan's here and there's no time to change anything. I grab my overnight bag from my bed and head to the front door before I completely back out. I open it to see Kohan standing there and all rational thought flees my head. In every day clothes Kohan could grace any magazine cover but when dressed up for a night out, he's sexier than any man I've ever seen. He's wearing tight black jeans that mold against his thighs and a grey shirt with the sleeves rolled up over his forearms. The combination isn't new but on him it just takes on a whole new level of hotness.

I must be staring too long because he coughs and when I look up he has that sexy little grin on his face. "Are you ready to go or do you want more time to look?"

I laugh and push him away from the door as I try to hide my embarrassment. I make sure the door is securely locked before following him to his car and get in.

"Are you ready?"

"As ready as I'll ever be. I might have changed outfits ten times and I'm still questioning my choice, but I'm ready."

Kohan hesitates for a few seconds before he starts the engine. Once it's running he looks at me. "You look really nice. It's unusual to see your hair styled but it works for you."

My hand goes up and runs nervously through my hair. I usually just leave it natural which means that it's slightly curly and sits over my forehead so it hides my scar. Tonight I cut the sides back a little so it sits over my ears. I really need to go to a barber to get it done properly but a home cut is all I was up for today. I got used to doing my own hair when I was with Micah because I wasn't allowed to go out without him. "Thank you, I took a little off the sides. I'm hoping it doesn't look stupid."

Kohan pulls out of my driveway and starts the five-minute drive to his house. "Definitely not stupid."

We are quiet the rest of the ride and I watch out the side window as we make our way to Kohan's house. I've never been there before and the area is new to me. We drive past a huge building and I point at it. "What's that?"

He looks in the direction that I'm pointing. "That's the

secondary school. Actually it's just the school. They built it for just the secondary pupils but when the school for the primary kids was damaged they moved all the pupils there. It soon became apparent that it was big enough to hold all the children so they stayed. . It's not a big town so two separate schools was a bit unnecessary."

I study the building and see that it is pretty huge. I still haven't seen the whole town but I wouldn't have thought there were that many kids.

"It's the same reason the newspaper offices are so big. When the building was constructed the council wanted to attract new businesses here. When the bypass was built companies weren't interested in moving here but the building was already finished. The town took the bottom floor for the library and rented out the others."

"I didn't realise there were so many stories about the place. Do you come from here originally?"

He indicates and turns down a street of little houses. "No, I grew up in Greenview. It's an hour away but sometimes feels like it's on the opposite side of the world."

I wonder if he's thinking about his mum. He mentioned that she lived there and I know that he hasn't got back to see her since her doctor's appointment. They're still waiting for a hospital appointment but were told that they would get her in for testing quickly. A sudden thought comes to me and I turn quickly to look at Kohan as he pulls into a little driveway and comes to a stop. "You could have spent the night with your mum. Shit, I'm sorry. We don't have to do this."

"Don't worry about it. She has a book club meeting at a neighbour's house so she wouldn't want me there anyway." He reaches out and takes my hand gently. "I want to go out with you." He squeezes my hand and climbs out of the car. I follow his lead and get out, walking up two steps to the front door he's opening. We step in and I look around the cosy little living room that the entrance opens into. It has wooden floors but it doesn't feel cold thanks to warm terracotta walls. There are pictures on the wall and the place doesn't feel much like a bachelor pad.

"I maybe should have told you before but I only have one bedroom. I'll take the couch or, depending how drunk I get, the floor."

"I'm not taking your bed, Kohan."

He just smirks at me and takes my bag. "We'll see."

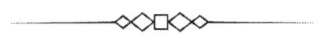

I down another shot of fireball and shake my head when the burn hits my throat. "These are soooooooooooo good." My words are slurred but I'm about three shots past caring. I'd never had Fireball before but Kohan assured me that I would like it and he was completely right.

"I'm glad you like them but that's the last one until you drink that pint of water."

I pretend to scowl at Kohan, or at least I'm hoping that's what my face is doing because I currently can't feel it. "Don't harsh my mellow, Bruh." I don't even get the whole sentence out before I snort rather unattractively.

Kohan just smiles at me and slides the water in my direction.

Sophie barges in between the bar and me, shoving the water across the bar. "You heard him, Bruh. Don't harsh his mellow." She grabs me by the hand and drags me towards the tiny dance floor at the back of the pub. Jason Derulo's '*Want To Want Me*' is just starting and I feel my hips start to move to the beat. I haven't danced in forever, and as I raise my arms in the air and grind against Sophie, I realise just how much I've missed it.

The alcohol has lowered my defenses and it's been a fun night. No one has caused me any problems and I haven't felt anything but comfortable. I think that might have something to do with the six foot three hottie that was sitting next to me at the bar. Kohan has been so attentive tonight and there have been many times where I just wanted to pull him in and kiss him. It has been a real struggle to keep everything platonic on my side, especially when I've caught him looking at me. A guy approached me while I was sitting at the bar, asking me if I wanted a drink, and I swear I heard Kohan growl until the guy left. I tried to convince myself that it was because he's looking out for me, but the possessive side of him was such a turn on. Maybe I should take Kohan's advice and slow down with the shots. Possessiveness shouldn't be a turn on for me. It's a red flag and I don't like it ... except ... with Kohan I do.

The song starts to change and I make a move to return to the bar until I hear the opening to Selena Gomez singing *"Can't keep my hands to myself."* I love this song and I *must* dance to it. I close my eyes and sway my hips a little more, not caring if anyone is watching. I decided earlier that this small pub is a safe place full of locals. No one has even given me a side eye since I arrived so I can relax and be myself.

I jump when arms wrap around my waist from behind but when Sophie looks behind me she just smiles so I relax. If it was anyone other than Kohan I'm pretty sure she would have attacked by now. Lips come close to my ear and speak louder than a whisper so I can hear what he's saying.

"Is this okay?" His breath warms my ear and it causes a shudder of pleasure through my body.

Even with something as simple as dancing Kohan is so considerate, asking permission before he goes too far with me. I relax into his hold and nod my head. With my permission he pulls me tight against his chest and starts to dance with me. My breath comes quickly as I feel him grind against me. His rhythm is hypnotic and all I can imagine is that we're naked and he's fucking me. My dick gets hard almost instantly and I would feel embarrassed but I'm not the only one who's feeling this spark between us. Kohan is rock hard and it's pushing against my arse.

The whole thing is too much but not enough. I struggle to catch my breath as the situation hits me all at once and I pull away. I give a tight smile to Sophie before telling her I need to use the bathroom. I can't look at Kohan because he's just too much at this moment. I need a minute to calm down and remember who I am. I need to decide if I can actually do this.

Chapter Seventeen

Kohan

I watch as Ares disappears into the bathroom and shuts the door behind himself. I don't know what I did to make him run but I wish I did. Coming to dance with him was a risk but when I saw him up here with Sophie I just couldn't resist. I have spent the last few hours trying to keep my hands off Ares and it's getting harder not to touch him.

When he opened his front door tonight it took everything in me not to push him back into his hall and kiss him until he forgot his name. When I saw him looking at me like he wanted to do the same I knew I had to get moving before I gave in to my urges. Watching him dance, swinging that denim clad arse, I knew I couldn't stop myself any longer. I was moving before I even thought of the consequences and that was a mistake.

Sophie hits me on the arm bringing me out of my thoughts. "Go after him."

"What?"

"You're such a fucking idiot some times. Ares likes you so go after him. If you don't you are going to miss your chance."

I want to believe what she's saying but there's no way that what's she's saying is right. "Again I say, what?"

She huffs and grabs me by the arm, dragging me towards the bathroom. It's down a hall at the quieter side of the pub and thankfully it's a single toilet with a locking door. It means that no one will walk in on Ares as he calms down. I'm pulled down the hall past the open doors of a few more toilets before coming to a halt outside the only closed door and Sophie knocks loudly before walking away. "You're welcome."

I'm about to chase her down and smack her when the door

opens just a little. I take it as an invite and slip into the small bathroom. Ares is standing with his hands against the sink and his head down. His back's to me but I can tell that he's overthinking something. I lock the door and lean back against it. I don't know if I should say something or let Ares start when he's ready so I just keep watching him in the large mirror in front of him. I feel better when he looks up and meets my gaze. He doesn't look sad which makes me relax a little. The look on his face is a little more confused and that's something I can hopefully help him with.

"I'm sorry." His voice is a little stronger than I expected it to be.

"Don't be sorry, just speak to me."

He goes quiet again but he doesn't look away. His stare is intense and it makes my jeans feel far too tight against my quickly rising dick. When he speaks he makes the problem a whole lot worse. "I want to kiss you so fucking badly and I don't know how to deal with that. You're my friend and I don't want to ruin that."

I start breathing quicker as I listen to him speak. Everything he says makes complete sense but my mind is stuck on the idea of kissing him. It's something I've been thinking about since the first night I bumped into him but I never thought he would feel the same. I've seen him look at me but with all the trauma in his past I never imagined that he wanted me. I thought all he wanted was friendship and now he's put kissing out there in the universe and I cant go back from that. "You won't ruin anything."

I swear I see him shiver and his eyes close slightly. He's told me how he feels but I know that he's new to all this and that he won't make a move, so I step in behind him, close but not touching. I leave the small distance between us to give him the chance to move away from me if he needs to. He doesn't flinch and that gives me confidence to close the final gap between us. As soon as my body touches his, heat spreads through me and my dick throbs. It was like this on the dance floor and I know that he's feeling the same result against his arse as he did before.

Ares eyes flicker and he drops his head back against my

shoulder. I turn so my lips brush against the side of his neck. I want to take things slow so Ares feels like he's fully in control of what's happening. His head rolls, giving me better access to his smooth skin and I run my nose along the length of his neck. He smells so fucking good. I don't know what aftershave he wears but I want to find out so I can buy him a lifetime supply.

His moan vibrates through my chest and I put my hands on his hips and grip them tightly. "I don't want to move too fast and scare you. I need you to show me the way."

The noise that comes from him almost sounds like a sob but when my eyes meet his eyes in the mirror I see nothing but heat. He pushes his arse back against me and I move instantly, thinking that he's feeling crowded. When he has enough space he turns around and leans his arse against the sink. "You're too far away."

Nerves suddenly attack and it takes me a moment to build up the courage to step forward. When I do, I decide that this is what heaven feels like. Having Ares' hard body against mine is like touching the sun. I close my eyes and try to memorise everything about him just in case this is the only chance I have. He's shorter than me, but not by much, and it leaves his hard on pressing against mine in a fucking mind blowing way. His body isn't built large, his frame small and toned, but I can feel the power in his muscles as they vibrate against me. His whole body feels like he can't control it and it worries me that it isn't caused by pleasure.

"Are you okay?"

Ares looks at me with lust filled eyes and nods his head. It's the only reaction that registers before the whole world vanishes in a cloud of ecstasy. I can barely stay standing when his lips connect with mine and it takes me a few moments to realise that I'm standing like an idiot while Ares kisses me. That's when I get involved, slipping my tongue in between his lips and against his. He tastes like cinnamon from the fireball and I can't get enough.

Thankfully Ares seems to be on the same page because he grabs me by the shirt like I'm about to disappear. Little does he know that it would take a rugby team to get me to move from here.

I growl as I become a little more aggressive in my kiss, needing more of his taste in my mouth. I've always liked kissing and Ares makes it so much better. I could spend hours just tasting him and letting his tongue do battle with mine to claim the kiss. Ares is more dominant than I thought he would be and I pull back slightly, letting him take this where he wants. I want him to enjoy this and have no regrets, so that means that he needs to be in control. His hands move from the front of my shirt but I don't pay attention until he grabs my aching dick through my jeans. I drop my head to his and try to focus on being able to breathe which gets even harder when the button on my jeans is popped open and my zip lowered. I hold my breath hoping knowing that my life is about to change forever. Ares hesitates slightly and I pull back to look at him.

"You don't have to do this. I'm more than happy just to kiss you."

Apparently that's all he needed to hear because his hand slips inside the top of my boxer shorts and wraps around my dick. *Holy fuck!* I meant to say that in my head but Ares laughs against my lips and I know that I haven't managed to keep it inside. I want to feel him, to pull those jeans down his thighs so I can see him fully but I'm scared to move. *Shit, I shouldn't be feeling like this.* I should trust him to tell me if it's going too far and I need to stop treating him like he's fragile. "I need to touch you and taste you, Ares. If you need me to stop, tell me. I don't want to treat you like glass and that's what I feel like I'm doing. Is that okay with you?"

Ares hand stops moving and he looks me in the eye. He looks a little scared but there's also determination in his expression. He slips his hand out of my boxers and leans back, putting a little space between us. "I don't know how to do this. I'm so lost in the darkness that I can't find my way out."

His honesty hits me straight in the chest and I reach out and cup his jaw. "Let me help you, Ares. Darkness is only scary if you're alone. Let me guide you through it. Let me be your light." My breath catches in my chest as I'm pushed backwards until my back hits the wall behind me. As soon as I stop moving my lips are attacked again and I take that as permission to take what I want.

Our coming together isn't graceful. It's a mess of hands and lips, and when Ares presses against me our now naked dicks press against each other. "Holy fuck, Ares."

He wraps his hand around our cocks, and even though he can't completely grip us both, the pressure has my knees wobbling. Thrusting gently into his hand I look down as we slide through his fingers and I don't think I've ever seen anything hotter. Watching our cocks rub together adds to the thrill that's already thrumming through my blood. I reach down and add my hand to his so we form prefect pressure the whole way round. I thrust again, adding some more speed as Ares stops moving, leaving me in charge of the friction. I move our hands up and down, and groan when his finger flicks over my head. It's not going to take much more before I come, its been a long time since I was with a guy and this is just too much pleasure to last a long time. "I'm gonna come, Ares."

"God, me too." His voice is as hoarse as mine and I'm glad I'm not the only one that's finding it hard to keep control. Ares' grip around us tightens as he kisses me again. This kiss feels different than the previous one, this time it's gentle, like he's happy to just kiss for the rest of the night. It's in complete contrast with the urgency that he's gripping our cocks with and moaning, and the combination is too much.

"Ares." I groan his name against his lips as I come all over our joined hands. Ares presses his forehead to mine and groans out my name as he adds to the mess I've left on our joined hands. As our hands still I look at Ares, studying his eyes carefully. I never dreamt that tonight would go in this direction and I doubt very much that he did, so I'm looking for signs that he's going to panic and run. I see nothing though except an orgasmic glow that's colouring his cheeks. He looks fucking glorious and I'm a little upset with myself for getting so caught up in my own orgasm that I missed him having his own.

Ares steps back and I can't help but watch him as he washes

his hands. He moves to the side so I can wash up, and tucks himself his jeans. I look down at my own body and see that my shirt hasn't escaped the mess. I take a paper towel and wet it, wiping over the bottom of my shirt to try and clean of most of the sticky mess.

Ares laughs and I turn to look at him. "I take it you will be tucking that in now."

I look back down and decide to give up. "I think you might be right. Oh well, tucked in it is."

"Don't worry, it will give me a better views of your arse."

I finish buttoning my jeans, making sure that the wet patch isn't visible, and turn to smile at Ares. He looks content and I can't help but feel a little smug that I did that to him. I don't want to cut the night short but I will if things are going to be awkward. "So what do you want to do now?" I give him the option to leave if he needs to.

"I think we should go back and get another Fireball, then get our groove on and dance with Sophie."

"I like that idea." I open the door and he practically bounces out of the bathroom. All I can think is that if anybody is watching us leave they are going to know exactly what we've been up to. Funny, I really don't care.

I stumble through the front door with Ares hanging onto my shoulder. The rest of the night at Westies had been such a laugh with us all singing and dancing together. Ares relaxed completely after our time in the bathroom and it was like he was a different man. We spent hours on the dance floor but it was basically just an excuse for Ares and me to touch each other, and we made the most of every second. I felt bad that Sophie kept making herself scarce but she assured me that she was perfectly happy to talk to the other people in the pub. We found her later in the night sitting on the knee of some guy, looking very cosy indeed.

Ares giggles as he heads across the living room floor. He's only seen this room so I'm not sure where he's heading so I rush to catch him by the arm. I lead him in the direction of my bedroom and he just laughs again and follows my lead. When I get us into the dark room, he stumbles over his feet as he collapses face first onto my bed. I shake my head at *Mr Can't Hold His Drink* and start undoing the laces on his shoes. I would try and get him to help but I think it's easier if I just do it myself. I throw his shoes to the edge of the room so he doesn't trip on them if he wakes in the night and start to remove the rest of his clothes. I lean down and try to get his attention by shaking his shoulder gently. He opens his eyes and looks sleepily at me.

"Do you want your clothes off?" He still just stares at me and I smirk at him. I had a few drinks after we went back to dancing, but not enough to feel more than a little relaxed. I didn't think that Ares had drunk much tonight but I must be wrong because there's no way he could be this drunk from the few fireballs I saw him drink, and whatever that blue cocktail was.

Ares eventually nods his head but makes no attempt to undress himself so I take that as permission to do it myself. It takes longer than I would like to get his jacket off and when I try to roll him onto his back to get to his shirt buttons he just flops like a dead fish. There's a part of me that's worried about how he will react in the morning when he realises how much he let his guard down tonight, but there's a part of me that's elated that he felt safe enough with me to do that. I'm beginning to notice that gaining Ares trust is becoming very important to me. I want to show him that the people who love you don't hurt you the way that Micah did.

I get to the last button of his shirt and pull it from his shoulders before rolling him onto his stomach again I tug it down his arms and throw it onto the chair next to my door when it's off. I turn back to face him and I freeze, confused by what I'm seeing. *That can't be right, it's the shadows from the streetlights that are making his skin look like that.* I step back without taking my eyes from Ares' skin and feel along the wall until I find the switch for the overhead light and turn it on. I close my eyes slightly against the sudden brightness but Ares doesn't flinch. I'm going to need a minute to deal with what I'm looking at and I have a feeling that if Ares saw my reaction he would run. Confusion flickers through my brain as I step closer and reach out, running my fingers over the uneven skin on Ares' back.

There are deep scars running across Ares' toned back, the edges of them rough as if they didn't heal right. I've seen people who've had terrible accidents and their scars are pale and, even the worst of them, are smooth to the touch. These are very different, they are thick and raised. It looks like he's been tortured. That thought has bile rising in my throat because I think I know who did this to him. *Was it Micah who put them there? Was Ares punished for some perceived misdemeanour and now has to live with the reminder for the rest of his life?*

I cover my mouth and run for the toilet as the need to throw up takes over. I manage to kick the door closed behind me as I collapse over the toilet and bring up the alcohol I drank tonight. When I'm done I reach up and flush before dropping onto the floor, sitting with my back against the wall. I grab the towel that's over the side of my bath and wipe over my face to get rid of the sweat.

Every time I think I know how bad Ares' abuse was, something happens and I see I don't know the littlest amount of what he went through. I've barely scratched the surface of the pain he's had to endure at the hands of that monster. This is why he cant trust me, trust anyone, and it's the reason that he fears that someone is always there to attack him. I can't imagine living like that, the constant worry of being back into a life that nearly killed me. Even Micah being in jail can't give Ares the peace he deserves. If I was him I think I would have locked myself in a room and never come out again. To live in that constant fear every moment of your life would drive me insane, I don't know how he does it.

I drop my head back against the wall and close my eyes when a horrible thought makes my stomach churn again. *Will Ares ever be able to trust me?* I don't know if he will ever be able to give me what I want from him, which is everything he can give me. I will take his scars and fears, his past and his future hopes, but I need him to be able to let me in. I need to make some decisions before whatever this is with Ares goes any further. Can I spend my energy and time on fighting for what I want when he might not be able to give me that?

Taking a deep breath I get up from the floor and wash my face at the sink, rinsing my mouth with mouthwash while I'm there. I return to the bedroom and wrestle Ares out of his jeans and manoeuvre him under the duvet to keep him warm. I strip down to my boxers and go to my chest of drawers and grab a vest to wear. I was going to sleep on the couch tonight but I don't want to leave Ares alone in case he's sick. When I have it on I climb into the other side of the bed and lie on my back, staring at the ceiling. Next to me Ares moans in a restless sleep and I look over at him. I don't think about my next move as I pull him towards me and lie him over my chest. He snuggles into my neck and throws his leg over mine. His heat is soothing and I let myself relax as I hold him tight.

I don't know what tomorrow or the next day will bring but I know that I want to try. I want something with this amazing man in my arms so I'm willing to fight, even if that fight is against the ghosts of his past.

Chapter Eighteen

Ares

Movement behind me pulls me out of my dream. As I start to become aware of the world around me, the dream itself fades but the memory of the pain and fear linger like a lead weight pushing me down into the bed. I open my eyes and find it difficult to focus as my head spins. Fear has me lying still even as the world moves around me. Disturbing Micah's sleep would earn me something worse that dizziness. I close my eyes and try to clear my mind but it's becoming really difficult.

Opening my eyes again the world is a bit more in focus and that's when I realise how stupid I'm being. Micah isn't here, I left him in the past along with all the pain. There's movement behind me again and my eyes go wide as I freeze, but for a very different reason this time. I look around when I'm sure the person behind me has gone back to sleep and I don't recognise anything. I can only see one half of the room from my position on my side but from what I can make out I know I'm not at home. *Where am I?* I don't remember anything from last night after my trip to the bathroom with … Kohan!

I turn slowly until I'm facing the person behind me. I let out a sigh of relief when I confirm that it is Kohan I'm sharing a bed with. I gaze at him as he lies there with his arm under his pillow and his face relaxed. God, I wish I could look at him forever. I don't think I've ever seen a guy as gorgeous as Kohan. That's why I gave in to my lust when he followed me to the bathroom, wanting to have one night that I got everything I'd ever dreamed of. The problem is I could see in Kohan's eyes that he wants more with me and I know now that I can't give that to him. I wanted to believe I could, that I could be the man who deserved someone like him, but I'm not, I know that now. That's why I drank so much when we went back to the bar. Having him so close to me, touching and kissing him, I needed the alcohol to get through the night. Having him close was messing with my resolve to walk away so I gave myself one night to enjoy it, to pretend that I could be everything that he needed before I put distance between us and become nothing more than his friend.

I slip out of Kohan's bed and grab on to the headboard as the effects from the night before hit me full force. I may have drunk a little more last night than I thought, but considering I haven't had a drink since I moved in with Micah, I think any is too much. When the world is level again I move quietly so I don't wake Kohan up. I need to get out of here before he wakes up, I don't want to explain why I'm sneaking out without saying goodbye. I might have made a decision about what I need to do, but that doesn't mean that I'm not above taking the coward's way out.

After picking up my clothes that were on the seat next to the door, I check inside a few rooms until I find the bathroom. I turn the light on and groan when the brightness makes my brain feel like it's being attacked by hammers. I close the door as silently as I can and turn towards the mirror. I cringe when I see the mess that's looking back at me. My hair is sticking up and my eyes are bloodshot from either lack of sleep or the alcohol, or possibly both.

A quiet humming in my ear catches my attention and I press my hearing aid gently to try and stop the noise. When I put the pressure on it slight pain spreads through my ear and I know that it's because I slept with my hearing aids in. I need to make sure I don't get so drunk in the future that I can't get myself ready for bed because there are certain things I need to do before I sleep, and one of those things is taking my hearing aids out. I found out quickly that the benefits of being able to hear while I'm sleeping do not outweigh the pain caused by having them in all night. I was told I could sleep with them in but I just can't. I don't know if I move too much or put too much pressure on my ears but the discomfort isn't worth it. I just made sure that all my smoke alarms are connected to vibration mats and everything else is connected to the lights. Truthfully, I only wear my hearing aids when I need to, or at least that used to be the case. I find myself wearing them a lot more now ever since I met Kohan. The silence doesn't appeal to me as much as it used to.

I take both hearing aids out and place them next to my shirt on the sink surround. I really want to turn the tap on so I can wash my face but I don't know how noisy Kohan's plumbing is. Instead, I grab a face wipe from the packet that's sitting on a small glass shelf and use that to try and wake myself up a bit. I look around and see a little bin under the sink and bend down to put the wipe in it. When I straighten up a hand lands on my shoulder and reflex has me lashing out. My fist connects with Kohan's face before my brain tells me that I'm not in danger. I pull my hand back and cover my mouth when I see blood dripping from his nose and down to his chin.

"Fucker." He shouts the word not at me, but more as a reaction to what happened, but I can't help shrinking away from him. Kohan has never shown me anything close to anger but my fight or flight response has me wanting to bolt from the room.

Kohan reaches out to grab tissues from the shelf behind me and I flinch, tensing my muscles like I'm waiting for him to strike me. He pauses with his hand at my side and stares at me, and I know that he saw the reaction. A few seconds later he grabs some tissues and pulls his hand back, cleaning his lips and pressing the tissues to his nose. He just looks at me as he tries to stem the flow of blood and I know I need to say something but I can't think what. I feel like shit that I thought he'd hurt me in any way, but the reaction is ingrained into me.

"I'm really sorry." I know it doesn't excuse what I've done but it's the only thing that I can think to say. All I want to do is to get out of here, even more than before.

Kohan's lips move and I remember that I'm not wearing my hearing aids when his words don't reach my ears. "I can't hear you." I point at them on the unit and he just nods at me.

I expect him to gesture for me to put them back in but he shocks me when he just grabs a wipe and carries on cleaning his face. When he's blood free he leans in and kisses me, a sweet little kiss, and leaves the bathroom.

I stand there shocked for a few moments before turning and grabbing my clothes. I dress as quickly as possible and head back into the bedroom. Kohan is back in bed but the light is on and he's looking straight at me. *So much for sneaking out without having to see him.* I put my hands in my jean pockets and bite my lip, not sure what to do now. Kohan turns to his bedside unit and grabs his mobile. A few seconds later my own vibrates against my hand in my pocket. I take it out and open the message.

Do you need a lift home?

I can't believe that I didn't think about how I was getting home so early in the morning. I suppose when I got outside I would have just walked the few miles to my cottage, and I would have been fine, well apart from the trip down the country road that leads to my cottage. I'm sure the darkness would have brought on a panic attack but I would have coped, I would have had to. Now I don't feel like walking in the dark but it's probably far too late, or early, for a taxi. Getting a lift home from Kohan makes my stomach churn with nerves because he'll want to talk, or will he if he knows that I can't hear him?

My head starts to hurt with all the thoughts that are rushing through it. I'm far too tired and still a little too drunk to be thinking about all this. All I want to do is go home, go to bed and sleep for about fourteen hours. Then I will wake up and forget that tonight ever happened. From us coming on each other to me punching him, I think it would be better if I just blanked it all out. I type out a response but don't look at him. I won't be able to hear when the message arrives on Kohan's phone and I'm perfectly happy with that.

It's okay. You just go back to sleep, I don't mind walking.

I start to wonder if I should just do us both a favour and walk out, but I see a shadow on the floor in front of me so I raise my head. Kohan is standing in front of me, obviously waiting until I see him so I don't hit him again, and when I look at him he moves forward. He carefully speaks and this time I can read his words.
"Not happening."
Even though I can't lip-read very well, if people take their time to speak I can usually make out a few words. Kohan is very clear in what he's saying and he leans in for a kiss before moving to his dresser, taking long shorts and a t-shirt out. I watch him getting dressed, wanting nothing more than to get back into bed with him and explore what he has under those clothes but that's a dangerous direction for my thoughts.

He only takes a few minutes to get dressed and slip on a pair of trainers before he turns to smile at me. *How can he make everything he wears look so fucking sexy?* Sportswear or dressed up smart, he looks perfect in it all. I can't take my eyes off him because the t-shirt he's wearing is slightly tight and clings across his stomach. It makes me wish that I'd paid more attention when he was naked.

He walks past me, touching my hand as he slips through the bedroom door. I follow him out to the hall, grabbing my jacket from the back of his chair as we leave his house. It feels strange being in his company and not being able to hear him. He's such a huge presence when he's with me, filling up the seconds with noise and fun. He opens the car door for me and I slip into the passenger seat and wait for him to walk around to his own door. When he gets in I'm thankful that it's dark as it means there's no way for us to talk. I know I'm being a coward but I just want to get home without having to say anything to Kohan.

Wondering what time it actually is I look at the clock on the dashboard and see that it's just after four o'clock. I feel really bad that I'm making Kohan take me home when he should still be asleep. I let myself feel better because I know I didn't ask him to drive, he told me he was. I look out the side window but there isn't anything to see in the darkness. It doesn't stop me from keeping my face away from Kohan so I can avoid any possible glances.

I'm pulled from my staring when the car stops. I look around and see that we are already parked in my driveway. I don't even remember passing the main road but here we are, and I can't avoid looking at Kohan any longer so I turn in my seat to face him.

"Thank you for the lift." I've practiced keeping my voice quiet when I don't have my hearing aids in as there's a tendency for me to shout when I can't hear myself.

Kohan reaches up and turns on the small console light above our seats so I can see him. "You're welcome." He says the words clearly again and I feel a lump in my throat. He does all these sweet things to make life easier for me and I can't give him a simple thing like my trust and possibly my heart. Okay, neither of those things are simple for most people and for me they are even harder.

I turn to leave the car, trying to escape before I need to talk anymore, but Kohan reaches out and grabs my wrist. I inhale slowly to brace myself before turning back around. Kohan gives me that sweet smile that usually makes my heart skip, but tonight it just increases the emotion that's building inside me. I don't know why I'm feeling so sad but I need to get out of the car before I make a fool of myself by crying.

"Will you call me?"

I nod my head not trusting my voice to make it out of my tight throat. I pull my hand away gently and get out of the car. I don't look back as I walk up the path to my front door but when I get there I look over my shoulder. He's still sitting there watching me, probably making sure that I get in safely. That's the final straw for my emotions and I quickly unlock the door and slip inside as tears fall down my cheeks. I have no idea why I'm crying but now that I've started I can't seem to stop. Once the front door is locked I quickly move to my bedroom and strip out of my clothes. When I'm naked I climb under the covers and pull them up to my chin. The coolness of the bed should feel refreshing but with the stupid tears still wetting my cheeks I don't enjoy it like I normally would. The ache in my chest makes me feel like I've lost something important to me and I wonder if it understands already that I won't be allowing myself to have any sort of intimate relationship with Kohan. The thought of him causes the ache to increase and I rub my hand against my chest to try and ease the pain.

What the fuck am I doing? I'm acting like I'm giving up a long-term relationship, like he's the love of my life and I've broken up with him. Or at least what I imagine a breakup would feel like. Splitting from Micah isn't exactly what I would call normal, that was more running for my life, so I don't know if this is normal. Escaping from Micah gave me more relief than heartache so this hurt shocks me. This thing with Kohan feels like I'm losing a part of me and it's making me feel stupid. I can't lose something that I didn't give and I didn't give Kohan my heart, except it feels like I did. When Kohan drove away tonight its like he took my heart with him. Maybe that's what the ache in my chest is, the empty space where my heart used to be? *Do I love Kohan?*

No, I can't be in love. I gave up the idea of a happily ever after when the last man I wanted to spend my life with nearly killed me. No, definitely not in love, even if Kohan is the kindest man I've ever met. His kindness is real, you can see it in his eyes and the way he treats people. He loves his family and friends with his whole heart so I know that he isn't faking anything. He would be the kind of boyfriend that people wrote books about and the kind of man that made you feel like you're the most important person in the world.

But no, I'm not falling in love with Kohan. Although, I think I am and I don't know what to do about it.

Chapter Nineteen

Ares

I sit and look out the car window as we pass through the built up area of Birmingham. I've been quiet since Roscoe picked me up and I know it has to be driving him crazy. Roscoe is the type of guy who has to fill every second when he's with someone, he hates silence of any sort. He's always been told that it's his ADHD that causes it but I think it's just him. He's always been a big talker and one of the reasons I begged my parents to let me move to the room on the top floor even though it was the smallest. I was happy just to be able to read without having Roscoe constantly talking in my ear. I don't think he realises he's doing it sometimes and that makes it harder to get him to stay quiet. So for him to sit here with me for so long without a word is a little bit of a miracle.

I decide that I need to start some sort of conversation, even if it's just to save us all from the amount he will need to talk over dinner to catch up. "I was thinking of learning to drive."

He looks over at me quickly before turning back to face the motorway ahead. "I think that's a great idea. It would save me having to come and pick your lazy arse up every time you want to grace us with your presence."

I bite the inside of my cheek and try not to smile. I know that he's just teasing me and I can't show that I find him funny, it gives him far too much power. "I thought I was helping you out by giving you something to do, saves you sitting at home all by yourself. Have you thought of getting a special friend?"

Roscoe bursts out laughing at my mention of 'special friend' and I smile to myself knowing I just won that round. I knew that using our gran's term for my boyfriends was guaranteed to break him.

Our gran was a sweet old lady but very old fashioned when it came to a lot of things. When I came out to the family she tried very hard to be as accepting as she could, but the first time she met Micah she said that it was nice to have a special friend to pass the time with. Even on that day we couldn't control the laughter that overtook us and I just hugged her hard while I had tears running down my cheeks. Now it's a joke between Roscoe and me, usually me telling him he needs to get a special friend.

"I'm sure Tina would be over the moon if I got a special friend."

"You never know, some women like that sort of thing."

The car swerves a little as he looks at me out of the corner of his eyes. "How the hell do you know what women like? I might not be fully up on everything being gay is, but I didn't think that you needed to know how to turn on a woman. Men yes, women not so much."

Roscoe has never been anything but supportive of me. Moments like this though I can't help but confuse the shit out of him. I laugh at him, only answering when he punches my arm. "I don't need to be able to turn on women, I'm not bi, but I have Facebook. Go into any hot man group and before long there will be pictures of guys kissing. Women like that sort of stuff. I don't mind though, it's a complete win/win for me."

Roscoe rubs his hand over his forehead. "Well shit, I did not know this. I don't think I will ask Tina about it though, ignorance is bliss and all that. I wouldn't want to start this discussion and then disappoint her."

"Disappoint her?"

"I love that woman and would do anything for her, live out any fantasy ... except that one. If I don't know about it then I can't disappoint her by not doing it."

A vision starts to build in my head and I block it instantly. There are certain ways I'm willing to think about my brother and that is definitely not one of those ways. "Let's change the subject shall we? You are my brother and you don't have sex."

He smiles over at me before being kind and changing the subject. "So why the sudden decision to drive? I don't think I've ever heard you talking about it."

I think for a minute and realise he's right, there used to be a good reason for me to not drive and that's now gone. "I was never allowed to drive. Micah saw it as a way for me to be independent so it was banned. Now, I think having that bit of freedom might be nice."

Bringing Micah into the conversation gets the same reaction from Roscoe it always does. His hands tighten on the steering wheel and his jaw ticks as he tries to contain his rage. I wish he could lose some of the anger but I know it won't happen. The hate that Roscoe has for Micah is heart deep and I think that if he were to see him again he would kill him. I feel bad for mentioning him and making my brother feel like this but I can't pretend that Micah didn't exist. If I'm to move on I need to be able to talk about him without having the world crash down around my ears "It would also save me from having to endure your company each time I want to see mum and dad."

The comment has the desired effect and Roscoe releases his death grip on the wheel. "Yeah, it would be nice if you weren't so dependent on me. I always have to let people know I might have to cancel plans if my loner brother calls."

God, if people could hear the shit we say to each other but little do they know that its this that got me through the last few years. Having Roscoe treat me normally made me feel normal, like I was just his baby brother. It's all love and sarcasm between us and it's just the way I like it. "As I said before, I've got to give you something to do."

We drive in silence for a few minutes and I go back to staring out the passenger window. Its only when we're entering Birmingham that Roscoe breaks the silence between us. "I think it's a really good idea by the way."

I look over, a little lost with the sudden conversation, until I remember what we were talking about. "Thanks. I just want to get back to being normal or at least as normal as I can be. Micah took so much from me and I don't want to give him that sort of power anymore."

"I'm proud of you, little brother." His voice is low but I hear it as clear as if he was shouting it straight in my ear. My throat tightens with emotion and I look out the window because if I look at Roscoe I'm going to cry.

About fifteen minutes later we pull into the driveway of our parent's home and I barely have my door open when mum is running out the front door and crushing me in a hug. "Oh my baby boy, I missed you so much." She pulls back and looks at me before scowling, giving me that disapproving look that only mothers can give. "You need to visit more or I'm going to start coming to you, and you know that means that I will have to stay over and cramp your style."

It's only about an hour's drive from mine to my parents but my mum isn't the best driver in the world so when she comes she needs to stay overnight at least once so she isn't making the two journeys in one day. I love my mum and spending time with her is never a problem, but when she comes to my house she cleans and that's never a good thing. After a short visit it can take me up to a week to find everything that she's *tidied* away.

Mum takes me by the hand and pulls me inside the house to the kitchen where my dad's reading the newspaper. He looks over the top of the paper and smiles at me. I take the seat next to him and he folds it up and puts it on the table in front of him. "Want a coffee?" He asks me this all the time even though he knows I don't drink the stuff, and even if I did, I'd never get my dad to make it. He makes his coffee so strong that I'm not sure how he actually manages to sleep at night.

"No thanks." Just as I answer him my mum puts a filled glass in front of me and I know instantly that it's Pepsi Max. My addiction is a long-term thing and there's always a ready supply in the house. I smile at her while I take a drink and she grabs a cup of coffee and sits opposite me.

"So tell us, how are things?"

The seat next to me is filled with my brother's huge body and he grabs the glass from me hand. As soon as he takes a sip I scowl at him. He knows that there's no way that I'll drink out of that after he has. My mum sighs as she gets up to get me a new glass.

"He's thinking of getting driving lessons."

My dad's eyebrows go up and I'm a little annoyed that he's so surprised. I'm not so much of a loser that I can't drive a car. "That's fantastic. Do you have someone who can teach you? It's a long way but I could come down and take you out."

I feel bad for being irritated at my dad, I should have known that even though he was surprised he would still be fully supportive. I really need to stop seeing the worst in everyone. "I haven't looked into it properly yet, but I will soon. It will probably just be someone local so I can go out regularly." *I wonder if Kohan would take me out?* He has his own car and I'm sure he wouldn't mind doing it. The thought of Kohan has heat spreading over my cheeks and I hope that it isn't noticeable. I know it is when my mum puts another glass in front of me and takes a seat, her eyebrows raising but for a different reason than my dad's. She doesn't say anything and for that I'm thankful, but I know she won't let me off the hook quite that easily. She will catch me at some point when we are alone and she will have a hundred questions.

My mum's always had this knack of reading me better than anyone else. She can take something as simple as a blush and know exactly why it's happening. I can guarantee that she knows that this one has something to do with a guy. I don't know how the hell she does it but she would be MI6's best interrogator if she wanted.

"I need to shoot. I'll be back in a few hours to take loser boy home." Roscoe gets up from the table and kisses me on the forehead before rushing for the door. I wipe the skin where he's left a wet spot and glare at the now closed door. He does that to me all the time and I hate it. I thought that once I grew my hair over my scar it would stop him but no, he's still a twat.

"How is everything else going?" My mum always has a hopeful look when she asks me that question, and for the first time ever I think I can tell her the truth. I've never lied to my parents about my struggles and they have always been there no matter how bad things got, so to tell them something positive for a change is great.

"Actually, everything's good." I take a mouthful of Pepsi Max to let them get over the shock of my words. Seeing the smile on both my parent's faces makes me feel like I've just given them a million pounds.

"Well don't leave us in suspense. Tell us what's happening."

"I'm really enjoying my job. Being able to get out and be independent is good for my confidence. I know I clean when the office is mainly empty, but I think it's a great starting point. I also met someone."

This has my mum nearly bouncing on her seat and I speak quickly before she becomes too excited.

"A friend, mum. I met a guy who's a friend. He's a journalist at the offices I clean and we've been spending some time together. He took me to the local pub and I had a really good time."

This doesn't help my mum lose any of her bounce and I know that she's already picking out a mother of the groom outfit in her mind. "I'm so happy for you, baby boy. It sounds like this young man is becoming important to you."

"Does he know about your past?" My dad asks, the ever-present voice of reason. I'm glad he's here to try and tamper down my mum's eagerness.

"Kohan, that's his name, knows. Obviously not all of it because I don't want to scare him off before I've time to actually get to know him, but he knows a lot."

"That's good. I'm a little surprised that you told him but I'm happy that you have someone else you can talk to. Someone that wasn't there at the time." I know what my dad's trying to say. Sometimes it's difficult for my parents to hear what I went through at the hands of Micah, and when I tell them anything I always try to leave out as much information as possible. I didn't to begin with and watching my mum's heart break became too much to handle. Now I give the minimal amount needed and no more. They went through the court case with me so they heard the things he did to me; I don't need to force them relive the whole thing over and over again.

"He's been a good friend. He doesn't judge, well not me anyway. I do think if he was ever to meet Micah there might be bloodshed." Kohan's never come out and said this to me but I can see it in his eyes when I tell him what I went through. I can see the anger and rage build when I speak. I've become an expert with that look because I saw it enough on my dad and brother's faces.

"I think I like this boy already." Dad winks at me before getting up to refill his coffee. Unfortunately that leaves me at the table with mum who apparently isn't going to let this opportunity pass.

"So this *friend*. Is he just a friend or do you think there might be something else?"

I pick at the small thread that's hanging off the placemat in front of me and think about her question. I have two options here: I can tell her that he's just a friend and stick with the plan that's in my head, or I can tell her the truth and ask her what the hell I should do. I need to talk to someone about it and not someone who is getting paid to listen. "I think I might like him."

She reaches out and grabs my hand to stop me from fidgeting. I finally look up and see that she has a sad smile on her face. "Why is liking him such a problem?"

"Because I don't know how to do this anymore. I can't trust my judgement when it comes to men." And finally there it is. The truth about why I'm scared to be with Kohan.

"You know how to do this, you just won't let yourself. I know that things with *him* didn't go well but that doesn't mean you have to spend the rest of your life alone. We've all misjudged someone but we learn from that and make sure that we don't make the same mistake again. It's just life, sweetheart, we all have to live it. Has this Kohan boy given you any reason not to trust him?"

I shake my head harshly needing my mum to know that Kohan isn't like that. "Nothing. I swear I've never met a nicer person in my life. He's sweet and patient, and lets me take everything at my own pace. He totally gets that things can freak me out and he tries to limit anything that would make me panic." I think back to the ways Kohan has gone out of his way to make me feel comfortable, even at work. They're all simple things but they mean a lot. I feel the corner of my lips turning up into a smile as I think about a few weeks ago at the offices when he needed to speak to me. He text me to let me know that he was there and when I turned I found him leaning against the wall a few feet back, waiting on me to notice him so I didn't get scared.

"Then you have nothing to worry about. Don't let one bad relationship ruin the future happiness that you deserve."

"Can I class what happened with Micah as a bad relationship? He nearly killed me." I regret the words as soon as they leave my mouth. My Mum's face goes white and the tears instantly build in her eyes.

"I know what he did to you, Ares. I nearly lost my son. Don't forget I had to sit by your hospital bed and pray that you woke up."

I try to grab her hands but she brushes me off and gets up, leaving the kitchen without another word.

My dad takes his seat again and looks at me with sad resignation.

"I'm sorry; I fucked that up."

He pats me on the shoulder. "I know that you want to get over this and get your life back, but you need to give your mum a little longer. You went through the actual abuse but it's still killing her that she didn't know. It's hard to know that your child is hurting and you didn't notice. We are meant to protect our kids and we didn't. Just give her a little time."

"I'm sorry, Dad, for everything. I brought all this into your lives and I will never forgive myself for putting you all through that."

My dad moves quickly and grabs me by the back of the neck. He pulls me towards him, looking deep into my eyes. "You listen to me closely, Ares. You did not bring this to our door so do not apologise. None of this is or was ever your fault. There is only one person to blame and he's behind bars now. If I ever hear you taking blame for anything he did to you I will be furious. Do you hear me?"

I nod my head because I don't trust my voice. My dad doesn't show emotion very often so when he does it means a lot.

He returns my nod and lets me go, picking up his paper and opening it again. "Did you hear about the new garage that's opening next to Tesco?"

And just like that the moment is over. I laugh before taking a mouthful of my drink, needing it to try and get rid of the lump in my throat. My mum returns with a smile on her face but her eyes are still red and it makes me feel like shit. She doesn't say anything as she goes about making lunch for us all. Soon the conversation is flowing again and we spend the next few hours catching up and making plans for my birthday. When Roscoe comes to take me home, I feel homesick before I even leave.

Chapter Twenty

Kohan

"I swear if you embarrass me I'll never let you meet anyone else ... ever." Carey is a bundle of nerves as we sit in the café next to his gym waiting for Duncan. He finally decided that I could meet his potential love interest after I pestered him for about a week. There was no way I was letting him off the hook about meeting the first guy that my brother has ever been interested in. I'm pretending it's for future reference to see what kind of guy revs my brother's engine but it's purely because I'm nosey.

"What the hell do you think I will do, pick my nose and eat it?"

Carey glares at me and I supress my laughter. This is becoming too much fun and I don't want to waste the opportunity to annoy him. Carey is usually really hard to rattle but today he's acting a lot like Damien. "I mean it, Kohan. I like this guy. I'm not even sure if you should meet him. Shit."

"What the hell, Carey? You need to calm down. I promise that I won't embarrass you in front of him."

Carey looks down and the move confuses me. I want to know what's going on in his head because he's not acting like himself. I lean forward until my head is almost touching his. "Talk to me, big brother. What's going on in that head of yours?"

He looks up and I can only see sadness in his eyes. "What if he likes you more than me?"

I flinch and I reckon my eyes must be the size of saucers. "What the fuck are you talking about? Why would he want me over you?"

Carey drops his head again like he's embarrassed and I'm not sure if I like seeing this side of my brother. He's always been super confident, especially when it comes to dating. "Look at you.

Then there's also the fact that you are the brother who is openly gay and knows what he's doing. I have no fucking clue what I'm doing here so I don't see why he'd want that. Maybe I should just go."

I'm about to lose my shit with my brother when a shadow falls over the table and Carey's head whips up to look at the guy standing next to us. As he gets up to greet the person I'm guessing is Duncan, I take a moment to look over him. He's tall, not quite as tall as my brother but there isn't much difference between them. He has really blonde hair with chunks of darker brown through it. It looks like he is naturally blonde but is trying to hide it a little with hair dye. He has a kind face and the way he's looking at my brother fills me with happiness. I reckon they could be in a room full of people and he wouldn't notice anyone but my brother.

They both turn to look at me, finally remembering that they're not alone. Carey looks as happy as Duncan does and when he blushes I know that this guy is probably a keeper. Anyone that makes my brother feel that way should be welcomed. "This is my brother, Kohan. Kohan meet Duncan."

I stand to be polite as I shake Duncan's hand. Something dark flickers across his face but it's gone before I can register what it is. He smiles as he tells me that it's great to meet me and I shake the look off as me imagining it. He's probably nervous meeting a member of Carey's family and it showed on his face for a brief moment.

We all sit at the table and I lean forward with my arms folded on the table. "So, Duncan, please tell me what your intentions with my brother are."

Carey drops his head to the table and groans but Duncan just laughs at me. "I don't have any intentions really, should I maybe get some?" Coming from anyone else the words would sound flirty but not from him. It's hard to explain but there seems to be an edge to his voice. It's maybe just the way he speaks, but his words come over slightly cold to me.

"I'm interrupting this sort of questioning. Kohan, stop being a dick or leave."

I laugh at Carey's attempt to get me to back off but I can't stop looking at Duncan. There's just something off about him, something I can't quite put my finger on. I decide to ignore it, convincing myself that it's just my imagination and the need to look out for my brother. "Tell me a little about yourself, Duncan."

"There isn't much to tell. I've not long moved here so I'm kinda new to the area. Carey was one of the first people I met, not that I'm complaining about that." Duncan turns and smiles at my brother which makes Carey blush again.

"What do you do?" I ignore the glare that Carey gives me because there's no way I'm not going to take the chance to find out as much as I can about the guy. I think he forgets about the grief he has given some of the men I've dated in the past, now it's my turn to return the favour.

"I'm not currently working but before I came here I was a personal financial advisor."

"Sounds important. Are you looking for work in the area?"

"Not at the moment."

Duncan seems to be answering everything without really giving me any real information. "Do you have a secret inheritance that you're living off?"

"Kohan, stop with the third degree."

Duncan reaches out and takes Carey's hand. "It's okay, he's just looking out for his brother. It's nice. But to answer your question, I'm on a sort of sabbatical. I'm taking a break from work to try and get things sorted. And before you ask that *thing* is a bad break-up last year. I needed to move to clear my head. I didn't expect to meet someone I liked pretty much straight away but I did."

All very good answers and they set my mind at rest. When he admitted to being unemployed I was worried that he would up and leave my brother or use him for money. I need this to go well for Carey, show him that being with a guy can be awesome. I don't want it to go completely wrong and Carey to think he made a mistake by taking a chance on a guy.

"Are you happy now?" Carey glares at me again but I notice he hasn't let go of Duncan's hand.

"Yes. But come on, remember when I brought home Matt? You locked him in the bathroom and wouldn't let him out until he told you everything you wanted to know."

Carey laughs and it makes me hate him a little. "I forgot about that. I'm pretty sure that guy pissed his pants before I was through with him."

"Not quite but I didn't see him again after that night. You scared him away and I'm sure he could have been The One."

This has Carey creasing himself. "Oh shut up, you know that you've found *The One* now. You just need to convince Ares of that fact." He winks at me and I give him the finger.

I turn to look at Duncan and there's no mistaking the look of anger that's on his face. He's glaring at me and I feel a little awkward. "Are you okay, Duncan?"

He blinks a few times before he smiles, his eyes clearing the cloud of anger that was there a minute ago. "Yeah, everything's great."

I would be happier if I believed him for even a fraction of a second.

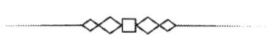

I sit in my car and stare at Ares little cottage. I haven't seen him since our night out and I'm pretty sure that's on purpose. He's answered any text I've sent him but hasn't started a conversation himself. Part of me thinks that if he is wanting to keep his distance from me then I should respect that and leave him alone, but the other, and more prominent part thinks fuck that. If I allow him to create distance between us then I'm going to lose all the headway I've made and I'm not going to let that happen. That's why I'm sitting here now in his drive building up the courage to go knock on his door.

I take a deep breath and grab the stuff I brought with me from the passenger seat before leaving my car and approaching Ares' front door. I press the doorbell and stand there wondering if he'll answer. I'm only waiting for a few moments before the door opens and Ares leans against the doorframe looking like every guy's wet dream.

"I don't care what you're selling, I'm not interested."

I hold up the tub of jellybeans I brought with me and I know the second that Ares spots them because his eyes light up. "Are you sure about that?"

He chews his bottom lip before he grabs the tub from my hand and disappears into his house. He doesn't shut the door behind him so I take it as permission to follow him. I was hoping that the jellybeans would distract him enough that I would be able to get inside to talk to him. I found bribery is one of the best ways to tackle some people, and with Ares jellybeans *always* work.

I reach the kitchen only to find him leaning against the unit with the tub already open. He picks out a couple of beans and puts them into his mouth, moaning as he chews.

"I would really like to know how you found out about my jellybean addiction."

The Pepsi Max thing he told me about but I had to work out this addiction on my own. It only took a few days to notice it. "Your trolley at work always had jellybeans on it and I noticed it was never the same packs so you must have been eating them. I started leaving some on there to see what you did and they always vanished."

"Have you ever thought of becoming a detective? You would be very good." He takes another handful of beans before replacing the lid and putting the tub on a shelf above the fridge. The shelf is full of other kinds of sweets but none of the tubs seem to be open. I thought it was a general sweet tooth he has but with his distaste of sweet drinks and these sealed tubs, I think it's just a jellybean craving.

"So men in uniform, that's what does it for you?" He has a sly smile on his face and I want so badly to go over and kiss him. I haven't seen him since the night at the pub but I haven't been able to stop thinking about how good he felt when I touched him. God, he felt so fucking good.

"Amongst other things."

"Other things?"

Now it's time to show my hand and see how he responds. I've thought about not making my attraction to him clear but no, I'm going to be a bit more obvious and see what happens. "I'm quite partial to quiet brunettes that sculpt in their spare time."

Ares cheeks go red which tells me he knows exactly what I'm saying. The silence stretches out between us but I refuse to make this easy for him by speaking. I want to know what he's thinking and being quiet is the only way for that to happen. "Would you teach me to drive?"

Okay, that's not what I thought he might say but he isn't running so that's a start. "I think that could be arranged. Just let me know when you want to go out and I'll make sure I'm all organised with insurance and L plates."

He nods and moves back to the fridge before opening it and grabbing some cans of soft drink. He doesn't ask what I want but I have a strange feeling I know what the drink will be. I let him carry on and I wander over to the shelves where he stores his sculptures. There are some new ones and I take a few minutes to look at them all. I move in front of the last shelving unit and stop dead. There's a new head sculpture in the middle and it's caught my eye. I want to pretend it's for a different reason than the obvious one but I can't do it. The face looks exactly like mine, it's almost like I'm looking in a mirror.

"That's my latest one."

I look at Ares over my shoulder before looking back at the shelf. "Its great. It's missing something though."

I feel Ares moving closer behind me, the heat from his body spreading over mine. "What?"

My breathing becomes a little laboured at his presence and I pray he doesn't notice. My body instinctively reacts when he's so close and it gets worse every time I see him. "The scar. All the others have a scar to show they're perfectly imperfect."

He must move closer again because when he speaks his breath blows across my neck. "I couldn't do it to this one. I couldn't mark something that was so beautiful."

I close my eyes and try to get myself under control because all I can think about is turning around and kissing Ares. He must know what he's doing to me; no one could be this naïve.

When he speaks again he sounds further away and I breathe a sigh of relief. Distance should make keeping my hands to myself a lot easier. "Pepsi?"

I walk over and take the glass out of his hand, taking a drink to keep my mouth occupied.

"So other than giving me a sugar high with the jellybeans, was there any other reason you came over?"

"Just wanted to see you. I felt that you were avoiding me and I wanted to make sure you were okay."

He looks down and I know that I was right in my assumptions. "I'm sorry. I needed some time to think things through. I needed to get my head straight."

"And how did that go?"

"Do you want to watch a movie?"

Ares' avoidance of my questions is getting frustrating but if I push him then he will just shut down. I need to let him lead this dance and hope that it goes in the direction I want. "What do you have?"

"I have a few DVDs but they're mainly old films. I have Netflix on my bedroom television if you don't mind watching something in there."

"Lead the way." I follow him down the hall to his room knowing that this is going to test my will power to its limits.

"I refuse to let you choose the next film."

I laugh at Ares reaction to having to watch Candyman. "I can't believe that you haven't watched it. I thought everyone had seen it."

"I don't do horror movies. I thought that it was going to be a movie about a sweet shop or something."

I laugh harder and Ares glares at me from his side of the bed.

"I'm going to be up all night because of it. You do know that means you're not getting to go home now, you have to stay and keep me company."

I turn onto my side and stare at Ares where he's lying on his back. "I can't think of a single problem with that."

He turns his head and looks at me. We've moved closer as the night's gone on and now there are barely a few inches between us. Even in the dark, with only the light from the television to illuminate the room, I can clearly see his eyes.

I take a risk and reach out my hand, brushing my fingers over Ares cheekbone. His eyes flutter shut and I continue my exploration until my finger runs across his jaw.

He opens his eyes again when I lower my hand and I see what looks like sadness in his eyes. "I don't know how to do this, Kohan. I want to, more than anything, but I'm scared."

"You don't need to be scared of me; I would never hurt you." Nerves start to make my palms sweat because this is so important. I need him to believe what I'm telling him and give me a chance to prove it.

"I know that, I really do, but I'm scared I'll hurt you." He looks as though he's going to cry when he suddenly gets out of the bed and leaves the room. I want to chase him but I give it a second. I will go after him but I want to give him time to deal with whatever happened in here before I expect more from him. After everything he's been through, I know that this whole thing is difficult for him, and I'm asking him to give me something that was stolen from him a long time ago. Trust.

I slowly get out of bed and head towards the light that's on in the kitchen since the rest of the house is still in darkness. I find him leaning over the sink with his head down. He looks so defeated but I don't let it put me off. Being with Ares is going to be a challenge and at times I'm going to have to push him out of his comfort zone. I'm willing to do that for him and I'll also be there to pick up the pieces.

I walk up behind him making sure that I make some sort of noise so he knows I'm here. I can tell he hears me because he raises his head but he doesn't turn around to face me. I stop when there's barely an inch between us and place my hands next to his on the worktop, again making sure that I don't touch him. "Is this okay?"

His body sways and he leans against me, his back pressing against my chest. He doesn't say anything but he's touching me and that's a good indication that he doesn't feel threatened.

I lean my head against the side of his, making sure my lips are close to his ear so he can hear me. "I know you're scared, I understand, but you can't judge me based on his example. It's not fair to me because I can't prove myself if he's always there overshadowing me. I want to be with you and I need you to see that. I thought I was happy to be just friends but after kissing you I won't be able to settle for just that. That night changed everything and I can't go back now."

Ares leans into me more and I know he has to feel the reaction that my body is having to him because it's currently pressing against his arse. All it takes is a simple touch from Ares and I'm aroused. "I can't give you what you deserve, Kohan. There's still so much darkness in my head, I don't want to put you through that."

"I want it all, Ares. I want the good and bad, because only

then do I have *you*. I want to see you laugh and smile when you feel safe, and I want to be able to hold you as the memories of the past threaten to drown you. I'll be the lifeline you need to get through this. I just need you to say yes."

Chapter Twenty One

Ares

"I just need you to say yes."

Kohan is putting this decision squarely on me and as I stand here feeling him against my back, his arms tightly around me, I can't find one argument not to trust him. He's asking permission to touch me, to pursue me, and for the first time in years I shut my head off and let my heart make the decision.

I drop my head back onto Kohan's shoulder and I know that he understands what I'm telling him without having to use words. His arms come around my body and I exhale on a stuttered breath as he presses his lips against my neck. We don't speak as Kohan just holds me and I don't think I've ever felt as safe in my entire life.

All too soon the erection at my back gets my body responding and the security morphs into arousal. I turn in Kohan's arms until I'm facing him and his eyes flicker closed briefly as my own erection rubs against his. When he opens his eyes again they are filled with lust and need and I know they must be reflecting what he can see in mine. I lean forward and kiss him, wanting to initiate the contact so he knows that I'm fully on board with this. We've already done so much but tonight there's no alcohol to hide behind and blame. No, tonight is going to happen because I want it to, because *we* want it to.

Kohan's lips are quick to respond but he lets me keep control of the kiss. I keep it slow and sensual, but when his hands slip from my waist to my arse, the kiss changes. It becomes desperate and needy, like neither of us can get enough of the other. I know that's what it's like for me because now that I've started kissing Kohan I don't want to stop.

His hands move up from my arse and slip under my t-shirt. It takes me a few seconds to come to my senses but when I do I freeze under his touch. I haven't allowed anyone to see or touch my back since it became scarred, and now that Kohan is touching it I know he'll feel the ugliness.

"I've seen them, Angel. The night I got you ready for bed and I don't care about them. They're part of you, the part that shows you're still here with me."

Tears burn in my eyes as he speaks against my lips, still kissing me in between his words. I've never had anyone accept me for who I am, scars and all, and I'm starting to realise what I've missed out on.

His hands continue their gentle massage of the skin and he goes straight back to kissing me, sliding his hands up my back until he has my t-shirt bunched up under my arms. "Can I take this off?"

I don't speak; I just raise my arms so he can pull the material up and over my head. The t-shirt is barely off when Kohan's lips are back on mine, making my brain cells melt with pleasure. I know I haven't kissed many men in my life but I doubt any would be as good as he is at it. His lips are soft but demanding and he manages to pull me into the moment, making my head stay quiet as I focus on only him. I reach out and find the bottom of his shirt, pulling it from his jeans so I can touch his skin. I have a sudden urge to feel him and to run my fingers along the toned muscles that I've been imagining since I met him.

Kohan groans into my mouth as I dig my fingers into his stomach. The slight touch on his body doesn't feel enough. I pull it up his chest and Kohan backs away while stilling my hands. I look at him, panicking that's he's about to leave but then I realise what he's doing. He unbuttons his shirt quickly and slips it off his shoulders, dropping it onto the floor next to mine. He grabs me by the back of the neck and pulls me into him until our chests connect. I'm grateful that he's holding me up as I feel him against me. His skin is hot and it feels like he's searing my body with his, and I don't want it to stop. God, he feels like fucking heaven and I can't hold myself back any longer so I reach out and start exploring his body with my fingers. Kohan takes it a step further as he lets his lips drift away from mine, kissing down my jaw and towards my neck.

I lean back against the worktop behind me, and when his tongue licks a spot behind my ear, I grip the edge of it hard to keep myself upright. Kohan's tongue leaves a wet trail as it brushes down over my shoulder and across my chest. My whole body is tingling like an electrical current is flowing over me. When he sucks my nipple into his mouth I cry out, finally looking down and following his movements. He watches me closely as he nibbles the skin on my chest and bites his way to my other nipple. He's looking for any signs that I'm not comfortable but he's not going to get one. I've never been so turned on in my life and nothing short of human disaster will make me stop him.

Kohan stands and cups my jaw. "I want to do something that I've been thinking about since I met you. I promise that I'll stop if you tell me to, but I want you to just enjoy it. Shut off that mind of yours and just feel. Is that okay?"

I nod mutely unable to form words. I don't know what he has in mind but I have a feeling I won't forget it. The breath races from my lungs when Kohan kneels on the floor in front of me. I suddenly know very clearly what he's about to do and nerves are threating to make me run. I grip the worktop harder to try and calm myself. I want to stop Kohan but it's not because I don't trust him. No, it's purely because I've never experienced this before. When it comes to sucking cock I'm an expert, Micah made sure I was, but I've never received a blowjob from anyone. I met Micah before I was able to explore my sexuality fully with anyone, and Micah was not the kind of man who would lower himself to do something like that. He would always tell me that he didn't bottom and there was certainly no way he would ever get on his knees for anyone. Now I'm looking down at a seriously sexy Kohan as he nuzzles his nose into my still clothed cock and I'm not sure I will last long enough for him to take me out of my jeans.

I close my eyes and drop my head back as he starts lowering my zipper. The click of the teeth vibrates in my balls. I try to think of anything that isn't what's happening right now but when Kohan pulls my jeans and boxers down I can't think of anything else. He nuzzles against my balls as my bottoms hit my ankles, and when his tongue flicks out and tastes them I flinch.

"Are you okay, Ares?"

I look down at Kohan and I know instantly that I've made a huge mistake. I groan audibly when I see him kneeling there in front of me with a trail of pre-cum glistening on his cheek. I've heard people talking about the person that is giving the blowjob having all the power and I thought they were insane. I never felt like I had the power with Micah. But, looking down at Kohan now, I know that he is completely in charge. He has the power to bring me to my knees and I fucking love it.

I nod at him again, wondering if he's finding it amusing that I've suddenly become mute. It's not humour I see in his eyes though, it's hunger and heat. He looks like he wants to eat me alive and I almost scream when he does just that. His tongue licks up the underside of my dick and it's the only warning I have before he takes me into his mouth. He almost swallows the whole length of me in one movement.

The whole thing is almost too much and I have to remind myself to breathe as white dots appear in my vision. I want to look away but I can't, I need to watch what he's doing to me. His eyes are closed and he looks like this is the best meal he's ever had. He alternates his movements, sometimes nibbling around my head before taking me deep into his throat. When he deep throats me, he swallows and the constriction around the head of my cock has my orgasm building quicker than I would like.

"Kohan, fuck. I'm so close. So fucking close." I feel proud of myself for actually managing to form some words to warn him. I expect him to pull back and finish me with his hand but he doesn't. Instead he takes my hands from their death grip on the worktop and puts them on the sides of his head. The move has me standing more and I grab onto his hair for support. Kohan stills his head and I'm confused to what he's doing. He must notice because he places his hands on my arse and makes me thrust into his mouth. With the first shallow penetration he moans and the vibrations add to the pressure that's already building at the base of my spine. He drops his hands and lets me take over. I start gently, only going deep enough to feel good, but it's not enough for either of us. Kohan completely relaxes and lets me thrust a little deeper, a little harder, and it's not long until I'm fucking his mouth with force.

I don't mean to treat him like that but with my orgasm about to explode from my body I've lost all sense and my body has taken over completely. The only thing I can feel is the tight heat from Kohan's mouth and with the sound of his moans in my ears, I let go. Bright white light explodes in my eyes and I'm sure I can hear someone calling out but with my ears buzzing I can't be sure. My whole being is floating somewhere and it's fucking amazing.

Hard suction on my sensitive dick brings me back to earth quickly and that's when I realise that I have my dick still pushed deep in Kohan's mouth. I pull out quickly, mortified at what I've just done. I know what it feels like to be treated so badly and I wouldn't want anyone else to feel that. "I'm so sorry."

Kohan stands but instead of looking pissed off he's smiling. He looks like he's just experienced the best thing in his life and I don't understand. "Sorry about what? That was amazing, Ares." He leans in and kisses me deeply. He tastes salty and I can't help but groan into his mouth when I think why. *Fucking hell, that is so good.* Micah would never kiss me after he came in my mouth and all I can think is he missed out on something special.

I pull back from Kohan and stare into his eyes. I keep waiting for common sense to catch up with me and the panic to start but there's nothing. Instead of running all I want to do is go to bed and hold Kohan for the rest of the night.

"You're scaring me a little here. Do I need to leave?"

I laugh before leaning in to kiss him quickly. "I'm actually thinking about how I don't want you to leave. I want you to spend the night and it's scaring me a little."

Kohan grabs me by the hand and pulls me before remembering that my jeans are around my ankles. I nearly land on my face but he catches me just in time. "Oops, maybe it would be safer if I did leave?"

I pull him tightly against me. "Don't even think about it."

Micah twirls me across the dance floor and I laugh as I get dizzy. This was a surprise night out for my birthday and it's been perfect. He didn't tell me where we were going, just to get dressed up and be ready to leave at seven.

The night started with dinner at my favourite restaurant and then he brought me here, to a jazz club that has a live band and dance floor. I feel like we've been dancing for hours and I never want to stop.

The song changes and Micah pulls me towards our table and as he looks back at me I pout a little. He smiles and it lights up his entire face. This is why I fell in love with him. He's the sweetest man I know, and even though he has temper issues sometimes, I know that he loves me and wants me happy. Before we reach the table I lean into Micah to make sure he can hear me.

"I'm going to the bathroom, I'll just be a minute." I kiss his cheek before heading towards the toilet. All the water I've drank tonight has my bladder ready to explode. I would have loved to have had a drink of wine with my dinner but Micah doesn't like it when I drink. He says that I shouldn't need alcohol to have a good time, and he's right. So I stuck with the water he ordered me when he ordered his own wine.

I push the bathroom door and it stops dead when it bashes into someone that's trying to leave. "I'm so sorry." The guy just smiles as he steps back and lets me past. "Thank you."

He doesn't say anything as he leaves and I hurry up and finish so I can get back to Micah.

I'm still bouncing as we enter the apartment and I twirl as I cross the open plan living room. "Tonight was so amazing. I haven't danced like that in so long."

"Go get a shower." He sounds angry but I dismiss the thought. He enjoyed tonight as much as I did and I know that I didn't do anything that would upset him. He's probably just tired after such a long night so I head to the bathroom to clean up.

I close the door to stop any steam escaping and step in front of the large mirror in front of me. My cheeks are red but there is real happiness in my eyes and Micah put it there. He spoilt me tonight and I want to thank him properly so I strip quickly and get into the shower. I turn on the water and step back quickly to avoid the cold blast. When the waters hot I get under the stream and turn my face up into it. While I wash myself I wonder what Micah will want tonight and I feel myself getting hard. I always feel like I'm the luckiest guy in the world when I look at him. He's sexy and sophisticated and he wants me. No one else, just me.

I quickly turn off the shower and when I slide the glass door to the side a fist connects with my face and sends me staggering backwards into the tiles. I slide down them until I'm sitting on the floor of the shower. I look up dazed to find Micah standing there, a look of rage on his face.

"Get up."

I struggle against the dizziness I feel until I'm standing in front of him. I don't know what I've done so it's better not to annoy him as much as possible.

"Do you think I didn't see you tonight?"

I hate when he questions me about things I don't understand. There is no right answer and when I get it wrong it makes him angrier. "When? What did I do?" This earns me another slap and I feel the skin above my eye split. It doesn't feel large so I'm hopeful that it won't scar. It's amazing how you can start to identify how bad an injury you've received is when you have had enough of them. At the start I just knew that everything hurt; now I know there are many different ways a body can hurt.

"You went to the bathroom with that man. Was it fun? Did it make you feel important to fuck someone while you're husband was outside waiting for you to come back?"

I try to think what guy He's going on about but the only person I can think of is the man I hit with the door. It couldn't be him though because I barely spoke to him. I must be quiet for too long because I'm pushed further back into the shower and my back collides with the tiles again. This time I stay on my feet but apparently that's not what he wants.

"I can't believe I treated you like a king tonight and still you acted like a fucking slut. Did he come in you? Is that why you raced to the shower?"

"You told me to shower!" It's out before I can stop it and Micah's face instantly darkens with his rage. I try to back away but I'm already as far into the corner as I can get. He grabs me by the throat and leans in close to my face, his eyes full of disgust and fury. I struggle to pull his hands off me but I can't budge him.

"That was really fucking stupid."

I don't have time to defend myself before Micah's fist connects with my stomach, knocking all the air out of my body. I struggle to breathe as he drops me on the floor. I can't move as the non-slip floor tile covering grazes the left side of my body. None of that pain registers as Micah kicks me in the side again.

Oh God. It feels like I'm suffocating as fire spreads through my chest and I try to get my lungs to inflate. Even as his foot *connects with my body again and again, my only focus is on my need to breathe. I need oxygen before he finally kills me.*

The kicking finally stops and I close my eyes, not wanting to see what Micah is currently doing. If I lie here quietly he might think I've had enough and leave me alone. I will my heart beat to slow down and when I finally manage to inhale some air to into my lungs I nearly cry in relief. If I can breathe then I can survive. Tonight is just Micah making a mistake, he must have thought he saw something and I will work hard to convince him that I didn't do anything with that stranger.

I'm so in my head that I flinch when something warm and wet hits the top half of my body and face. I keep my eyes closed as a few more drops hit me, and when I breathe in through my nose, the smell tells me exactly what it is.

"There, that should keep you warm for the rest of the night. I think it's better if you just sleep in here tonight, I don't want your cheap arse in bed with me."

The overhead light goes off and I'm left in the dark with Micah's drying cum on me. I should feel ashamed but I just don't have the energy to care.

Chapter Twenty Two

Kohan

A noise pulls me from sleep and it takes me a few moments to remember where I am. I lie still for a few moments but I can't hear anything so I decide it must have been something outside. I'm about to go back to sleep when the noise sounds again. I roll over to see Ares thrashing about under the sheets. He's clearly having a nightmare and I wonder what I should do. When he emits a painful cry, I decide to wake him up, and so I reach out and gently shake his shoulder.

He sits up instantly and looks around the room frantically. When he looks in my direction he scurries away from me, falling off the bed in his haste to escape. "No, I'm sorry. I didn't do anything, please don't hurt me."

My heart is in my throat and it takes everything in me not to start crying at the fear in Ares' eyes. There's a light in his back garden that shines in his window and lets me see him clearly as he moves backwards into the corner and hides his head in his hands. I take a couple of deep breaths and look up, blinking a few times to try and clear the tears in my eyes.

When I have myself under control I slip slowly from the bed, making sure my movements won't scare Ares. I don't exactly know what he was dreaming about but I have a good idea. "Ares? Hey, it's me, Kohan." I slowly sit in front of him, crossing my legs and making sure I don't touch him.

There's no response from Ares so I try again, talking to him gently to see if I can get him to come back to me.

"Are you okay, Angel? Do you need anything? I want to help you but you need to talk to me, tell me what you need."

He finally raises his head slowly but I don't think he's fully back from wherever he went yet. It takes another few minutes before he blinks and actually sees me. It happens suddenly and it shocks me when he actually speaks. "I'm sorry, Kohan."

"Can I touch you? Is that okay because I need to hold you."

He doesn't say no so I don't waste any time in pulling him into my lap and wrapping my arms around him. He's shaking and his sobs start quietly but they're soon painful and loud. My heart aches for him. I've never wanted to hurt someone as much as I want to hurt Micah. I want to hunt the fucker down and feed him his own balls. I don't think I'll ever know everything he put Ares through and I don't think I want to know.

Ares finally settles and I move us to the bed where I pull him into my arms and hold him again. I will sit here all night if I have to, anything to make him feel safe and protected.

"This is what I get for trying to be normal. I can't be and I shouldn't pretend I can." His voice sounds hoarse from his crying.

"It was a nightmare, nothing more. We all have them." I get no response so I keep talking, hoping that he will listen to what I'm trying to say. "I told you that I would hold you together and that's what I'll do. I want to be with you and it will take more than a few bad dreams to run me off. I don't scare easily and you'll come to realise this."

"Kohan, I can't hear anything you're saying. I can feel your chest moving so I know you're speaking, but I don't have my hearing aids in."

I cringe when I realise what an arse I've made of myself. Of course he can't hear me, he doesn't sleep with his hearing aids in. *I know this.* That means when I asked to hold him he hadn't actually answered me because he hadn't heard me. I'm lucky he didn't freak out when I grabbed him. I really need to remember these things in the future. "I'm so sorry, Ares."

"Still can't hear you."

I laugh nervously this time because I'm totally messing this thing up. How can I get it so wrong?

Ares must sense my tension because he turns in my arms, switches on the bedside lamp and he looks at me. "Do you want me to put them in?"

I shake my head but I still feel like an idiot. How do I think I can help him move through his past if I can't even get this bit right? I don't realise I've looked away until Ares cups my face and tilts it up towards him. He looks deep into my eyes before he speaks. "I can read your lips if you keep it simple and slow."

"I'm sorry." Nothing could be simpler than that. He must understand me because he shakes his head.

"This is my fault not yours. You didn't know I would go off the deep end like a fucking freak."

He makes me forget the anger I feel towards myself when he talks about himself like that. I make sure he can see my lips clearly as I talk clearly and slowly. "My boyfriend isn't a freak." Ares eyes widen and that's when I realise what I've said. *Shit, I didn't even think about it.*

"Your boyfriend?"

"Well I know that … you know… it's just the start …" My words are cut off by Ares' lips and I'm glad that he saved me from making a bigger fool of myself.

Less than half an hour ago Ares was in the grips of a painful nightmare and now he's kissing me like his life depends on it. I should stop him and make sure that he's feeling better but as his tongue slips between my lips I lose all thought.

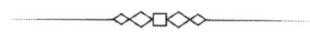

I groan and try to hide from the bright light that's threatening to pull me from my sleep. I pull the pillow further over my head and try to get comfortable again, and it's working until lips start kissing down my spine. As soon as they touch me I know that there's no way in hell I'll be able to get back to sleep. I relax into the mattress, or as relaxed as my painfully hard dick will allow, and just enjoy the journey they're taking.

Just as I think it's getting to the good bit my pillow is pulled off my head and Ares leans over me, kissing me on the cheek. "Good morning. I made you coffee but maybe you should brush your teeth first. Morning breath isn't my favourite thing."

I don't think before I turn quickly, grabbing Ares and rolling us so I'm on top. I go to grab his arms to pin him to the bed when there's a flicker of panic in his eyes, so I change tactic. Instead, I lower my head and nibble his neck. He seemed to like it when I did it last night, and going by the reaction that's happening under me, he likes it this morning. "Feels like you don't mind my morning breath after all." I grind down on him to prove my point which makes him moan.

"Okay, so maybe some things trump morning breath." He tilts his head back to give me better access to his neck and I make very good use of it. I lick and nibble the sensitive skin while I thrust against his erection, making sure my own bumps against his in long strokes. Ares moans again and I use that as my cue to have a little fun.

"What the fuck?"

That's all I hear from Ares as I get up off him and head towards the bathroom to brush my teeth. I'm risking a serious case of blue balls, especially after not coming last night, but I decide that it's completely worth it. "You told me to brush my teeth. I'm doing as I'm told."

I enter the bathroom and walk to the sink where I run the water and splash some cold water on my face in an attempt to calm myself a little. Blowing Ares last night had turned me on to the point where my dick had been in pain but I was willing to live with the discomfort. I want last night to be all about him to show him that he was worth the time to pleasure. I don't know what his sex life was like with Micah but I would put money on him not getting much from it. Last night was about showing him how things were going to be. Then after his nightmare we'd spent what felt like hours kissing and holding each other. It had been innocent and gentle, but like any other time that I touch Ares, my dick had spent the whole time rock hard. Now for the third time, I'm sporting a boner without a way to give myself relief and I'm very close to locking the door behind me so I can jack off in the shower.

Instead, I grab the unopened toothbrush that Ares must have left lying next to the sink and open it so I can brush my teeth. I add toothpaste and scrub at my teeth until my mouth is filled with foam. I bend over to spit out and rinse, and when I stand up again my eyes connect with Ares who is now standing behind me.

He looks so fucking sexy his boxers hanging loosely on his hips. I take a minute to let my eyes wander over his body, wishing he was completely naked, before I look back to his eyes. They're filled with lust and it makes my already hard dick twitch inside my own underwear.

Ares doesn't speak as he takes two steps forward, his eyes never leaving mine. When he's directly behind me he kisses my shoulder and runs a finger down my spine. My entire body erupts into goose bumps as I shiver at the sensation. His finger doesn't stop as he reaches the waistband of my boxers and when he starts to drag them down he uses both hands to push the material down my legs.

My breath comes out shaky as I stand naked in front of Ares for the first time. I can feel his stare as he looks over my body. I've never seen Ares this in control and it's doing strange things to my insides. Excitement and longing races through me and it takes everything in me not to collapse on the floor in a melted blob of lust. I'm not exclusively a top but with the men I meet I usually always end up in that position. There's just something about Ares being in control and having power over me that turns me on more than usual.

"You are so fucking beautiful. There isn't a part of you that isn't perfect." His hand brushes over my arse and I have to fight the urge to bend over for him. The urge almost becomes too much when he slides a finger in between my cheeks. He parts them slightly and his eyes drop down to where I know he must be able to see everything, making my hole clench in anticipation.

"Oh god, Ares." I drop my head to my chest because I can't watch him anymore. Spending the last twelve hours hard without any release has me approaching an orgasm without anything touching my dick. The only problem with closing my eyes is that I can feel everything a hundred times more: the brush of his finger, the heat from his palms as he runs them around my waist before cupping my balls.

This has my eyes flashing open, meeting his again over my shoulder. Ares presses himself into my back and that's when I notice that he's completely naked now. I don't know when he did it, but when his erection settles in between my arse cheeks I forget to think about that. He breaks contact for a second and I watch as he drips saliva onto his cock to ease some of the friction as he continues to pleasure himself between my arse cheeks.

"You make me want something I've never had before."

I don't know if I'm meant to answer him but his statement has me interested. "What do you want, Ares?"

He looks away from where his cock is pressing against me and meets my eyes. "I want to fuck you. I've never topped before but you make me want to."

I want to give him a really intelligent answer and tell him that when he feels comfortable with that I would be willing to work through it with him. But, the only thing that's going through my head is *fuck yes*. "Yes. Anything you want, Ares. Anything." I'm proud of myself for managing to get any words out when all my blood is firmly in my aching cock.

He leans into me making me bend over slightly and my world focuses in on just him. There's only this moment and what's happening; the rest of the world could implode and I wouldn't notice. The hand that was gently massaging my balls moves and I expect to be bent fully over the sink so he can take me but instead he leans his chin on my shoulder and grips my dick. "Maybe next time. I want to see you come this way. I want to be able to remember what you look like."

His hand starts stroking me in time as his dick fucks my arse cheeks and the dual sensation is too much. My orgasm builds quickly and it doesn't take me long before I'm alternating between fucking his hand and thrusting back against him. I feel a pool of stickiness at the base of my back and it's all the evidence I need to know that Ares is enjoying this just as much as I am.

Our eyes never waver from each other but our breathing changes, becoming erratic and noisy. When he flicks his finger over the head of my dick I groan long and low, and Ares' movements behind me become muddled and out of sync for the first time. I'm glad I'm not the only one struggling to hold on for a decent amount of time. I think I'm doing well with controlling my orgasm right up until Ares presses the tip of his cock directly onto my hole. He doesn't enter me but the pressure alone is enough to tip me over the edge. I come with a force I didn't know I had and cover the sink in front of me. I grip the sink so I don't fall over and when Ares uses his free hand to jerk himself off until I feel him coming on my back, I'm glad I have a tight hold. The look of sheer ecstasy on his face is even better than the intense orgasm I just experienced and to know that I did that to him makes me almost giddy.

It takes us both a few minutes to recover and my thighs are starting to cramp when I finally have to stand upright. I don't want to do it because after he came, Ares leaned his head onto my back and I liked the intimacy. I don't say anything as I clean my mess off the sink but Ares' laugh pulls my attention. I turn the tap off and turn to face him. Seeing Ares happy after being with me will never get old. I know it's only happened a few times but each time makes me feel more comfortable. I trust him to know what he wants and to tell me when I go too far, but I also fully expect him to put distance between us after every encounter. Not that I blame him. "What's so funny?"

A little blush colours Ares' cheeks and God I just want to reach out and touch him. I wonder if his cheeks are as warm as they look but I don't know if we're there yet. "I just think it's funny that you're worried about cleaning the sink when your back is covered in …"

It's adorable that he can't bring himself to say it and the last bit of tension that was in my shoulders vanishes because he's finding humour in the situation. Maybe he isn't going to run this time. "If you think I'm cleaning that off myself then you're mistaken. You made the mess, you clean it."

His blush deepens but he leans over the bath and turns on the shower. "After you."

I like this Ares. I feel like I'm getting a glimpse of who the real Ares is, the one that I'm seriously crushing on. This Ares is fun and cheeky with a sexy, dominant side that turns me on more than anyone has before. There have been times he's looked at me with so much passion in his eyes that I've wanted to drop to my knees. I don't think he even knows he possesses that power.

I step into the shower and shudder when the freezing water hits my skin. I look down I see he has the water turned fully cold. I turn and glare at him. "I don't need a cold shower."

He leans around me and adjusts the temperature before stepping in behind me. "Sorry, but the last shower I had needed to be cold." That thought catches my dick's attention but I try to ignore it. I want this moment to be about just being together and not to do with sex.

I step under the now warm water and turn my face up into the spray. I can feel Ares' presence behind me but he isn't touching. I flinch when something cold connects with my back but relax as it warms quickly. I drop my head as Ares' uses the sponge to massage my back and shoulders. His touch is always welcome but the deeper massage after such an intense orgasm is making my muscles turn to jelly. I turn as pressure on my hips urge me to face him. I clear the water from my eyes and watch as he gently washes the front of my body. He's taking a lot of care and his actions steal a little bit more of my heart. I think it would be really easy to fall in love with Ares and the more time I spend with him gets me closer to it.

"Do you have any imperfections? Seriously, there is nothing, not even a blemish."

I reach down and brush his now wet hair away from his face. I see him look away as the scar on his head comes into view but I don't let him hide from me, not now. I lean down and kiss the faint line that dissects his eyebrow and I feel him relax. "There's a lot that isn't perfect about me, you just don't see them. It's funny how that works, how others don't see our imperfections the way we do." I hope that he hears what I'm trying to tell him. I don't see his scars the way he does and I need him to know this.

Ares looks up at me, his eyes full of tears. "Is that true?"

I kiss him with everything that I feel for him but can't explain. I keep it soft but I show him how much he means to me. I pull back but don't go far as I lean my forehead against his. "I only see you, Ares. Only you."

His arms wrap around me and I follow his lead, engulfing him in my warmth as we stand there under the warm water. This moment makes the struggle between us worth it. Moments like this are what I'll fight for.

Chapter Twenty Three

Kohan

I rub my head and try to keep my temper in check. I remind myself over and over again that it's wrong to lose it with my mum, she's ill and doesn't know what she's doing all the time, but it's becoming increasingly difficult. We decided after her scans at the hospital that we would get a nurse to come in during the day when no one could be here. We thought that it would be the safest option but now I'm rethinking it.

Her visit to the hospital was a few weeks ago and even though it was good to get a proper diagnosis, it wasn't the news we were hoping for. The CT scan had shown that an area of mum's brain had been affected by blood loss. They think she'd suffered several minor strokes and this had affected the blood flow to certain areas of her brain. That news alone had nearly knocked us on our arses but then the neurologist had followed that up with the news that the dementia isn't the only problem that she found. No, she thinks that mum is also suffering from the onset of Alzheimer's and that it's only going to get worse. The confusion and mood changes may be due to her dementia, but the forgetting names of the people around her point to Alzheimer's.

Dealing with one thing would have been bad enough but with everything else we need to come up with a better plan of attack. My mother's father suffered with Alzheimer's and we saw the devastation it caused to the family as he faded away. Mum made us all promise that if she developed it we would put her into a care home where nurses could look after her. Of course we all agreed because there was nothing wrong with her at the time. Now that the situation is very real it's more difficult to carry out her wishes.

"I'm telling you, she's trying to kill me."

I roll my eyes and place the tablets back in front of my mum. "She isn't. The doctor said that these would help you with the forgetfulness. Remember the nice lady at the hospital? You said you trusted her."

One of the symptoms of Mum's dementia is paranoia. We should have known that something was wrong when she told us that her neighbour was taking pictures of her. It started maybe two years ago and the doctor thinks it was probably around the time she had her first stroke. We thought she was just lonely and that living without dad was making her a little eccentric.

"Yes, I liked her. She had nice hair."

I resist the urge to roll my eyes again and put the pills into her hand. "That's good, now take your tablets." She doesn't argue this time and I sigh in relief. I think my brothers and I need to have another talk about this. Even with the medication I can see a decline in Mum's behaviour. I'm only here today because her community nurse called in a panic because Mum locked herself inside the bathroom and refused to come out. She was still in there when I arrived after the long drive and the nurse was beside herself. She hadn't been able to get a hold of any of my other brothers so it was me or the police. I'm glad she called but it's not really a practical arrangement since I live so far away. One of my brothers should have been on hand since they live within a few minutes of her.

I watch my mum over the table and I feel the sadness threaten to devour me. She was always such an outgoing woman and full of life. She helped out with all the local charities and filled her days with friends and family. Now she struggles to remember what day it is and it's only going to get worse. She wouldn't want our lives to be effected by her decline in health but it's so difficult to make the decision to look for a home.

Checking my watch I see that I really need to get home. I have a deadline that I can't miss and an article that's only half written. Even if I leave right this second I'm going to be writing through the night to get my article finished in time for printing tomorrow. I grab my mobile and try Damien's number. He answers on the second attempt and it pisses me off.

"Yo bro, how's it hanging?"

His cheerfulness just adds to my already rising anger. *If he can answer the call for me where was he when the nurse called?* "I'm at Mum's and I need you to come over."

"No can do. I have a night out with Heidi that I can't miss. Wait, why are you at Mum's?"

I pinch the bridge of my nose so I don't give in to the urge to rip him a new one. Damien is our number one opponent when it comes to Mum's care. Every time we try to make a plan he blocks it and he's also the last one that is willing to help out. "I'm at Mum's because she had an episode. Now I need to get back to work so you need to come over."

"I told you I can't."

That's the final nail in his coffin and I get up from the chair and move to the back bedroom so Mum can't hear me. I don't know how much she understands at the minute but I refuse to argue about her in front of her. As soon as the door closes behind me I let him have it. "I don't give a flying fuck if you have a night out planned. I had to drive over an hour to get here because no one would answer his or her phone and the nurse was panicking. You will get over here and look after your fucking Mum since you're the one who's constantly fighting against us putting her into a home. You can't have it both ways, Damien. You can't be the son who refuses to get care for their mum and then not be willing to give the care yourself. I am leaving now and I suggest you get over here so she isn't alone for too long."

I don't give him a chance to reply before I hang up on him. He'd just come up with some bullshit excuse and I'm over it. It's about time Damien stepped up and did something.

The nurse text me to tell me that Damien had turned up about fifteen minutes after I left. He's going to be pissed off at me but I'm past caring. I am sick of everything falling on Carey because I'm not there and I refuse to drive up every day because the others can't deal. As much as I hate the thought of putting my mum into a care home it might be the only option. Her disease is progressing faster than we first thought it might, even the neurologist isn't happy with the sudden decline. They want mum to go back for more tests but this time it will require a few nights stay. We are just waiting on a date for her to go in but the thought scares me. If her doctor is worried then we definitely should be.

I sit back in my desk chair and stretch my arms over my head to try and ease the tightness in my shoulders. It's dark outside the window so I must have been hunched over for a few hours now. I got back just before six and came straight to the office so I could get my work done. I need this article to be written and edited before eight o'clock tomorrow morning. It is going to be a horribly long night. I close my eyes and lean my head back on the seat, promising myself that I will just close my eyes for a few seconds.

Gentle kisses on my cheeks wake me and I sit up quickly, wondering what the hell is going on. When I open my eyes I see a smiling Ares standing in front of me. I blink a few times as I try to work out how the hell he got into my office without me knowing. That's when I see the clock and see that it's after midnight. "Shit, I fell asleep."

"I saw that when I went past an hour ago but I thought I would let you nap while I finished up cleaning." He hands me a takeaway cup that I didn't notice before and the smell of coffee hits my nose. "So I got you this and thought I would help you get finished. Tell me what you need."

A smile plays at the corner of my mouth. "I need you to sit in that chair and make sure I don't fall asleep again."

He rolls his eyes but moves to the chair I pointed to. Instead of taking a seat he picks up the chair and brings it to place next to me. He sits down and smiles innocently at me. "So what now?"

"Now I need to finish this article before the morning."

"Well come on then. Maybe if you didn't procrastinate it would be done by now."

I feel my stomach drop when I think about why the story isn't finished and the conversation I'm going to have with my brothers. It's not a chat I want but it needs to happen, sooner rather than later.

"What did I say?"

"What are you talking about?"

"Something I said was wrong and it made you sad. I want to know what it was."

I thought I had hidden my emotions better than that, but apparently I hadn't. Either that or Ares is getting better are reading my mood. "It's just …" I pause and Ares reaches out to hold my hand. It gives me comfort knowing that he's here for me, sharing my problems and helping me to cope. "My mum isn't doing so well and I think we might have to think about her living arrangements. I was with her today because she was having a bad day."

"I'm so sorry, Kohan. I didn't realise it was so bad and here I am trying to tease you." He looks so contrite but I don't want that. If he had known what I was going through he would never have said what he did. It's my fault for keeping him on the outside.

I turn my hand and hold his hand properly, entwining my finger with his. "I should have told you. I need someone that I can talk to about this and I want it to be you."

Ares pulls his seat closer until our knees are touching. "So talk to me. Let me help with your problems for once."

"My mum has been diagnosed with dementia and the onset of Alzheimer's. We have hired a nurse to keep an eye on her when we can't but she's getting worse. Its progressing a lot quicker than we thought it would, even the hospital is surprised. We have to take her in for more tests but they think she is having mini strokes without anyone knowing. We thought she was just being eccentric but we were wrong. It's all tied in. Now I don't think we can keep her at home and it's killing me."

Ares pulls me into a hug and I sit there and just absorb the comfort. I missed this part of being in a relationship. No matter how much I love Sophie, it's just not the same. "I'm so sorry you're going through this, sweetheart. I wish I could do something to take away some of the hurt."

The use of the name Sweetheart makes everything a little bit better. As horrible as this thing with Mum is, having Ares on the same page as me about how he feels is perfect. I feel like I'm not the only one that's trying and that makes everything worth it. "Just having you here is helping. I just need to talk to my brothers about what to do but we need to get the results from the hospital first. What do I do if we need to put her in a care home?" My voice breaks and Ares pulls back until he can look me squarely in the eye.

"You do what needs to be done with courage, and then when you get home you let me hold you while you break. You're not the only one who can be strong. Let me help you as much as you help me."

I've always wondered when people know that they have fallen in love. Is it a gradual thing or is it one specific moment in time? For me it's now. It's looking into Ares' eyes as he gives me more than he realises. "Thank you."

He gives me that smile that makes me putty in his hands, and leans forward to kiss me. "Thank you for letting me in. Thank you for treating me like an equal. Thank you for treating me like a man."

"You're all man, Angel, so there's no other way to treat you. And you are my equal … actually that's a lie. You're better than me in every way and that's how I will always think."

"If you are hoping to get laid soon then you're going the right way about it."

Laughter fills the room and it eases the emotions that were brewing just below the surface of our conversation. "That's good to know."

Ares kisses me quickly on the lips before letting go of my hands and turning back to my desk. "Right, let's get this shit done."

With that we spend the next few hours writing and editing, and it's one of the best nights I've spent in my office.

I climb into my bed just as my mobile starts to ring. I'm tempted to leave it but I know I can't just in case there's something wrong with Mum. I can't exactly complain about my brothers not answering their mobiles if I ignore mine.

Thankfully it's on my bedside unit so I don't have to do anything more than turn my head and reach out to grab it. "Hello." My voice is muffled by the pillow I'm lying on but I don't have the energy to put more effort into moving.

"Well don't you sound like a barrel of laughs?"

"I'm not in the mood, Carey. I was up all night working because of my little visit with Mum yesterday."

He's silent for a few minutes before he speaks. "I heard about that. I'm sorry I missed the call but I was at work and couldn't have my phone on."

I'm not pissed at Carey because he's always with mum. Well other than when he can get someone else to look after her for a few hours so he can see Duncan. It's the only time he gets to have anything that resembles a normal life and I don't begrudge him that. "It's fine, just made it a long night at work."

"This maybe isn't the best time to be talking about a night out then?"

Again, if it was anyone else that was asking I would have hung up by now, but not Carey. He doesn't get out much these days so I know I'm going to agree with this no matter what. "Just text me the details and I will make sure I'm there."

"Aren't you trusting? I also want you to bring your boyfriend, almost like a double date." I can hear the excitement in his voice and it makes me smile. We've never been on a double date and there's one problem with his plan.

"Well send me the info and I will check with Ares. I don't know if he will be up to a night out but I'll ask." I have told Carey a little about what Ares went through with his ex so I know he understands what I'm saying.

"No worries. Let me know ASAP so I can tell Duncan."

"Later." I hang up just as a message comes through with all the information. Carey must have had the whole thing typed up before he called. *Sneaky fucker.*

I groan and sit up in bed, wondering if Ares is still awake. I type out a message to him and send it. If he isn't awake now I will have a reply by the time I get up.

Carey wants a night out and you're invited. It will be in Greenview and with his new man. Let me know if you think you would feel comfortable doing it and I will let him know. Xx

It's the first time that I've put kisses at the end of my message but it seems right now. I want him to know that I'm taking this relationship thing seriously. I jump a little when the message tone goes off. I didn't expect Ares to still be awake but his name appears on my screen.

I'm up for it. I might need you to hold my hand all night … and there might be some freak-outs but as long as you're prepared for them I'm in. xx

Ares is always quick to point out his flaws and he hasn't worked out yet that he isn't managing to scare me away. I'm fully prepared for anything he throws at me.

"I'm a good boy scout. I'm prepared for anything. Xx

I close my mobile and put it on my beside table. I'll give him all the details when I see him later because I'm just too tired now to deal with it.

Chapter Twenty Four

Ares

I add the bubble bath to the running water and inhale the aroma of bubble-gum. After spending the night helping Kohan finish up his article, I slept until the middle of the afternoon. The rest of the day is mine and I plan to do nothing but relax.

While the water is running I walk back to the kitchen and grab the bottle of wine that I bought at the store the other day. One thing that my night out with Kohan told me was I enjoy having a drink so the next time I went to the store I grabbed a bottle so I could have the odd glass at night. Today feels like the perfect day to finally open that bottle. I will class it as a reward for saying yes to the night out with Kohan and his brother. My heart had been racing as I typed out my response but now I'm glad I agreed. As scary as it feels going out for the night to somewhere unknown and with people I have never met, I'll have Kohan there to make sure I don't have a meltdown.

I grab the bottle and a glass, and make my way back to the bathroom. I pour myself a glass and place it on the edge of the bath before turning on my iPod. There are very few things I do to treat myself but a relaxing bath is one of them. Usually there isn't wine but bubbles and music are something I love. I grab a little box of matches and light the candles I have sitting around the sink. I can feel myself getting hard as the memories of what filled that sink not too long ago invade my head. I haven't been able to use it without remembering Kohan leaning over it. That sight is going to live with me the rest of my life.

Lights start to flash and I groan at the interruption. I turn of the running water and head out into the hall. I'm not expecting anyone today so I slowly make my way to the front door. I use the small window at the side of the door to look out to see who's ringing the bell and my smile is instant when I see Kohan standing there with another tub of jellybeans. I swear this man is going to make my teeth fall out. I open the door and grab him by the front of his t-shirt and pull him inside, kissing him before the door is even closed. Feeling so relaxed with someone is a new experience and I'm finding I'm really enjoying it. I thought Micah had ruined me for everyone else but I'm beginning to realise I'm wrong. There might be hope for Kohan and me yet.

"I am going to bill you for all the dental work I'm going to need if you keep bringing me jellybeans."

Kohan puts the tub on the table inside the front door and grabs my hips to pull me tighter against him. "If this is my reward for bringing you them I'll start saving now."

I laugh against his lips, not wanting to put any space between us. Kissing Kohan has become one of my favourite pastimes and I don't want to miss a single second of doing it. I make a note to call Adam for an appointment because I'm sure he'll love to hear all the details of me finally grabbing life by the balls. "Not that I'm complaining, but why are you here?"

"I missed you. Do I need a better excuse?"

I shake my head, happy that there isn't a real reason he's here. It makes me feel that this thing between us is real, it makes me feel like I'm important.

"Are you busy?"

"I was just about to relax… want to join me?" Suddenly having a bath with Kohan seems like the best idea in the world.

"Lead the way, Angel."

I take Kohan's hand and lead him down the hall towards the bathroom. When we walk through the door his eyes widen before a sexy grin lights up his face.

"I think I arrived at the right time. One question, who's gonna be the big spoon?"

I remove my t-shirt as a response and it only takes a moment before Kohan is stripping out of his clothes as well. When I'm naked I step into the warm water and sigh as it rises up my legs. I stay standing while Kohan finishes getting naked and steps into the bath behind me. "So you're the big spoon then?"

Kohan laughs before pulling me down into warm heat. I lean back against his chest and sigh as the water covers me up to my chest. Kohan uses his hands to scoop water onto the bits of my skin that aren't underwater and it's the sweetest thing. "How was your day?"

I close my eyes and lean my head back onto his shoulder. "Lazy. I slept most of it and when I woke up I just wanted a bath. Yours?"

"The same as yours, well apart from I hadn't planned on the bath."

I sit up and grab the glass of wine that's sitting on the bottom end of the bath. I take a drink and turn to hand it to Kohan.

"If I drink I won't be able to leave."

"Then take a lot."

His eyes twinkle over the edge of the wine glass and I don't think he's ever looked so attractive. There are times that Kohan looks younger than his twenty-six years and when he looks at me like that it's one of those times. "Are you trying to get me drunk so you can have your wicked way with me, Angel?"

My stomach summersaults with nerves as he asks me that question. I've never topped for anyone before and it's not something I thought interested me, but when I look at Kohan I want nothing more than to slip inside his body. "Is it a problem if I am?"

"No, I just want you to know that I don't need to be drunk for that to happen."

And just when I thought I had control over my body he says something like that. My breath stutters and my dick is instantly hard. "Good to know." I turn my back to him and lie down on his chest again. I can feel his erection poking into my back and I relax knowing that I'm not the only one who's turned on. I blame Kohan for my constant arousal because since I met him I haven't been able to control my body.

We lie together for a few minutes in silence before Kohan speaks. "Am I being too forward?"

I run my nail along the top of his leg and see goose bumps rising on his skin. "Its only too forward if it's something I don't want."

His fingers glide up and down my arm, mimicking the motion of my own fingers. "I don't want you to do something you aren't ready for. I don't know what he did … what I mean is, I don't want to push you into anything. I'm happy with what we've done so far and if that's all you can give me then so be it."

I still don't look at Kohan because it's easier to say all this if I can't see his face. "I want more. I want it all with you. I didn't think that I would be able to give you as much as I have but I also think I need to tell you something before we go further."

I feel Kohan tense under my body and I hate that I'm making him feel like that. I want to get out the bath and pretend this conversation didn't happen, but instead I do what Adam has been encouraging me to do since I started seeing him. I keep going even when I feel like running.

"I won't be able to look at you when I tell you and I would prefer if you just listened. Is that okay?"

"Anything you need, Ares." He wraps his arms around my shoulder and rests his hands over my heart. I would think that the move is an accident but Kohan doesn't do anything without thinking. No, I'm sure that this is a way for him to show support without being too obvious.

I place my hand over his to help give me the confidence I need to do this. Taking a deep breath I start to tell him some of my darkest secrets that I have never told anyone before. "I met Micah when I had just left secondary school. I was at a gym when he spotted me. I had spent my teenage years being picked on for being scrawny and I wanted to add some muscle to my body. I had been working out for about a year when Micah spotted me and asked me out. He told me how sexy I was, how much he wanted me and totally won me over. I craved the attention he gave me because no one had ever said those things to me before. I'd come out in school but I hadn't done much more than kiss another boy. Micah changed all that. He showed me what I had been missing, even though I see now that it was very one sided. What that means for you, Kohan, is that I can pleasure you a hundred different ways but it also means I don't know how to be more than an object for you to use. I want more than that with you but it might take some time for me to get there." I lean up and grab the wine from where Kohan's put it and take a large mouthful. I wish that the bottle was closer but maybe it's better if I stay sober for this next part.

"The first time Micah raped me was also the first night that he hit me. He came home after a night out with his friends and a simple denial of sex turned into a slap. Then it turned into something much worse."

I feel Kohan's hands grip mine tighter and for a split second I consider stopping but I don't. He needs to hear this if he wants to understand me.

"I remember the whole thing so clearly. When he walked in I could smell the alcohol on him. He'd been out for what he called a work meeting but I knew that meant the guys from his office were going out drinking. That night they had ended up at a strip club, and since Micah was the only gay guy it was a straight one. He joked that he has seen more vaginas that night that any other time in his life and I needed to make him forget. He pinned me to the wall and started groping me through my clothes, and normally it wouldn't bother me but he was just so drunk. I pushed him away and told him to sleep it off before walking to our room. Turning my back on him was a huge mistake." I take a deep breath to calm myself down a bit. Reliving this is hard but I'm determined to get it all out.

"I had just walked through the door into our room when he pushed me from behind and I smacked into the wardrobe. I was shocked, and honestly, I thought I must have tripped. When Micah grabbed me by the back of the neck and threw me towards our bed I knew that I hadn't. He was a lot larger than me, not like a body builder but strong enough to overpower me. God, I wish had I had ran, just got straight off that bed and got the fuck out of there, but like a fool I sat there and tried to make sense of what was happening. I actually sat there and watched him take a handful of ties from his drawer before walking over to me. The first slap shocked me but it was the second that told me that my life was about to change."

"I struggled so hard as he turned me onto my stomach but he was just too big. I was so fucking scared when he tied my wrists to the headboard but I kept telling myself he was messing around, that any minute he would let me go and we would laugh about it. The laughter never came. Fuck!" I wipe at my eyes to get rid of the tears that are falling. I swore that I wouldn't waste any more tears on Micah but the memories still really fucking hurt.

"You don't have to do this, Angel."

I lift our joined hands and kiss Kohan's knuckles. "I do, I need you to know."

Kohan kisses my head but doesn't say anything else, letting me compose myself before I carry on.

"He used a knife to cut my clothes off me and I spent every second of it thinking he was going to stab me. Every time I managed to see his face he was smiling like he was enjoying it. Lying there naked, not knowing what he was going to do was the hardest thing and I couldn't get the words out to ask him to stop because I was crying so hard. I don't know if it was because he had been drinking or if he just wanted to hurt me, but he pushed inside me without any preparation and the pain nearly made me black out. The whole time he was taking me, he was growling in my ear telling me that I was his and he would do whatever he wanted to me, that I'd asked to be treated that way by saying no and I would learn. Thankfully he didn't last long and soon he was getting off me. I thought my nightmare was over but it wasn't. He left the room and I thought he had gone to the bathroom to clean up, the only thing is he didn't come back. I lay there tied to the bed until he woke up on the couch in the morning. My hands had gone numb and there was blood and cum dried onto my thighs. He was so sorry when he finally cut me lose. He said it was the alcohol that made him do it and that he would never do that when he was sober, told me that he was ashamed of himself and he wouldn't blame me if I left him. I should have but I bought the whole thing. He managed to distract me from everything he put me through and I stayed for more."

Kohan's whole body is tight and he has me in a death grip but it's comforting. Having him hold me is actually helping me from breaking down like I have in the past when I told people just a little of what I told Kohan.

"It's why I don't like being pinned down and I felt I needed to explain that before we went any further. You've never come close to making me feel like I'm being forced into anything but if I ever freak out just know there's a reason. You seem to see it though; you can sense when something isn't working and you change what you're doing. That in itself makes you different." I finish talking and wait to see what Kohan says but then I remember that I asked him not to speak. "I can hear your brain racing. This is now your chance to ask me anything and I will try to answer it."

Kohan kisses my temple and still remains quiet. I know it won't last forever and I try to stay relaxed as I imagine what he's going to ask. "What happened to your back?"

Okay, that's not the first question I thought he would ask but I suppose since he's seen the scars I should have guessed. I would want to know about any scars Kohan had. "I was late with dinner."

"What the fuck?" There's the tell-tale anger in his voice that I'm used to when people hear about what I experienced. I pat his hand to try and calm him down.

"Don't waste your anger on him. He's in jail so there's no point wasting all that energy on him." This is what I've been finding since Kohan came into my life. I've accepted my past for what it is, the past. It can't hurt me physically anymore and even though sometimes the memories catch up with me in my dreams, when I'm awake I refuse to give them power over me anymore. I spoke to Adam on the phone at the end of last week and he told me this is a very important part of my recovery. Realising that I have the final say over what I feel is the big breakthrough I needed.

"That's easier said than done, Ares. I want to kill the man with my bare hands." He takes a deep breath and I feel him exhale slowly. "Please carry on."

"Are you sure you want to hear this?"

He nods his head.

"Micah had told me he would be home at seven and he wanted his favourite pasta dish made for his arrival. I had fully intended to be ready for him but I got distracted by a book. I didn't notice the hours slipping away as I read about the life the characters had, dreaming that I could live like that, get back out into the world and meet people. When the front door slammed I realised my mistake and I tried to make it right. I might have managed but he'd had a bad day at work. He lost his shit instantly and after screaming at me and threatening to punish me, I tried to escape. I knew something bad was going to happen and I didn't want to deal with it. The first slash of the belt hit me between the shoulder blades before I reached our bedroom. You've seen the rest of the scars so you know it didn't end there."

Kohan covers my mouth with his hand and leans his head against mine. "I changed my mind, please don't tell me anymore. I just don't know how you survived."

I lean into him and his hand drops to my neck where he places it loosely around the base. Whereas this move usually makes me feel frightened, this time I just feel wanted.

"I can't promise you I know everything, Ares, but I can promise you this: I'll never hurt you like he did. The only time I will put my hands on you it will be to make you feel amazing. No pain unless it something you want and specifically ask for."

"Thank you." The words feel inadequate but it's the only ones I have. He will never realise how much he has changed my life and I will never be able to tell him because I don't have the words to explain it.

―――◇◯□◇―――

"I know I bill by the hour, Ares, but this tends to work better if you actually say something."

I look at Adam but the words still won't come. I called for an appointment because I needed to talk to him, try and settle the fears that have been threatening to take over the last few days. I thought the afternoon in the bath with Kohan had given me the breakthrough I was looking for, but since he went home I've felt like I'm floundering.

"Okay let's start with something simple. Why are you here, Ares?"

"I'm scared." I didn't know that what I was going to say but it explains clearly how I'm feeling. "Tell me what you're afraid of."

"Start with something simple why don't you?" I remember the first time I came to visit Adam I was scared to say anything wrong. Now that we have relaxed into an easy companionship, he puts up with any attitude I throw at him.

"I'm waiting."

Struggling to not give him the finger I try to put into words what I'm thinking. "Everything is going well, too well. Kohan seems too good to be true and I'm constantly wondering when I'm going to lose it all."

"Why do you need to lose it? Why can't you be happy with someone who's treating you properly?"

"Because life doesn't work that way."

Adam writes something on the pad in front of him before looking up at me. "You need to tell your parents that then."

I hate it when he starts being all cryptic and shit. I wish he would just come out and tell me what he's thinking. "Tell them what?"

"That they shouldn't be happy together and something needs to change. Maybe they could divorce before it all goes wrong."

"No one likes a dickhead, Adam. That isn't what I meant and you know it. I just meant that ..." I don't know how to explain it. Now that Adam's blown the arse out of my argument I'm at a loss. "Shit never goes well for me."

"No, your relationship with *Micah* didn't go well for you. What happened to the guy I spoke to last week? He was brimming with confidence and couldn't wait to tell me that he was finally seeing the positives in life. He was willing to take some risks to get what he wanted and what he wanted was Kohan."

I get up from the sofa and walk to the large window that covers the back wall. "Kohan's different from anyone else I've met. He sees me, like really sees *me,* not the scars or my past. He makes me feel less out of focus, like I can finally see a future for myself."

Adam's voice comes from behind me, but the distance doesn't cause it to lose any of its volume. "Nothing you're saying sounds bad to me. I think you are worried about letting go of the past. It's become a safety net that you can use to keep people at a distance. Will this thing with Kohan last forever? Possibly not, but that's life. You just have to take a chance and hope for the best."

I come back over to the sofa and sit down. "I don't know how I went from being optimistic one minute to doom and gloom the next."

"Old habits are hard to break and your go to escape is to see the worst in everything. You've been through a lot and sometimes your brain will take a second to catch up. It's completely normal and what you need to do is not let it get to you. Accept the uncertainty and move past it. Everyone doubts themselves but they learn how to cope with it. That's your next step: to learn to take a deep breath and carry on. Go on this night out with Kohan and his brother and allow yourself to have fun. Wanting to laugh again doesn't make you a bad person. It doesn't make what you went through less traumatic; it just shows that you are more powerful than your memories."

I need to remember what Adam is saying to me because I

have a feeling that over the next few weeks I will need to remember his words to get me through the bad days.

Chapter Twenty Five

Kohan

I check my watch again as my brother shuffles in the seat next to me. We arrived about forty minutes ago and are still waiting for Duncan to arrive. He texted Carey to say that he was sorry but he would be a little late, something to do with a family member and that he would explain when he got here. I thought it was nice for him to text so Carey wouldn't worry, but it's done the opposite, making him worry more. I love my brother with every part of me but if he bounces his knee against mine one more time I'm going to pin him to the seat.

Ares squeezes my knee under the table and I know he can see the frustration on my face. This is also the night where my brother is getting to meet my boyfriend for the first time and he has pretty much ignored him since he arrived.

"So Kohan tells me that you like to work out." I smile at Ares as he tries to engage Carey in conversation, and he couldn't have picked a better subject. There's nothing my brother loves to talk about more than his work out routine, but it doesn't really grab his attention this time.

"Yeah I do."

I grind my teeth as Carey pretty much blanks Ares. I know he's worried about Duncan but it doesn't give him the right to be an arse to Ares. It took a lot for him to come out tonight and I expect more from my brother. I kick him under the table and he turns to glare at me.

"What?"

"Could you get your head out of your arse for just a minute?"

Ares takes this as his cue to give us a few minutes alone. He stands and kisses my cheek after telling me he's going to the toilet.

I know it's a lie but I appreciate a moment with my dickhead brother.

I wait until we're by ourselves before giving it to him it with both barrels. "Could you be any ruder to Ares? In case you've forgotten, you asked him to come tonight and you have barely said two words to him."

"I'm worried about Duncan, okay?" He grabs his bottle of beer from the table and takes a drink. I want to grab the bottle from him and throw it across the bar but instead I take a deep breath before carrying on.

"I get that, but I also know that if I was ignoring Duncan like this you would be pissed off. It took a lot for Ares to be here tonight and you treating him like shit is pissing me off." It takes everything in me not to reach over the table and shake my brother.

"I get it okay, but I'm distracted. Once Duncan arrives I will apologise and it will all be fine. I just wanted tonight to go well and it's going to shit already."

"Well that isn't my fault and it certainly isn't Ares. When he comes back I want you to say sorry and actually have a conversation with him, one that contains more than four words."

Carey looks like I'm asking him to sell an organ but I try to stay calm. I know that Carey has been going through a lot recently between all the stress with mum and the whole being bi thing, so I'm trying to give him the benefit of the doubt. With every flick of his eyes to the door while I'm talking to him he's making it harder to give him that.

I'm about to say something else when Carey grabs his mobile from the table in front of him. As he reads a message his face drops and I know that the night is probably going to end a lot earlier than we planned.

"Duncan's really sorry but he can't make it. Something to do with his ex, he said he'll try and explain later."

He types something out on his phone and I take the opportunity to look towards the hall that Ares went down to go to the bathroom. I thought he would be back by now but he must have seen us still talking and gave us more time. I hate that it's his first night out here and he has to avoid coming back to the table. I had great plans of dancing with him and enjoying the feel of him against me as we spent hours building a sweat on the dance floor. Now I'm stuck with a mopey brother and I don't have any idea where my boyfriend is.

The corner of my mouth curls up but I try to hide it from Carey. I started thinking of Ares as my boyfriend after the night we spent together. I let it slip out after he had his nightmare and I haven't changed his title since then. I've wanted to repeat it again and again to see how Ares would react to it, but I haven't been brave enough in case he rejects it.

The last week it's felt like Ares has been a completely different person. He still has the important traits that make him the man I met, but there's a fire inside him now that I find hot as fuck. He's developed this take charge attitude that's completely adorable, especially when it's directed at himself. I've seen him talk himself through difficult situations, like walking into the bar tonight, and I love watching him build up his confidence.

"Do you just want to call it a night? I'm think I'm gonna just bail." Carey sounds so sad and I should tell him to stay out with us and that we can still make a great night of it, but all I can think of is getting Ares on that dance floor and then home. If Carey stays with us then we will have to include him and make sure he doesn't feel left out, so dancing would be a no no. Still, I can't just bail on my brother when he's feeling shit.

"Why don't we stay for a little while longer? You can be nice to Ares and get to know him so the next time you won't be a dick."

Carey glares at me but it doesn't have any anger in it so I know that I've got to him. "Shit, I'm sorry. I don't know what's wrong with me tonight. I've been a complete fucking stress head for about a week now. I was worried that's what scared Duncan away tonight, but if it's his ex then I can understand."

"He mentioned his ex before; I take it that it wasn't a particularly good break up?"

He grabs his bottle and finishes his drink. I look around to see if I can see Ares yet but there is still no sign of him. I won't be getting another round until he's here so I don't offer to get Carey another drink just yet.

"His ex was a complete dick. He was always cheating behind his back and then blaming Duncan when they argued about it."

I feel so sorry for Duncan because I can't imagine how it feels to know that the person you love is cheating on you. I would never do that to someone and I definitely wouldn't want them to do it to me. It would break my heart if Ares ever did that, but after everything he's been through I don't think he would ever cheat on anyone. "That's shit. It seems that our men haven't had the best of luck when it comes to their exes. Makes you want to meet them so you can show them the error of their ways."

Carey tilts his empty bottle in my direction. "I'd raise my bottle to that, little brother, but it's empty so I will be right back." He gets up from the table and I check my watch. Ares has been gone for far too long now and I'm starting to worry a little. He's a grown man but I if something has overwhelmed him then he might be having a panic attack in the bathroom.

I'm about to get up from the table to check on him when I feel my mobile vibrate in my pocket. I grab it and see Ares' name on the message notification. My mind wanders back to the last time we were in a bar together and I wonder if he needs some company back there. The thought has a huge grin on my face before I open the message but that smile disappears quickly when I read what he's sent.

I'm really sorry but I had to go home. I left a while ago in a taxi and I'm safe. Please don't ruin your night for me, will see you soon.

The message is short, abrupt and really fucking confusing. Why would he leave without me when we are here together? If there was something wrong he could have come and got me; I would have left in a heartbeat if he had needed me. I drove us here tonight and the plan was to spend the night at mine. I press reply and type out my own message, hoping that he will reply before I get in my car.

Ares

My mobile goes off in my hand and I jump at the noise. I've had it in a death grip since I messaged Kohan and I should have known that he would reply. I'm surprised that he didn't call but glad he didn't. Against my better judgement I open the message and read it.

> *Did I do something? Please, Ares, just tell me where you are so I can come and get you. Don't leave like this.*

Tears build in my eyes as I read it and a huge part of me wants to tell the taxi driver to turn around and go back, but I can't. I had a moment in that bar and I can't risk going back there.

I'd spent about ten minutes in the back hall to let Kohan speak to his brother. Before we arrived he had told me that Carey was the nicest of all his brothers and I would get on great with him. After about half an hour of trying to get him to talk to me I knew that Kohan was close to blowing his top. I made myself scarce so the brothers wouldn't feel awkward and I didn't think that Carey would appreciate being called out in front of me. I could see that he was distracted by his boyfriend being late but Kohan was pissed at him.

When I couldn't stay in the back hall any longer without risking being reported to management, I started making my way back to the table. That's when time stopped and I was frozen to the spot. It took me a minute to make sense of what I was seeing, but when my senses came back to me I ran. I didn't stop until I got to the taxi rank outside the club and slipped into the first car I saw, pushing the guy who was about to get in out of the way. I could hear him shouting at me as I closed the door but I just told the taxi driver to drive.

Now that I'm sitting here common sense is coming back to me. I should have gone back to the table and told Kohan what I saw, or who I thought I saw, but I panicked. My brain is telling me that it wasn't Micah that I saw in that club, it couldn't have been. He's locked away in a cell and that's where he'll be for the next seven years. They say everyone has a twin out there somewhere and I must have seen his. Now that I'm picturing him in my head he was slightly different. His hair wasn't as blonde as Micah's was, no this guy had darker lowlights making his hair thicker. He was also built bigger than Micah. Micah's body was large, but this guy obviously likes the gym because his muscles were huge.

I shake my head again and can't believe that I'm still trying to convince myself that it couldn't be Micah because of the way he looked, completely missing the fact it couldn't be him because he's in prison. *Get it together Ares. Shit, I am finally losing it.* This is what I get for trying to have a normal life; my crazy has multiplied and caught up with me.

I look down at my mobile and start typing out a response to Kohan, telling him that I'll meet him at his house. After I'm finished I stare at it and I can't seem to press send. The way I panicked when I thought I saw Micah has my head all fucked up and I think I might just need some time to sort it out. It's too late to call Adam but I could write down everything that I'm struggling with and call him tomorrow. That seems to be the best idea for everyone involved so I press delete until the message is gone. I will make it up to Kohan when I see him next, starting by explaining everything.

I put my mobile back in my jacket pocket and try to relax back into the seat. There is still about ten minutes to go before I get home and I close my eyes to try and will the time to go quicker. I'm hoping that Kohan will do as I ask and stay away tonight but I'm not convinced. He is the kind of guy who will be worried and that usually means that he'll ignore what I said. My only hope is to reach my cottage before he does and hide. I know it's not grown up or mature but I can't face him tonight knowing how stupid I've been.

I had been so confident at the start of the night. I was going to spend the whole time showing Kohan that I wanted to be with him and that I wanted more between us than the friendship that I was pushing. I don't know where this thing between us will go, but I know that I want to try to be more than his friend. I want to be his love, his boyfriend, whatever title he wants to use. I don't know if we will get our happily ever after but that's what I want.

That's what I was going to prove to Kohan tonight but instead I messed it all up. Just when I was feeling that life was finally going my way, that the universe had decided that it was going to pick on someone else, I had to go and lose it over a stranger in a bar. If I was to go back now I would probably see that the guy looked nothing like Micah. I am starting to think that my stupid imagination was having a laugh at my expense and I saw something that wasn't there. Shit, I know it wasn't there. There was no possible way for Micah to be in that club unless he had escaped and I'm pretty sure I would have heard if he had.

"That's us here, son."

I open my eyes and look around my dark little road. The taxi has pulled into the paved area that it classed as my driveway and I look towards my dark front door. Normally I would have left a light on but since I wasn't planning on coming home tonight I left the house in complete darkness.

"That's twenty eight pounds please."

I lean forward and struggle a little to get my wallet out of my pocket. I should have moved it to my jacket before I got in but I wasn't thinking clearly. I take a tenner and a twenty-pound note out and hand it to the driver. "Keep the change. Thanks for getting me here, I was sure that I would need to give you directions from the high street."

"Nah, son, my sat nav is pretty good. These houses have been here long enough now that they are easy to locate. I went to this farm house once and I swear my sat nav told me to drive through a river to get there." He chuckles to himself and I smile for the first time in what feels like hours.

I open the door and step out onto the paving stones. I'm walking past the driver's side when the window goes down.

"Are you going to be okay out here? I can easily wait until you are safely inside."

The thought warms my heart and it makes me realise even more that there are kind people in this world. I was unlucky to meet one of the nasty ones but I can't judge everyone by how Micah treated me. "It's fine. You get going so you can catch the people coming out of the club. Thanks for driving me so far."

He nods his head. "No worries, you take care now." He puts his window up and I watch as his back lights disappear into the distance.

When I turn towards my house I realise my mistake. I should have gotten him to point his headlights at my door so I could see where the hell I was going. *Oh well, can't change my mind now.* I pull my mobile out of my pocket and use the flashlight to make my way to my front door. I'm halfway up the path when a message comes in and I see Sophie's name. I think about ignoring it but I know that she would turn up at my door. My message to Kohan may keep him away for the night but I know Sophie would have no problems ignoring what I ask.

> *Kohan is shitting himself. Tell me you're home and I will keep him away, if not then you're on your own.*

I don't want to tell anyone I'm home but it will lead to so many problems if I don't. Maybe if I tell her I'm safe and where I am, she will be able to keep Kohan from coming over as she's promised.

> *I'm home but don't want company. Tell him it's not him, I promise its not. I had a moment and need to sort my head out. Tell him I will call tomorrow because I want to see him ... I just can't tonight.*

I hope that will make Kohan feel better, or at least good enough to just go home when he gets back to Tonbridge.

You have twenty-four hours to sort this or I'm kicking your arse ... and you know I can do it.

I laugh at her response even though I shouldn't be finding anything funny in this situation. Sophie has a way of making me feel better but I have no doubt that she could hurt me if she really wanted to.

I close my phone and walk the rest of the way to my front door. I manage to get my front door open after struggling with my phone and keys more than I should have. I turn the flashlight off and press the light switch next to the front door. Nothing happens and I flick it a few more times even though common sense says the bulb is gone. I turn to face the dark hall and try to remember where I put my spare bulbs.

Fear explodes through me when I'm knocked back into my front door by a large body. A hand covers my mouth and another pins my throat so I can't move. The shadow of the person holding me is all too familiar and my body freeze in pure terror. The shadow moves slightly, leaning into me and I can smell his aftershave. It's the same aftershave I can still smell in my nightmares.

"Hi, Ares. Did you miss me?"

Chapter Twenty Six

Kohan

Sophie grabs my mobile out of my hand and hides it behind the cushion on the sofa. "You are not calling him. He said he would be in touch today and you need to make him chase you."

I hate that she makes a little bit of sense but I still struggle with her until I get my phone back. "I don't care. Something happened and I need to make sure he's okay. It was a big step for him last night and something must have freaked him out." I hardly slept a wink because I was worrying about what had happened. Even after she'd invited herself over and told me to give Ares some space I couldn't relax. Sophie managed to keep me company but as is normal, she fell asleep within a few hours even though she had bitched at me until I put on series one of Shadowhunters. She's lucky that I'd found Alec hot or I would have been pissed off.

"He's a grown man, Kohan. I know that you feel like you need to protect him but he's been dealing with the fallout from his ex for a long time now. Put your sword away and stop trying to play his saviour."

"Fuck you, Soph. I am not playing his fucking saviour, but I do care when my boyfriend is struggling with something. You might let the people you love suffer but I don't." I can feel the anger I've been feeling since last night trying to break free and I take a deep breath so I don't unleash it all on Sophie.

"Back. The fuck. Up. Boyfriend? The person you love? Whoa, when the hell did this happen?"

I feel my face start to burn and I know that it must be bright red. I might have let my anger say some things I wasn't ready to say out loud yet, and Sophie being Sophie picked up on them. "I didn't mean ... it was just ..."

"Uh hu ... you didn't mean it and all that shit. Now tell me the truth or I'm giving you a purple nurple."

I roll my eyes at her but squeal when she moves towards me. Sophie is a mean bitch when she wants to be and it wouldn't be the first time she's left my nipple bruised for weeks. "Fine, calm down. We both know that I want a relationship with Ares, I just haven't got far enough to actually tell him yet that I have started one with him. I don't see the problem with him not knowing and I'll tell him soon. The love thing is ... well it kinda sneaked up on me. I didn't know that's how I felt until I just said it then. I knew I liked him, like really liked him, but I didn't think it had gotten *there* yet."

She smiles indulgently at me and I get up from the sofa. There is no way I'm sitting here and spilling my guts to her when she's in one of these moods. I hear her steps follow me to the kitchen but before I can tell her to go away my mobile goes off in my pocket. I take it out and stop instantly, causing Sophie to walk into my back.

"Give a little warning next time. Jeez." She walks around me into the kitchen and opens the fridge door. "Do you want something to drink?"

I don't really hear her as I reread the message from Ares. I wondered what he would say when he got in touch but I thought it would be sorry and then we would talk over what happened last night. Not this. Never this.

I'm really sorry but I can't do this. I think it's better for everyone if we call this off before it goes too far. Thank you for everything you've done and I might see you about.

That's it? Just thank you and goodbye? No explanation or hint of what went wrong. No way. If he wants to break this off with me, he needs to do it to my face. He has to look me in the eye and tell me that he is finished with me completely.

"Are you okay?" Sophie walks in front of me and I hold out my phone so she can see the message. "Holy shit. That's it?"

I shake my head as I take my mobile back and put it in my pocket. "No, that's not it."

I bang on his front door again and press the doorbell. I know he's in there and he *will* answer. I walk around onto the grass and look in the living room window hoping to catch a glimpse of him but there's no sign of life. Common sense might tell me to go and come back later on but I need to see him. I don't understand what happened between last night and this morning, and I need him to explain it to me. Ares told Sophie that he was fine and he would see me today. Well he better bloody see me because I'm not going anywhere.

A bang from inside catches my attention and I walk to the side of the house. Ares bedroom is towards the back of the house and I would put money on the noise coming from there. I step over the small hedge that divides the front garden from the back and walk slowly and quietly across the grass. I don't hear any other noise but I know that I heard something and I'm not leaving until I find out what's going on.

When I reach the window that I know belongs to Ares bedroom I try to look in but the blinds are fully closed blocking me from seeing anything. I press my hands against the windowpane and get closer hoping there might be a small gap that I can see through but there's nothing.

"Ares." I don't know if it will make a difference but I hope that hearing me might get him to come to the door. "Please open the door. I don't know what's happening but I'm not going to leave until you speak to me. I want to know what I did wrong. Tell me and I'll try to fix it. Please, Angel, please just open up."

I lean my head against the window and realise that this might actually be it. I might be losing the man I fell in love with and I have no idea why. My mobile goes off and I ignore it. There's no one I want to talk to apart from Ares and he's hiding from me.

My mobile goes off again and I growl in frustration as I take it from my pocket. I'm not in the mood for anyone today but I need to check in case it's about Mum. That's the only thing that would make me leave here today. My eyes go wide when I see Ares' name on my screen and I struggle to get my phone unlocked in my hurry to see what he's written.

Front door.

Two words and my hopes soar. He's willing to talk to me and I know that I can convince him that whatever went wrong can be fixed. I run around the front of the house, jumping the hedge this time in my haste to see Ares.

When I take the two small steps to the front door it opens a crack and I come to a halt. Ares face appears slightly around the door but I can't see all of him. What I do see is enough and it makes my heart break. His eyes are red like he's been crying and I want nothing more than to hold him. I take a step forward but he closes the door a little more.

"You need to go, Kohan. You … you can't be here. I …" A sob escapes him and I put my hand against the front door so he can't shut it.

"Let me in, Ares. Talk to me, tell me what's wrong."

He looks at me with pain and fear in his eyes, and anger starts to build inside me. I have never seen that look on Ares face before and I want to know who put it there because I know it can't have been me.

I push against the front door and his fear turns into panic when I manage to open it another few inches. His face comes fully into view for the first time and there is no way for him to hide the huge bruise that covers his cheek.

"What the fuck, Ares? Who did that too you? Who hurt you?"

"Go away, Kohan, please. You should leave and forget about me. I …" He scrunches up his face and I swear I hear another voice from inside the house but when Ares looks at me I forget all about that. The determination I was getting used to is back and it gives me hope, well that is until he speaks again. "Go away or I will call the police. I don't want you, Kohan, so go."

The door in front of me closes and I stand there in shock, staring at the plain wood. I wanted him to tell me to my face that it was over and that's what he did. Now I have to try and man up and do what he asked.

Ares

"He never takes the hint does he? I could tell he was going to be a problem the first time I met him."

I lean my head against the front door and try to fight the urge to throw it open and go after Kohan.

"I wouldn't do it if I was you, Ares. Just think of all the pain I could put your boyfriend through."

The fear is the only thing that has me turning away from the door and quietly making my way back into my bedroom. I sit on the edge of my bed, flinching slightly as the pains in my body from last night's lesson make themselves known.

When Micah pushed me against the door I was hoping that I was dreaming the whole thing even though I knew I wasn't. A small part of me was happy to know that I wasn't losing my mind by seeing him in the bar, but the biggest part was filled with body numbing fear. I tried to run, I tried to get away so I could get help, but the extra layer of muscle that Micah's added to his frame made it impossible to win that particular fight.

I woke up this morning lying on the bathroom floor, my body covered in bruises that I don't remember getting. I must have passed out or been knocked out and I'm thankful for that fact. I just wish that the numbness was still there because my body is screaming out in pain with every move I make.

Micah walks until he's standing right in front of me and I keep my head down, refusing to look anywhere other than at his feet. "Look at me."

I keep my head lowered. Micah may think that I'm the same man he knew before but I'm not, I'm stronger thanks to Kohan and I won't bow down to him and do as I'm told. He may bruise my body but I'm determined to be strong.

My hair is grabbed and my head pulled back roughly until I'm looking up at Micah. "I said fucking look at me. I think you've forgotten your place and I need to remind you."

"How are you even here?" It's the one question that's been in my head all morning but I wasn't brave enough to ask. One thing that I learned from being with Micah so long, even silence won't keep me safe so this time I will use my voice.

"Didn't your lawyer tell you? I was released over a month ago on a technicality. Apparently one of the statements wasn't filed and signed correctly so my lawyer got me released pending a new trial. How did you not know this?"

A month? He's been out there for that long and I didn't know? My body goes cold as I think of all the times he could have come back and hurt me, and no one told me that I needed to keep myself safe. I would have thought that I would have been the first person they called when the case dissolved, or at least within the top ten. Why didn't my lawyer tell me or at least let my family know so they could tell me?

So many questions but I have no way of finding out the answer. I doubt that Micah will allow me to call the law office to find out what the fuck happened. "So they just let you out? How did you find me?"

"Oh, that was the easy bit. I just spent a few days outside your parents and I knew that you'd turn up at some point. It was just a case of following you back here." His hold on my hair tightens and I close my eyes at the pain. "I have to say that I was pissed to see that you had someone sniffing around you already." He drags me up to standing and pulls me close to his face. I feel his breath on my lips and I can't hide the shudder that runs through me. "What did I tell you? You're mine, Ares. No one else can have you."

I use my hands to push against Micah's chest, putting some distance between us. I fight against the pain in my head until he finally lets go of my hair. "I'm not yours anymore, Micah."

I see the instant the anger rears its ugly head and I realise that I've pushed him too far. All the years I was with him I never spoke back, never told him that I wasn't his, and seeing him now I think that it was maybe safer that I hadn't.

The backhand he delivers sends me twisting backwards and I fall onto the edge of my bed, the wood of the base catching me in the middle of my back. I cry out in pain but it doesn't deter Micah. He walks calmly over to the iPod speaker I have set up on my dressing table and presses play. This was always his trick to drown of the sound of a beating when he knew that the neighbours were in. Today I think it's in case Kohan is still outside.

My heart aches with the thought of Kohan, about the look on his face when I told him I didn't want him. He'd been so worried about me even after I pushed him away and I wanted to tell him I loved him. I would have but Micah had spoken behind me, telling me to get rid of him before he killed him, and I believed he would. So I told Kohan to leave and not come back, and now I will never get the chance to tell him that I love him more than I've loved anyone else in my life.

"After we've done this I want you to start packing. We'll be leaving this shithole soon and I don't want to hang around longer than I have to. We are going somewhere new where no one knows us and we can start over."

I feel a cold sweat spread over my skin when he mentions after we're done. I don't want this to happen, but no matter how much I want to tell myself I'm stronger, I don't know how to stop it. I can't fight back against Micah, I never could.

As Snow Patrols *Run* starts playing I close my eyes and listen to the words. It's an appropriate song for this moment and I feel tears running down my cheeks. Every single word sung makes me think of Kohan, about the life I'm going to miss having with him, and I feel the actual moment I give up. I can no longer run and I resign myself to the fact that I'm going to live my life in pain and fear, but for once it doesn't threaten to break me. I feel nothing but numbness.

"The tears won't help you, Ares. You know the punishment for disobeying me."

I open my eyes and stare blankly at Micah. "I give up. You can do whatever you want to me, you win."

Micah looks confused when I speak, almost like he's not sure what to do with me when I'm not scared and begging. "What kind of game are you playing, Ares?"

"No game. I'm just done. You've taken everything away from me, I've nothing left to fight for." I struggle to my feet and stand in front of him. Whatever he's about to do to me I will face him eye to eye. There will be no more cowering at his feet.

"Is this about him? Kohan?"

Another tear runs down my cheek when he mentions his name and I want to tell him that he doesn't get to speak about him. I don't ever want to hear Kohan's name tainted by his voice.

"It is. Oh god, I can't believe that the thing that's going to break you is giving up a loser who thought he had you." He moves quickly and grabs me around the throat. It's his favourite thing to do to me, the one that gives him the most control, and with his increased strength he moves me quickly. I grab his wrist with both hands as he drives my whole body backwards. My knees hit the edge of the mattress and I fall quickly onto my back, Micah's weight crashing on top of me.

I wince in pain as he leans on the bruises he gave me last night but I don't cry out, refusing to give him the satisfaction of hearing me scream. His hand tightens on my throat briefly before he lets go and stands up. I spend a few seconds breathing deeply now that the weight on my chest is gone. I close my eyes and imagine I'm anywhere but here. I'm lying on a beach with Kohan, or at the movies with Kohan, or just about anywhere as long as it's the man I love with me.

The man I love. That's exactly who Kohan is and I feel blessed that he gave me his time and patience. My life is better for having him in it, and no matter what happens now Micah will never be able to take that away from me. I feel myself smiling despite what's going on around me.

Fingers working on the buttons of my jeans pull me back to reality quickly and the numbness that I felt a few minutes ago leaves me. I don't want to have sex with Micah and my fight or flight response kicks in. I pull at his hands and try to get him off me. Another backhand to the face stops me for a few minutes but soon enough I'm back to fighting.

I can see Micah's anger rising but I don't care. He can beat me all he wants but I won't give him this, I won't give him my body again. Micah grabs me by the front of the t-shirt and pulls me slightly off the bed. His right hand pulls back and I only have a few seconds to register what's about to happen before his fist connect with my face. Pain explodes through my nose and I instantly feel wetness running down the back of my throat. Another hit has my head crashing back onto the bed as he lets me go, all fight is instantly drained from me.

My body is manhandled until I'm lying on my stomach and I feel my jeans being pulled from the bottom half of my body. I moan as a heavy weight leans on my back and my legs are spread.

"Fight all you want, baby, it just makes me harder. Now be a good boy and take your punishment, I know how much you love it."

Chapter Twenty Seven

Kohan

It's been three days and four hours since Ares broke my heart, and it's been that long since I had a shower. I tip the bottle of vodka up and I'm a little surprised to find it empty. I throw it across the room in the general direction of the bin but a loud thump tells me it landed on the carpet instead.

I roll off my arse and onto my knees, grabbing the table in front of me to try and get to my feet. I need to open another bottle before I become too sober and start thinking again. I use the wall to walk towards the kitchen but there is a loud bang on the door before I get halfway there. I groan before doubling back to tell whoever it is to piss off.

I pull the door open and I'm met with a very pissed off looking Damien. I squint at him convinced that I'm seeing things. "You aren't good looking enough to be a hallucination."

He pushes me back and slams the door when he's in. "You fucking stink."

"Well hello to you too." I decide to go back to my original plan of heading to the kitchen but I'm grabbed by the arm and dragged towards the bathroom.

"You need to get a shower and clean clothes. Emile has gone to get coffee and will be back in ten minutes. That's how long you have to get ready."

Damien needs to slow down if he expects me to be able to keep up with him. He can't just turn up at my door and start demanding shit from me, nope, not going to happen. "Well Emile can come here in a hundred hours if he wants but I have no fucking plans to go with you. In case you didn't hear, I got dumped and I am going to go pickle my liver a little more." I snort at my own joke and turn to leave but Damien doesn't let me.

"You have no idea what day it is, do you?"

"I do believe it's Monday … Friday! Thursday?" *Fucking hell, how hard is it to remember what bloody day of the week it is?*

"Unbelievable. You pushed to get Mum a hospital appointment, made sure that we would all be there when she went in and now you're bailing. I'm sorry you aren't getting your dick sucked now but there are more important things happening in the world."

Now I totally understand Damien's anger towards me. I can't believe that I let my own shit get in the way of remembering about Mum's hospital appointment. There's nothing in the world that's more important than that. I turn without saying a word and Damien grabs me again.

"Where are you going?"

"I'm going to get a shower and get dressed. I will be out in five minutes so be ready to go." It's amazing how sober you can suddenly feel when you realise that your pain isn't the only important thing happening around you.

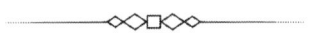

Good to my word I'm in the back of Emile's car within five minutes. Damien pushed a large takeaway cup of coffee into my hand as soon as I got in and I've been nursing it for the past fifteen minutes. My drunken numbness is starting to fade which means everything I felt from the day at Ares' house is starting to seep back in. Seeing him with that bruise on his face, knowing that he's hurt and doesn't want my help, it cut me deep. The worst thing though was when he told me he didn't want me. God that fucking hurt. It didn't sound like him but since I heard the words come out of his mouth there was no mistaking them.

"You need to get your head out of your arse before we get to the hospital."

I turn and blink blankly towards Damien who's driving. "I'm fine."

"You aren't fine and it's going to upset mum. The last thing we need is for her to get stressed before we leave her."

"I said I'm fine." The words come out on a growl and I see Damien looking at me in the mirror.

Emile turns in his seat to face me with a sad look on his face. "I heard about the break up. I'm sorry that it happened."

I nod and take a drink of the now cold coffee to try and swallow the large lump in my throat. My feelings about losing Ares are still very raw and as much as I want to talk about it, I don't.

"I know that you had some strong feelings for him, little brother."

"Who told you?" Now that I think about it, I'm not sure how any of my family knows since I came straight home from Ares' house and started on my first bottle of wine. The only person who knows is Sophie and she would have no reason to call my family.

Emile's cheeks heat and his eyes flicker away. He's showing all the signs of a guilty conscience and I don't know why. "Um ... Sophie mentioned it when I called her. I didn't know it was a secret."

"Why were you calling Soph?" In all the years that she's been my friend I don't think they have ever reached out to her and why would they now?

"It was just ..." He won't meet my eyes and my mind is now in overdrive. My brother wouldn't be that stupid would he? Would Sophie really do that?

"Are you fucking Sophie?" My voice comes out much louder than I intended.

Damien turns and glares at Emile. "You had better not be cheating on Maya or I'm gonna kick your arse."

Emile is now beetroot red and he's holding his hands up in front of him in defence. "I'm not sleeping with Sophie. Shit, there is only one woman in this world that I want and I bloody married her. Back off both of you."

As happy as I am that he isn't sleeping with my best friend it doesn't really answer my question as to why he was calling her. "Then why did you call her?"

"It was …shit… can we just pretend I'm having an affair?"

Oh, this must be good if he's willing to throw himself under the bus so we don't find out the real reason. Now I need to find out what is going on.

"Oh no, you are not getting out of this that easily. Spill it, E, because you aren't getting out of this car until we know." I'm glad I have Damien on my side and we both sit in silence as we wait on Emile to answer.

"Fuck the both of you. Its Maya's birthday soon and I want to get her something special. I thought that maybe Sophie could help me with that."

"I'm nearly buying it, but what can she help with that we couldn't?"

Emile rolls his eyes and drops his head so we can't see his face before mumbling something under his breath.

"Nope, didn't get that so try again."

'I want to get sexy photos taken and I thought that she might know a good photographer. I didn't want to ask you, butthead, so I went to her. Happy now? Want your phone so you can let the other two know how pathetic I am?"

We all sit in silence for a few moments before Damien and I burst out laughing. *Holy shit.* The thought of Emile getting boudoir pictures taken is the funniest thing I've ever heard and the more I picture it the harder I laugh. It's not long before tears are streaming down my cheeks.

"Laugh it up fuckers."

Emile's pissed off tone just makes the whole thing funnier and I'm finding it hard to breath. "Did you … oh shit … did you have a theme? Leather chaps or feathers?" I barely get the question out and it makes Emile turn in his seat and cross his hands over his chest.

"This is why I don't tell you anything."

I try to calm myself down because hurting his feelings wasn't my intention. "I'm sorry. I'm sure Maya will love it, and if Sophie can't help you let me know. I know some people too."

"Yeah, thanks. Can we just focus on getting to the hospital before Mum needs to get settled?"

The mood in the car changes quickly. No matter what else is happening in our lives we need to focus on Mum. She is going through so much just now and that needs to be our focus. These tests are important and the results will change our lives, I just don't know if it will be for the better or worse.

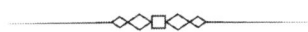

"Do you want to talk about it?"

I look over to Jensen who's sitting on the other side of mum's hospital bed. She finally fell asleep about forty minutes ago after we managed to get her to swallow a sleeping tablet. She cried from the minute we arrived and only settled once I promised to stay until she woke up. Jensen was the one who offered to stay with me so I could get a lift back to mums house. I thought he would need to rush home to Thea and Henry but he said it was fine. Jensen is probably the brother I spend the least amount of time with but it's easy to be in his company. He's relaxed and easy going, and that affects the people around him.

"About what?"

He laughs and I know I'm not fooling him with my act of ignorance. "The weather. What the hell do you think I'm talking about? The break up, do you want to talk about it?"

I lean forward until my elbows are leaning on my knees and I let my head fall forward. This last week has been so fucking hard but at least I was numbing everything with alcohol, being sober isn't helping with the pain. Helping mum settle blocked everything out for a while but since she fell asleep I have been sitting here thinking about Ares and how much I miss him. "There's not much to say. He asked me to leave so I did."

"Did he mean it though? If I got a pound for every time that Thea told me to go away I would be able to buy her the diamond wedding ring she deserves."

I look up at him in surprise. I was sure that his story with Thea was a simple one. They just seemed to click and that was it, instant family for my big brother. "Thea told you to leave?"

"Hell yeah, too many times to count." Jensen smiles at me and I'm betting he's remembering some of those times in his head.

"Why?"

"She was scared. She had to protect Henry even if it meant she missed out. It took me a long time to convince her that I could love our son as well as her."

I love listening to Jensen talking about his relationship with Henry. I don't think I've ever heard him calling him Thea's son, it's always their son or his son. It gives me hope that if I decide to have a family one day that I will feel that love for a kid even if they don't have my blood.

"Ares doesn't have a kid who's he's trying to protect though."

"What is he protecting then? There's always a reason and I think if you took a minute you might see that he really didn't want you to leave."

I lean back in my chair and think over everything that happened the last time we were together. We were having a great time at the club even though Carey was being a dick. Ares kissed me and went to the bathroom and that was the last time I saw him. There were no clues that anything was wrong and he was smiling as he walked away. Did he have second thoughts in the short space of time he was gone? No, because he messaged Sophie to say that he wanted to see me the next day, that he had a moment and just needed time to himself. *He wanted to see me.* Those words are stuck in my memory from the message he sent her. It's not the words of a man who wanted to get rid of me.

Then the next day he was gone. Even when I saw him face to face he didn't change his mind. I didn't manage to get him to see how good we are together. No he just walked away without any feelings. Except there were feelings. When he opened his front door he looked like his heart was breaking just as much as mine was. I never did understand why he looked so sad when he was the one walking away. "He was crying when he opened the door. He looked so fucking sad that it broke my heart."

"That doesn't sound like a guy that really wanted you gone. Did you say anything to him, fight for him?"

I look down as guilt attacks me. "No, I did as he asked and walked away."

"Seriously, Kohan."

I rub my hands over my face as Jensen's words make complete fucking sense. Ares spent his life being dismissed like he was nothing more than a favourite toy. Then when the time came for me to tell him how much I cared, how much I wanted him, I turned and walked away. What if all he needed was a few words from me telling him how important he was to me, that I wanted to spend the rest of my life with him no matter how bad his scars were. "I know right. I seriously fucked this whole thing up." Another thought comes to mind and I speak before I really think it out clearly. "And he had a black eye."

Jensen sits forward in his chair, glaring at me like I've made a huge mistake. "A black eye? And you didn't ask him what the hell happened?"

"He told me to leave." My voice is quiet and I know that Jensen must hear the guilt that's present too. I can't believe that I walked away knowing that Ares was hurt. I'm about to tell him how stupid I was when my mum wakes up.

"Joe?"

I stand up and approach the side of the bed, taking my mums hand in mine while I speak gently. "It's Kohan, mum. Everything is okay."

She struggles to get up and Jensen helps her by raising the back of her bed with the buttons on the side. She looks around, confusion clear on her face. "Where's my Joe?"

I hate this part of her memory loss because when we have to tell her that dad is gone I swear it's like he's just died all over again. I take a deep breath, preparing myself to explain it to her again. "Dad passed away, mum. Don't you remember?"

Tears fill her eyes and she shakes her head in denial. I hold her hand tighter and hope that it's enough to give her some comfort.

A moment later a nurse enters the room and approaches the bed. "Oh, Mary, what's wrong?"

I take a step back and let them have some space. She talks gently to my mum and the tears quickly stop before a smile appears on her lips. This is why I think we need to look into care facilities for mum. As much as I love her, I know that we aren't qualified to deal with her condition. If love was enough to help her then she would be in the best hands, but that isn't all she needs. The only thing we can do is get her into the best facility we can and visit her all the time so that she doesn't forget us.

A queasy feeling sits in my stomach as I realise that no matter what we do, mum's going to forget who we are. There will be a day in the not too distant future that she will look at all her sons like they're strangers and I'm not sure how I will cope with that. How does Damien explain to his daughters that Grandma doesn't know who they are, and how will Henry cope when he can't sit on her knee and listen to her stories? These thoughts have tears burning my eyes and I need to step away for a moment.

I walk to the window and look out over the parking lot below us. The sky is dark but I can see clearly with all the lights surrounding us. I jump a little when Jensen puts a hand on my shoulder and grips it tight.

"It's hard on everyone but we'll cope." He sounds so positive that I want to believe him.

"I don't know if I can watch her fade away."

"You have no option in that, Kohan. If you love mum you'll be there while she goes through this, and if one day she looks at us as strangers then we will try and help her remember."

The tears that were threatening to fall finally win and they roll down my cheeks as I stare out of the window.

"Thea and me will always be here for you, just like the rest of the family. It's going to be hard for everyone but we have each other."

More tears fall but it's for a different reason this time. This time it's because I feel very alone. As much as I love my brothers, it's just not the same as having that special person. All my brothers, apart from Carey, have the person they love to help them through this. When they go home after a hard day they have someone that will hold them close and tell them it's okay to break apart. They have that anchor. I have no one because the man I love doesn't want me.

Chapter Twenty Eight

Kohan

I glare at the three people in front of me in the queue and pray to anyone that's willing to listen for them to suddenly vanish. The person being served is telling the barista her life story and I don't have the patience for that today. I just want to get my coffee, preferably in a bucket, and go back to the office so I can attempt to catch up on everything I've missed. I glare at the back of the woman's head and hope that she can feel my hate. I'm so behind on my assignment because of everything with Ares and Mum.

I lost days to my drunken stupor and I missed some important interviews. Thankfully Sophie saved my arse by calling these people and telling them that I wasn't well. Everyone was really understanding, telling her to tell me to feel better and just call to rearrange everything.

Then I was with my mum for two days as she settled into the hospital for her four day stay. I thought that we would be there a few hours and then I would head home but I had been wrong. When she woke up on the second day she had panicked because she didn't recognise anyone including me and my brothers, so we had a meeting with her doctor about extra tests that were needed. Even Damien, who was still a little shocked that she didn't know who he was, had agreed that it was for the best. The next few hours were filled by form signing and further discussions on what would happen when it was time to take her home. We reluctantly decided that it might be best to look for a residential care home so Mum could get the constant care she needs. That was two days ago and we are still waiting to hear back from the doctors.

I couldn't take any more time away from work so Jensen drove me home last night. After a grovelling phone call to Mr

James I got an early night so I could be in at work early to do some work. Obviously I wasn't early enough if the queue when I turned up at the coffee shop is anything to go by. I check my watch and see that's its now after eight and I'm about to say something when what the woman is saying catches my attention.

"I don't know who he is. All I know is that quiet boy down Smithy Road has moved some man in with him. It isn't someone from town even though I thought he was dating that reporter."

The whole café seems to go silent as nearly all the eyes in the place turn to look at me. The woman must notice that she's said something wrong and when her eyes meet with mine she looks shocked. She turns away quickly and says something quietly to the server before rushing away. The noise starts again gradually but I'm lost in my own head.

I know that they're talking about Ares because there's no one else it could possibly be. Who does he have living with him? I'm so fucking confused because I thought that I was important to him. Was I just a stopgap until he found someone better? That doesn't make a single bit of sense with everything I've learnt about Ares. He's quiet and slow to let people in, he wouldn't give anyone that sort of trust straight away, would he?

I leave the coffee shop without actually getting my order and start walking aimlessly down the pavement. I don't know what to make of what I just found out and I don't know who to talk to about it. I can't get over the fact that Ares has moved someone in with him. It's been less than a week since he told me he didn't want me and I walked away. He did look sad that day, sadder than I'd ever seen him, but I don't believe it was because he was cheating on me. But that voice I thought I heard when we were talking; was that the voice of the guy who moved in with him? What about the bruise on his cheek? How would he …

The large body that I walk into doesn't move and I feel like I'm falling until hands grab my arms.

"Careful there."

I look up and come face to face with Duncan, my brother's boyfriend. "Duncan?"

"Kohan, nice to see you again." The words are polite but I sense that undercurrent of anger that I noticed the first time we met.

"What are you doing in Tonbridge?" My brother never mentioned that Duncan had any connection with the little town and I'm sure if he did, Carey would have said something.

"Personal reasons."

I wonder if it's to do with his ex but again I'm not sure why that would bring him here. I would know if there was someone in the town that had cheated on their boyfriend. Town gossip has its uses. "Carey missed you the other night. Did you get things sorted with your ex?"

Yeah, there is a definite look of hate in his eyes as I speak. This is the part of Duncan I thought I saw last time but put it down to me being over protective. Now, I know that there's another side to this guy and I don't like the thought of my brother being involved with him. "Everything is great with him. Look I need to go." He doesn't even say goodbye as he walks to a small sports car and gets in. I watch as he drives away in the opposite direction of the main street. He's heading towards the quarry and I know that there is nothing down that way apart from the three little houses.

Something is bugging me and I can't quiet put my finger on it. It feels like there's something really obvious that I'm missing. I grab my phone from my jacket pocket and call the one person who might be able to give me some answers.

"Hello?"

"Carey, have you seen Duncan recently?" He's silent on the other side of the phone and it doesn't fill me with confidence.

"No, not since the night he bailed. He hasn't been at the gym and won't answer his phone. I drove past his house a few times but he hasn't been in. Why are you asking?"

He hasn't been seen since the night at the club, the night that Ares vanished from my life. I can almost see the finished puzzle and it's driving me a little crazy as I stand in the middle of the pavement and make people walk around me.

"Why are you asking, Kohan?"

"He's here."

"What are you talking about?" He sounds as confused as I am.

"Duncan, he's here in Tonbridge."

I tilt my head as more and more realisations race through my mind like a mini movie: Ares running, his sudden disappearance from the world, the bruises, Duncan being here when he doesn't need to be. *Duncan driving towards Ares house like he knew the way.*

I'm running before I realise what I'm doing and I nearly drop my phone in my haste. I can hear Carey shouting at me but I can't stop to answer him. I need to get to Ares. It all makes so much fucking sense now and I am pissed that I didn't see it before.

I run around the corner onto the dirt track that leads to Ares' house. This is when I finally stop and lift the phone to my ear.

"Carey?"

"Shit, Kohan. What is happening?"

"I need you to call the police and send them to Ares house. He lives on Smithy Road." I hope he can hear me through my panting because I need to go. I'm about to hang up when he catches my attention again.

"Kohan, tell me what's going on."

"It's Micah."

"Ares ex?"

"Yeah. Duncan is Micah."

Ares

I hear the front door slam and I have to hold back the sob that his presence always brings. It's been less than a week and we're already back where we left off. I'd convinced myself that I was strong enough to survive anything that Micah could put me through but I'd been wrong. It was like he was on a mission to make up for the time he lost while he was in prison and I suffered like I never had through our relationship. Even now my body feels like part of it is on fire and I feel the belt marks on the back of my thighs as I sit in the corner of the living room.

The first time he used me for his pleasure had dragged me back into the life I thought I had left behind. Pain had ripped through my body but it hadn't hurt as much as the memories of Kohan's touch, the touch that Micah was erasing from my body. Now I spend my days trying to remember the gentle caresses that Kohan put on my skin, the sweetness of his lips against mine as he told me how much he wanted me. It's funny that you only realise how wonderful something is once you lose it, and now that I've lost Kohan I wish I hadn't hesitated to be with him. I should have grabbed onto what he was offering with both hands and never let him go.

Footsteps come closer and I wipe my eyes roughly as the memories of Kohan rip a bit more of my heart out. I try not to picture his face when I told him I didn't want him but I'll remember that until the day I die.

"Your boyfriend is a pain in my arse. He's sticking his nose in where it doesn't belong. That's going to get him hurt."

There's only one person that Micah can be talking about and he suddenly has my full attention. I get up from the chair I'm sitting on and walk over to where he's pacing. He's in front of the window and every few seconds he pulls back the curtain to look outside. I have spent most of the time since he got here in darkness with all curtains and blinds closed so that the world can't see in. I've been tempted to run when he's left the house but he warned me that he would find me, he would always find me, and until he did he would hurt the people closest to me.

"What are you talking about?"

He turns towards me and I can't help but shrink back at the intensity of the anger in his expression. "You know. The guy you let fuck you. He's pissing me off and if he doesn't back off I'm going to make sure he does."

My stomach plummets at the thought of Kohan being hurt. *Micah wouldn't actually do that, would he?* I know that thinking he wouldn't is crazy but I have to hold out hope that's he's just trying to hurt me. "He's your boyfriend's brother. He cared for me. Why would you want to hurt him?" I don't know where the bravery is coming from but I need him to leave Kohan alone. A slap across my jaw makes my head fly back but I stand tall, determined that he will hear what I'm saying.

"He wasn't my boyfriend, he was the person I needed to get closer to you. I can't have a boyfriend when I'm married. You might have forgotten that we're still hitched but I haven't. I took my vows seriously and if that arsehole doesn't stop pushing, he will see how seriously I take them."

I feel a trickle of something tickling my lip and I wipe at it, looking down briefly to confirm that it's blood. I rub it on my jeans as I continue talking. I know that I will regret it soon but I just can't stop myself. "I can't believe that you used Carey like that. He was completely innocent in all this."

"I suggest you shut up and back the fuck off."

I should listen to his tone and do as I'm told but a twisted part of me wants to push his buttons and get a reaction from him. Maybe that's what Kohan actually did for me. He gave me the strength to not just lay down to the abuse, not when he's threatening someone I love. "Not until you promise to leave Kohan alone."

He stalks towards me and the courage I had a few moments ago vanishes as I step back to keep some space some between us. "Do you have feelings for him? Did you like it when he dropped to his knees in the kitchen and sucked your dick?"

I feel my cheeks heat as he speaks because he's admitting to watching us. That night in my kitchen was a special moment between Kohan and me, and Micah is reducing it to something filthy and voyeuristic.

"Do you really think he meant those things he said? Please, Ares, how could he want a pathetic loser like you? A guy that hot wouldn't want anything more than a quick fuck from someone who has no idea what he's doing."

I know what he's doing; he's trying to break me down so he can hurt me without trying too hard. The thing is he's managing it so easily. He's taking all my doubts about Kohan and myself and saying them out loud. I never believed that someone as perfect as Kohan would want me and Micah is confirming it all.

"I'm the only person who could love you, Ares. I broke you so I think it's my place to keep you. The sooner you realise this the better. Stop acting like you can fight against this. We are meant to be together forever and no one will ever come between that."

"You're wrong, Kohan had feelings for me?" My voice comes out a lot weaker than I intended and it sounds like I'm asking a question, like I need Micah to tell me that he did. I want to be strong but I just don't think I can.

"He had you convinced, didn't he? Shit, Ares, be realistic. He was out to fuck you and nothing more. You should know that no one else wants you, only me."

Tears fill my eyes and I try to blink them away. I don't want to give him the satisfaction of knowing that he's hurting me. I got used to dealing with the physical pain years ago but the mental pain has always been the thing I struggle with. I've never been able to build up the wall I needed around my head and heart so it's been easy for Micah to make me suffer. I think this is why I needed so much help from Adam; I honestly think the mental anguish I went through will stay with me forever.

Micah reaches out and runs his fingers over my cheek and it takes everything in me not to flinch at his touch. I hold firm as his fingertips tickle down over my jaw and out over my neck. When he reaches the back of my head he runs his fingers through my hair, suddenly gripping it tightly and tilting my head back. It's something that he does a lot as it gives him complete control over my movements and makes the difference in our height even more obvious. "You are mine and there is no changing that. The only way to get away from me, Ares, is in a body bag. The only way."

Tears flood my eyes again but this time I don't stop them falling. I don't care if he sees how weak I am, I'm not hiding it from him any longer. If the only way to get out of this hell is to die, then so be it.

Micah must see something in my eyes because he leans in, his voice almost a growl when he speaks. "Don't do anything stupid."

I stay silent and we battle each other in a silent stare off. I think he is about to speak when there's a knock at the front door. My stomach drops to my knees at the noise. I don't want anyone to have to face Micah and I hope that he ignores it like he's done all week.

He doesn't, instead he walks over to the door and looks through the peephole. He turns with a smile on his face and I know that this isn't going to end well. Micah only ever looks that happy when he's about to teach me a lesson.

"Looks like we have a visitor." He opens the door and the ability to breathe leaves me when I see Kohan looking at me from the top step.

Chapter Twenty Nine

Kohan

  I come to a stop in front of Ares' cottage and rest my hands on my knees. The run along his road isn't a long one but with the panic I'm feeling it took more energy than it should have. I didn't know what to do once I reached his house, common sense told me to wait for the police that Carey had called but I wasn't sure how long they'd be. The problem is I don't actually know if Ares is in any immediate danger but there's no way I'm going to leave him inside on his own just in case. Now that I've worked out who Duncan is so much makes sense: the underlying anger when I met him, the fury in his voice when his mask slipped. There is no way I can leave Ares in there with that man.

  The curtains are all still closed so I don't know what I'm walking into, but the car in the driveway tells me that at least Duncan … shit, Micah is here. I'm not sure if I would feel better if I knew Ares was somewhere else, but then that thought scares me. Micah could have taken Ares anywhere and done anything to him and I would never know. Going by what Ares has told me about I know that Micah has a sadistic streak that's a mile long. No, staying outside is not an option.

  I knock on the door and wipe my hands on my jeans to dry them and get rid of some of the sweat that's there. I pull my bag strap off my shoulder and place the bag on the ground. I won't need it while I'm in there no matter what happens and I'd rather not have something hindering my movements. I'm envisioning a fight when I get inside and that thought alone should have me running away. I'm not a fighter even though everyone looks at me and think I should be. I'm sure I could hold my own in a fight if my life depended on it, but I have as much grace as a bull in a china shop so fighting has never been high on my list of things to do. I just hope I can keep Micah talking long enough for the police to get here.

When the door opens my eyes instantly connect with Ares and it's a struggle not to rush straight to him. There are more bruises on him today and there's fresh blood running down his chin from his lip. The sight of him makes me want to cry but I turn that emotion into anger, anger that I direct at the smug looking man who's holding the door open.

"Come in, Kohan. Let's all get to know each other better."

I don't get a chance to move before Micah grabs the front of my jacket and drags me into the house. As soon as I'm past the threshold the door slams behind me. I stumble towards Ares but manage to catch myself before I fall. He puts his arms out like he's going to try and catch me but he pulls back quickly, his eyes looking over my shoulder. I know that Micah must be standing there but I refuse to acknowledge him.

"Are you okay, Ares?"

His eyes flicker to me and he smiles a little. He can't hide the fear in his eyes though and that makes me even more determined to get him out of here.

"He's fine. I don't know what he told you about me but know that I would never hurt him, well not in a way that he didn't deserve." He sounds so smug and I want to do nothing more than turn around and punch him square in the face. Instead, I keep my voice steady and speak with as much control as possible.

"I didn't ask you." I keep my eyes on Ares as I speak but we all know who I'm talking to. "When I want the opinion of his abusive ex boyfriend I'll make sure I come to you."

This gets a laugh from Micah and I hear him moving behind me. I stand my ground as he moves in close behind me and stage whispers in my ear. "That's husband, fucker. Get it right."

My eyes get wide with shock and I look to Ares to deny what he's saying, but the look of horror on his face tells me that it's not a lie. "You didn't tell me he was your husband."

Ares shakes his head and takes a step towards me. He looks as though he's about to throw up and I wonder if I want to hear what he's about to say. "I didn't want anyone to know how stupid I had been. It was bad enough that I stayed with him when he was just my boyfriend, but for people to know I actually married him. I couldn't let you know."

I'm so focused on Ares that when a hand comes out and punches him in the jaw I actually jump. Blood splatters over the side of his face before his legs give out on him and he collapses to the floor. I move quickly to try and help him but Micah grabs me by the arm and pulls me across the living room. I try to fight back but he's incredibly strong. It looks like all the time in the gym has paid off.

I watch Ares as he shakes his head like he's trying to clear the stars that must be invading his vision. I don't know how he isn't passed out cold after being hit that hard. Then a sickening thought hits me, he's probably used to it.

"That wasn't a very nice thing to say, Ares. I've gone to a lot of trouble to find you after what you did. I could have easily walked away when you put me in prison but I knew that it must have been your family who made you do it. What you just said though, that makes me think that maybe you don't feel the same as I do and that's a problem." Micah's grip on my arm tightens and I try not to flinch as his nails dig into my skin. Even through the few layers of fabric I can feel bite of pain on my skin.

I continue to watch Ares as he gets off his knees and stands slowly, taking his time to straighten his body. He's so fucking brave and I'm standing here doing nothing as he takes Micah's abuse.

"I put you in jail, Micah. Not my parents and not my brother. Me, just me." His voice is quiet and he sounds like he's struggling and considering the red mark on his face that's progressively getting darker I know he must be in a shit load of pain.

Micah laughs but I can't hear any humour in it. I turn to look at him and I wish I hadn't the second his fist connects with my face. Pain explodes through my head and I fall backwards. My hip is the first thing that lands and I feel the impact vibrate through my body, making me bite my tongue. The taste of blood distracts a little from the pain I'm in and I'm thankful to have something to focus on.

I can hear shouting and I blink to try to clear my vision. I see Ares trying to pull Micah back from me but it's like a kitten trying to fight with a mountain lion. Micah pushes Ares' chest and he almost flies across the living room until his back slams against the wall opposite them. He slides down until he's sitting and I can hear his laboured breathing over the ringing in my ears.

Rolling onto my side becomes a bigger struggle than I anticipated but I need to get to Ares. I'm worried that all the hits to his head are going to really damage him. I'm just getting to my hands and knees when I'm kicked in the ribs and my whole body leaves the ground. My breath explodes out of my lungs, and when I land on the carpeted floor I'm struggling to breathe. *Holy shit.* Again, I wonder how Ares survived this. If this was what he felt every time there is no wonder that he is still traumatised by it.

"I don't know where you think you're going. I think you should just stay where you are, and that's away from my husband." Micah sounds far too calm in this situation. I would have thought that he would sound angry but there is nothing. He sounds emotionless and it's scaring the shit out of me. If he is disconnected from what he's doing then there's no way for me to talk him out of it.

"I don't know where you think you're going. I think you should just stay where you are, and that's away from my husband." Micah sounds far too calm in this situation. I would have thought that he would sound angry but there's nothing. He sounds emotionless and it's scaring the shit out of me. If he is disconnected from what he's doing then there's no way for me to talk him out of it.

I grab a hold of my ribs and turn again, needing to get off my back so I can sit up. I need to get to my feet because I am at a disadvantage down here. Micah must realise this too because he kicks my hand out from under me and I land back on the floor. Moving quicker than I thought possible I roll away from him and get to my knees. It takes me longer to get to my feet than I would like but I get there before Micah decides to come after me again. In fact, he looks like he's waiting for me to get up and I falter a second, trying to work out what his plan is.

He moves closer to me and I try to take up a fighting stance, which is difficult while holding my aching ribs. "I think you've wasted enough of my time, Kohan. It's time for you to stop being a problem."

I barely have a second to work out what he's saying when he rushes me. I expect to be knocked to the floor and winded again but what I get is something much worse.

Fiery hot pain slices through my side and I gasp in shock. Micah backs off and I look down, my hands flying to the area that's hurting. I press my fingers to my side but flinch when the pain becomes too much. I blink a few times when I look at my hands and think that I must be seeing things but I'm not. There's bright red blood dripping from my fingers and I can't quite work out why. Pulling my shirt from my jeans I move it out of the way so I can see the skin on my side.

My legs collapse from underneath me the second I see the large laceration. I'm still kneeling when Micah comes and stands in front of me, a small blade dripping blood in his hand.

"You were a problem, but not anymore." He pulls his hand back to hit me but all the energy is draining out of my body along with the blood. I sag to the floor, my hands limp at my side.

I use what little energy I have left to turn my head to face Ares who seems frozen to the spot. His face is ashen white and his cheeks wet as tears run down his cheeks. His eyes are like saucers and when he looks deep into my eyes I can only see fear. I can't let him watch this, I need him to get away so he'll be safe, so I do the only thing I can think of.

"Run!" The word comes out loud and strong but uses the last ounce of effort I have left.

When Ares doesn't run I want to scream but I don't have anything left, and when I hear Micah moving beside me I know it's going to be over soon. That's when Ares moves, fast and sure, and places his body between Micah and I. I want to push him away and tell him to save himself but my vision is starting to fade.

"Stop, Micah. I'll come with you, I promise. Just leave Kohan, please don't hurt him more. Just give me a minute with him and I will leave with you, no questions."

"Prove it."

I watch helplessly as Ares leans into Micah and kisses him gently. Apparently it's not enough because Micah grabs him and kisses him with ownership like he wants me to see that he's won. Ares relaxes into Micah's hold but you can still see tension in his fingers as he digs his nails into the palm of his hand. He's doing this to save me from any more harm but I still want him to be free. He can't give himself over to Micah no matter what happens to me. Micah has already taken so much from him and I can't allow this final nail in Ares' coffin.

"Ares, please don't do this." The words come out on a gurgle that I feel deep in my chest. The pain I'd felt has faded and I would be happy except the whole side of my body has gone numb. I need to get Ares out of here before I pass out.

The two men split and with a simple nod of his head, Micah gives Ares the go ahead to speak to me. Ares instantly drops to his knees and I blink a few times as he lowers his face over mine, kissing my lips like it might be the last time. I can taste the salt from his tears as they drip down his face. When he speaks his voice is so low that only the two of us can hear them.

"I need you to listen to me, Kohan. As soon as I get away from him I'm going to call an ambulance, but I need you to hold on." He takes his t-shirt off and presses it to my side. I thought the pain had vanished but I gasp as the pressure hits me.

"I can't let anything happen to you, this world needs you. You're too good to die for me. Just hold on until someone gets here. I can't stay with him no matter what so when I know that you are safe I'll be going. He told me I could only get away if it was in a coffin …"

His words cut off and I suddenly know what he means. My heart starts racing in my chest and it only makes the pain in my side worse. "Ares, no."

He leans down and kisses me again to silence me.

"Time to go."

Ares flinches when Micah speaks and I reach out to grab the hand he has on my side. He covers my hand and squeezes, it feels so final that tears start to fall down my cheeks.

"Please don't cry, Kohan. You'll be fine, I promise. No matter what happens next I need you to know something really important. I love you. I think I always have but I was too scared to admit it. But I do, I love you."

Darkness starts to seep into the centre of my vision and I struggle to hold on. I want to tell him I love him but my eyes are becoming heavy. I can see his lips still moving but my head is filled with white noise and it's drowning everything else out. My thoughts are screaming the words for me but he won't be able to hear me. When I can't fight the inevitable anymore I give in to the bliss of the darkness but I repeat in my head over and over.

I love you Ares and I always will.

Epilogue

Kohan

I sit up upright in bed, sweat trickling down my back as I try to calm down my breathing. It's the same dream I've had since the day I was stabbed and it doesn't seem to be getting any better. I lean forward and rest my arms onto my knees and drop my head. I thought that after nearly a year I would be past dreaming about it but apparently my brain has other ideas.

I'm tempted to get up and go to the kitchen for a drink of water but the cool breeze coming from the open window is so nice. It's cooling the sweat from my back and even though it makes my skin a little itchy, it's relaxing. I look at my watch and see that it's barely two in the morning. I haven't even been asleep three hours but I know that trying to get any more sleep tonight is a lost cause. Once the memories of that day hit me there's no escaping the fear and pain.

I jump when a hand touches my shoulder but I relax instantly when warm lips leave tiny kisses on my shoulder.

"Did you have another one?"

I turn and kiss Ares on the head before resting my cheek on him. "Yeah, same as always."

He pulls me back onto the mattress and rests his head on my chest. I look down into his eyes that are illuminated by the street light outside. I run my fingers through his hair and it sticks up at funny angles once I'm finished.

"Talk to me."

I trace the scar on his forehead. I know he hates it when I do that but it's a reminder of what we've been through and survived.

"It's just the same as every other dream. But in the dreams I lose you, Ares."

The dream changed after I'd had them for a few months, morphing into something that shatters my heart every single time. In my dream I watch as Micah plunges the knife into Ares heart. It's usually that act that wakes me up in a panicked state, just like tonight.

He takes my hand and runs it over his face, neck and down over his shoulder. It stops when he presses it against his heart. "I'm here with you. He tried to take me away but he didn't. We escaped and almost fully intact."

The scar on my side tingles like it does every time we talk about that day and how we nearly lost each other. I barely made it to the hospital in time due to blood loss. The stab wound itself wasn't large but my spleen had been nicked which caused the blood loss. I spent a few hours in surgery and then about a week in intensive care. The whole time I was lying in that hospital bed my only thought had been Ares.

"Do you ever think about it?" I don't have to clarify what I'm asking because it's a variation of the conversation we have nearly every time I have a nightmare.

"Not so much now. The court case felt a little like deja vu, only with me being the criminal."

"Shut up, you were never a criminal. It was self-defence and that's why it was thrown out on the first day. His family might have thought that you took his life out of spite but the law knew better."

Going through the court case with Ares has been so fucking hard. He had spent nights crying about what happened that day, and the thought of losing him for defending us both scared me. But four months after the incident Ares was found not guilty of murder and not guilty of manslaughter. It was a bittersweet victory for us when we saw his family breaking their hearts over the ruling. It's been difficult for Ares to come to terms with killing Micah, but after many sessions with Adam he's accepting that he had no other choice.

I was passed out when it happened but Ares told me that Micah had gone for him with the knife that he had stabbed me with. Ares thought Micah was going to stab me again so he tackled Micah to the ground. When Ares pulled back to punch him he saw that the knife was sticking out of Micah's chest. Micah died before the police arrived and Ares was arrested. They kept him in jail for three days but when I woke up in hospital he was sitting by my side looking like the sexiest guy I had ever seen, even with his bruised face and bust lip. All I cared about was the fact he was alive.

The police were really sympathetic to Ares plight, especially once they found out why he was never told about Micah's release. Apparently the crown prosecution service dropped the ball when it came to contacting Ares about Micah's release. They told us a story about a misplaced file and a member of staff being off ill but all I heard was how badly they had fucked up. It had been overlooked for months and it had left Ares defenceless against his abusive ex.

"I know, but it's over now and we have the rest of our lives together. I wish we hadn't had to go through all that, but we are here." Ares looks deep into my eyes before leaning down and kissing me. We didn't have the best start to our relationship and things have been difficult between us but I wouldn't change a single thing. Okay that's a lie, I would maybe take away the stabbing and death. Truthfully though, all these things brought us closer and more appreciative of everything that we now have. We never take a single day together for granted because we know that we aren't guaranteed a tomorrow. Our bruises might have faded now and we both have scars that will never vanish but we work every single day to outrun the darkness that threatens to overtake us and drag us down.

"I like being here." I run my hand down his spine and cup his perfect arse, feeling his gentle sigh against my lips.

"I like you being here too." He moves his body until he's lying on top of me and I open my legs to let him lie in between them.

Feeling his body against mine still gives me a rush of lust and I tilt my hips until I feel his cock rub against mine. I slip my finger in between his arse cheeks and rub his hole, loving the groan that it elicits. "Do you like me here too?"

Ares drops his head to my shoulder and pushes back against my finger. I let him take over as he alternates between making sure our cocks rub and pressing my finger into him. I'm not really penetrating him because since his abuse by Micah, he's been struggling with allowing me that last thing. I don't care if he never gives me the chance to fuck him like he does to me, but I can see that it bothers him. I know he wants to be able to share everything with me but I remind him that we will get there eventually. We have the rest of our lives together to try it but even if he doesn't like it, I won't love him any less. I think nearly losing him has made everything more than just being with him a bonus. If I can spend the rest of my life just holding Ares then I will die a very happy man.

"I want you." His voice comes out breathy and it has my dick twitching against his.

"You know I'm yours."

He lifts his head and looks deep into my eyes, almost like he's seeing into my soul. "No, I want you. I'm ready."

I panic and say the first thing that comes into my head. "No you're not."

Ares starts giggling at my response and I don't blame him. I would laugh right along with him but my heart is beating in my ears at the thought of finally being inside him. I don't want to rush him, and I truthfully would be happy if he was never ready, but imagining what he feels like is at the top of my list for wank material.

"I think I know when I'm ready, and it's right now."

"You're just doing this to distract me from my nightmare."

"Fuck you, Kohan. If that were what this was I would have done it months ago. I want to do it because I love you and I'm ready. Now get the lube and shut up."

I just stare at Ares for a few minutes, a little shocked at his outburst. "That wasn't exactly romantic you know."

He hits me on the chest and rolls off me to let me get to the drawer next to our bed. I put my hand in the drawer but instead of grabbing the lube I take out the small black box that I put in there the other day. I didn't know when I would need it but I wanted it there just in case.

I exhale deeply but as quietly as I can so I don't give away my sudden nerves. I don't know why I think doing this now, in the middle of the night when we are both naked, is a good idea but it feels like there has never been a better time.

"I'm growing old over here. Do I need to start without you?" The humour in his voice tells me that this is it, this is the perfect moment to do this. I wanted to do it when it was unique and we would both remember it, and I think this fits both of those criteria.

"Here, get yourself sorted out." I throw the ring box over my shoulder and Ares yells in surprise but catches it in his hands. I turn and lean back on the headboard while I watch him.

He sits up with a puzzled expression on his face as he turns the little box over in his hands. He then turns his eyes up to me but looks no less confused. "What's this?" His voice has lost the confidence it had a few minutes ago and I think that's because he knows exactly what this is.

"Open it."

He slowly raises the lid and I turn on the lamp next to the bed so he can see clearly. His eyes widen and I can't help but smile because I know what he's looking at. Two matching black bands that I picked out because they were simple and beautiful. Sophie had tried to get me to get rings with rainbows and diamonds on them but that's not us. Our love doesn't need to be a big show, these rings are just a small symbol to show the world that we belong to each other. In our hearts is where the real fireworks are and that's just for us to see.

"I don't know what to say." Ares looks up at me and a single tear runs down his cheek.

"I hope you will say yes, and just on the chance you do, read the inside of the rings."

He picks the slightly smaller ring out of the box and reads the inscription that I had engraved there.

You're the only one who makes my heart sing

I take the ring from between his fingers and slip it onto his finger. "I love you, Ares Masterson, and I want to spend the rest of my life with you. I didn't really believe in love until that night I ran into you at work but I knew then that I needed to know you. Will you spend the rest of your life with me, listening to my stories and letting me love you?"

Ares launches himself at me and wraps his arms around my shoulders. I feel his back shake with the quiet sobs he's trying to control. I run my hand up and cup the back of his head and my finger catches the back of his hearing aid.

I smile to myself as I realise that I don't even notice them anymore. The fact that he could hear me tonight didn't enter my head, because even when he isn't wearing them he still seems to know exactly what I'm saying. "You put your hearing aids in?"

He pulls back with a smile on his face. "Always for you. You are the only thing that's worth listening to in this world. You make the silence less appealing, you make me want to hear." He turns and grabs the second ring and pulls it from the box. I hold up my hand in front of me and he starts to slip the ring onto my finger. He stops before he gets to the first knuckle and pulls the ring off again. He looks on the inside and screws up his nose. "It's blank."

"I thought maybe you could get something put in there. Something meaningful."

He looks deep in thought before a small smile tugs at the corner of his lips. "I could do that." He pushes the ring fully onto my finger and leans in to kiss me. It's a kiss that's full of love and passion, and my dick instantly takes notice.

"Does this mean you say yes?"

"There is no other answer, Kohan. I love you more than I thought possible. You saw through my scars. *You saw me.*"

I wrap him in my arms and pull him close to me, the heat from before taking a backseat to the love I feel for this man. I didn't think I would ever deserve the sort of love my mum and dad had for each other, but I found it and I won't be stupid enough to let it go.
"Am I allowed to know what you're getting engraved for me?"
He bites my bottom lip before sitting back on my legs. He cups my face and runs his finger along my lip to soothe the pain he caused. "I could put so many things, and as much as I want to keep you in suspense I'll tell you." He looks down at the ring on his finger before speaking softly as his gentle eyes meet mine. "You listened when I needed someone to hear me."

THE END

Bonus Scene

Ares

I watch as the light fades from Kohan's eyes and they close. Painful, blinding panic rushes through me as I stare down at his lifeless body. A loud sob escapes me and I drop my head to his chest. It takes a few moments for the motion of Kohan's chest to catch my attention. When the information finally filters through my grief soaked brain I turn my head until I can hear his heartbeat. I close my eyes and let the sound sooth my frazzled nerves. This is the last moment I'll spend with Kohan and I want to remember this sound for the rest of my life. The strong regular sound calms my own heart rate and it feels like my heart tries to mimic his, almost like it wants to have that connection.

I'm pulled from my place of peace by a hand in my hair, dragging me back along the floor. I grab onto Micah's wrist to try and stop him from pulling the hair out by the roots but he doesn't ease up at all until he stops near the front door and lets me fall onto my back. I look up into the angry face of the man who has starred in my nightmares for far too long now. I look over to where Kohan is lying on the floor, blood pooling underneath him, and I know that now is the time I need to finally stand up for someone else. No, not someone else, myself. I've been pushed around far too long and now Kohan is relying on me being the man he thought he could see.

Struggling to my feet I move to stand in front of Micah. My entire body is crying out in pain and my first instinct when I meet the rage in Micah's eyes is to run, but I can't. I need to call someone to help Kohan, I need to make sure he's safe. "I need to call someone."

Micah laughs without humour and steps closer to me. Every part of me wants to step back but I force myself to stand tall and keep eye contact. "And you think I will just allow you to do that?"

"No, but I didn't ask your permission. I'll call an ambulance and then we will leave. I told you that I would go with you if Kohan was safe, he isn't yet." I turn to walk towards the house phone but I don't get very far before Micah grabs me by the arm and turns me roughly towards him.

"No, you can call from the car once we're out of this town."

I pull my arm away, suddenly feeling a lot more confident than before. I grab my mobile from my pocket and quicker than I thought possible I write out a message to Sophie and send before Micah grabs my phone and smashes it against the wall. It doesn't matter though because I know that the message is sent and she won't ignore it.

999 Kohan hurt. My house. Send help.

I close my eyes and smile, a moment of peace spreading through my body as I realise that this whole thing is nearly over. I just need to keep Micah distracted until Kohan is safe and then I can leave this fucked up life of mine knowing that the man I love is safe. That's the most important thing, that Kohan walks away from this and lives a long happy life. I know that I'm not destined for the happily ever after, but if I can give it to him I will.

"Who the fuck did you text?" The anger is rolling off Micah in waves and it gives me more satisfaction than I thought possible. I've spent the last four years trying not to anger Micah but now I refuse to do it. He's caused so much pain that it doesn't actually scare me anymore. I'm deaf and my body is covered in scars, leaving grotesque memories on my skin, so there really isn't much more he can do to me. He can hit me, break my bones, or lock me away, he could even cause so much damage to my body that it finally gives up, but nothing will hurt more than walking away from Kohan.

My eyes automatically seek out his unconscious form as I think of him, and even in his damaged state he's the most beautiful man I've ever seen. I truly thought that I had the chance of a happy life, of finding that happiness that my parents and brother found, but now I know it was never meant to be. What I do have is memories of happy times, of sharing tender times and finally trusting someone to love me. Those memories will get me through what's about to happen.

The words are on the tip of my tongue, the ones where I tell Micah that it doesn't matter who I messaged, when I hear sirens in the distance. The relief nearly makes me collapse to the floor because now I know that Kohan will make it. The ambulance will get here and stop his bleeding before taking him to the hospital.

The backhand across my face takes me by surprise and I spin in place, hitting my forehead off the wall hard enough that it dazes me. I put my hands against the wall for stability while the fuzziness in my head fades. I can hear Micah behind me shouting about messaging the police and how we need to leave before they get closer, bringing with them his return to prison. I blink a few times and take a deep breath. That's when I notice the silence and that scares me. Micah and silence is never a good thing.

Turning slowly I look behind me and the world stops. My vision zones in completely to where Micah is kneeling next to Kohan, the knife that he previously used pressed against Kohan's throat.

"We can't leave any witnesses."

Instinct take over and I don't think about what I'm doing when I lunge across the living room towards Micah. He must hear me or see my movements because he twists in my direction, the knife out in front of him. In my heart I can tell that this is the end for me. That when I land on Micah he will push the knife into my body and my life will drain away from me slowly, but if it buys the police time to get here then it's worth it.

I connect with his body and the momentum slams his back to the floor with me on top of him. A sharp pain erupts in my side but I stay where I am, pinning Micah to the floor. This will be my legacy that I'll leave in my family's memory, that I was finally strong enough to stand up to Micah. The pain starts to fade and I wonder if I'm going into shock. I've never been stabbed, but I know that when Micah broke bones the pain only lasted until the adrenaline kicked in and then that hid the agony. If I'm going into shock I need to use it to my advantage now to get Micah under control.

Looking down at Micah I notice two things at the same time. Number one is the struggle that I was expecting isn't actually happening. Micah is lying under me, his body stiller than I would have thought possible. The second thing I notice is the paleness of his face. His skin has lost all colour and his face is contorted into a grimace, a sheen of sweat appearing on his forehead. Something is wrong and my brain is struggling to make sense of all the information I have.

There's shouting outside before the front door bursts open and my house is suddenly filled with uniformed policemen. There's shouting and a minute later paramedics appear and move instantly to Kohan's side. I'm grabbed from behind and pulled up to my knees by my arms. "Don't let him up. He's trying to kill my boyfriend. He shouldn't be here, I have a restraining order." I don't even know who I'm talking to but the words explode from me as I feel the handcuffs click over my wrists. Being pulled to my feet is a struggle but the hands on my arms help me. I finally look down at Micah and I suddenly know why I have handcuffs on my wrist. I understand the stillness of his body and why he looked so pale.

My eyes go wide and my mouth drops open as I take in what I've done. The knife that I landed on, the one that I thought had stabbed me is embedded in Micah's stomach, pushed deep enough that some of the handle is under the skin. There's blood all over him, much more blood than I thought possible; but it looks like its stopped flowing, which can't be a good sign. I look at his face but I can't see him there. His eyes are empty as they stare blankly at the ceiling, everything that made him Micah missing from those beautiful eyes that showed me so much emotion in the past.

The paramedics wheel Kohan passed me, telling the police they need to get him to the hospital before he bleeds out, and I know I need to focus. I need to get this mess sorted out so I can get to Kohan's side and be there when he wakes up. I just don't know how to do that. I've done the unthinkable and I don't think that I'm going to be able to walk away from this. Even in his death, Micah has stolen my chances of a normal life. I feel the tears falling down my cheeks when I admit to myself that I just killed a man … and I'm not even sorry about it.

Domestic abuse helpline contact information

This book was never meant to follow the path it did, it was meant to be happy and full of rainbows and unicorns, then my voices spoke loudly. I was worried to cover such a delicate topic but once the story started flowing I realised that I needed to do it. I wanted to tell people that domestic abuse doesn't only happen to women, that it doesn't just happen in heterosexual relationships, that anyone is at risk and you shouldn't suffer in silence. I've seen what can happen to someone who suffers at the hands of another and it's not something I want anyone to go through.

If you or anyone you know is suffering please try to get them to get help. There are many groups out there that know how to deal with domestic abuse and they are only too willing to help.

U.K.

National LGBT Domestic Abuse Helpline

T: 0800 999 5428

E: help@galop.org.uk

http://www.galop.org.uk/news/galop-to-run-national-lgbt-domestic-violence-helpline/

Stonewall

http://www.stonewall.org.uk/help-advice/criminal-law/domestic-violence

Refuge

0808 2000 247

http://www.nationaldomesticviolencehelpline.org.uk

U.S.

Domestic Abuse Hotline: 1-800-799-SAFE (7233)

Gay Men's Domestic Violence Project: 1-800-832-1901

Suicide Prevention Hotline: 1-800-273-8255

The Trevor Project: 1-866-488-7386

Substance Abuse and Mental Health Hotline: 1-800-662-HELP (4357)

www.glbthotline.org

www.safehousecenter.org

http://gmdvp.org/gmdvp/

Acknowledgements

Now to the people who helped me write this book. Who soothed me when I cried because the words broke my heart.

Nicola: Every book seems to get darker and you are right there behind me telling me to hurt them more! Yeah, people don't know how twisted we actually are … or maybe they do! I love you lady and I'm thankful every day that you are my person.

Claire: You are my sounding board and for that you are never getting to leave me EVER! You provide support and laughter when I need it, and I don't think you realise how important you are to each book. Thank you!

Ellie: Making my words awesome again…that is your superpower!

My beta readers: Michele, Amy, Robyn. Thank you for reading the story before it made any real sense!

Cindy and Michele: You double checked it all and showed me how many mistakes I actually miss. You are both worth your weight in gold … Thank you!!!

To anyone who has read and shared this book….thank you!!! Without you I wouldn't be able to do what I love.

Other information

Leaving Marks series:

Leaving His Mark ~ Out now

Leaving Her Mark ~ Out now

Clay ~ Coming soon

Hard To Love series:

Worth The Fight ~ Out now

Make Me Trust ~ Out now

This Isn't Me ~ Out now

Standalone Novels:

Undercover ~ Out now

Someone To Hear Me ~ Out Now

The Roommate Series:

Asher

Keep up to date with all my news:

Website: www.authortamckay.com

Facebook: https://www.facebook.com/pages/Ta-Mckay-Author/1462902633937350

Twitter: https://twitter.com/tamckayauthor

Amazon author page: http://www.amazon.com/T.a.-McKay/e/B00JFF1R80/ref=sr_ntt_srch_lnk_1?qid=1411487268&sr=8-1

Goodreads: https://www.goodreads.com/author/show/7750967.T_A_McKay

Made in the USA
Columbia, SC
09 May 2017